COLLECTORS, CATS & MURDER

A Dickens & Christie Mystery - Book IV

KATHY MANOS PENN

MANOS
PENN & INK

COLLECTORS, CATS & MURDER

A Dickens & Christie Mystery
Book IV

Kathy Manos Penn

Also by Kathy Manos Penn

Dickens & Christie Series

Bells, Tails & Murder

Pumpkins, Paws & Murder

Whiskers, Wreaths & Murder

Collectors, Cats & Murder

Castles, Catnip & Murder

Bicycles, Barking & Murder (2022)

https://www.amazon.com/gp/product/B085FSHQYW

Would you like to know when the next book is on the way?
Click here to sign up for my newsletter. https://bit.ly/3bEjsfi

*To Banjo, who inspired the
easy-going lovable personality of Dickens.
I couldn't ask for a better canine muse.*

I don't know what lies around the bend, but I'm going to believe the best does.

— -ANNE OF GREEN GABLES

CONTENTS

Cast of Characters

COLLECTORS, CATS & MURDER
CAST OF CHARACTERS
The Americans

Aleta "Leta" Petkas Parker—A retired American banker, Leta lives in the village of Astonbury in the Cotswolds with Dickens the dog and Christie the cat.

Henry Parker—Handsome blue-eyed Henry was Leta's husband.

Dickens—Leta's white dog, a dwarf Great Pyrenees, is a tad sensitive about his size.

Christie—Leta's black cat Christie is sassy, opinionated, and uppity.

Anna Metaxas—Leta's youngest sister lives in Atlanta with her husband Andrew, five cats, and a Great Dane.

Sophia Smyth—Leta's younger sister is married to Jeremy and lives in New Orleans.

Bev Hunter—Bev is Leta's Atlanta friend who fosters dogs.

Prentiss—A journalist from the States, he and Leta ...t it off when he stayed at the inn.

The Brits

Martha and Dylan—The donkeys in a nearby pasture look forward to carrots from Leta.

Libby and Gavin Taylor—The Taylors are the owners of the Olde Mill Inn.

Gemma Taylor—A Detective Inspector at the Stow-on-the-Wold police station, she's the daughter of Libby and Gavin and lives in the guest cottage behind the inn.

Paddington—Libby and Gavin's Burmese cat is fond of Leta.

Beatrix Scott—Owner of the Book Nook, she hosts the monthly book club meeting.

Trixie Maxwell—Beatrix's niece works in the bookshop.

Wendy Davies—The retired English teacher from North Carolina returned to Astonbury to look after her mum and has become good friends with Leta.

Peter Davies—Wendy's twin and owner of the local garage, Peter is a cyclist and cricketer.

Belle Davies—Mother to Wendy and Peter, Belle lives at Sunshine Cottage with Wendy.

Tigger—Belle and Wendy's cat is a recent addition to Sunshine Cottage.

Rhiannon Smith—Rhiannon owns the Let It Be yoga studio where Leta and Wendy take classes.

Jill and Jenny Walker—Jill works at the Olde Mill Inn, and her sister Jenny is a barista at Toby's Tearoom.

Toby White—Owner of Toby's Tearoom, he gave up his London advertising job to pursue his dream of owning a small business.

Constable James—Constable Jonas James works with Gemma.

Brian Burton—A DCI stationed in Stroud, Brian is Gemma's boss and Wendy's boyfriend.

The Watsons—John and Deborah live next door to Leta with their little boy Timmy.

Barb Peters—Barb is a barmaid at the Ploughman Pub.

Brian Peters—Barb's cousin Brian is the gardener for the Olde Mill Inn and several country estates.

Caroline—Caroline is the cook at the Manor House.

Ellie, the Dowager Countess of Stow—Ellie lives in Astonbury Manor and is active in village affairs.

Matthew and Sarah Coates—Ellie's son and daughter-in-law, the Earl and Countess of Stow, live on the estate in a large cottage close to the Manor House.

Teddy Byrd—Teddy is the elderly proprietor of Bluebird Books in Chipping Camden.

Fiona Linton—Fiona works part-time at Bluebird Books.

Albert Porter—Albert is Teddy Byrd's driver and does odd jobs at Bluebird Books.

Pris Price—Pris manages Bluebird Books for Teddy.

Gilbert Ward—Gilbert is a collector of Sherlock Holmes memorabilia and a friend of Dave's.

Alastair Porter—Alastair is the proprietor of Alastair's Attic in Manchester.

PETER'S
GARAGE

SUNSHINE
COTTA

PLOUGHMAN
PUB

THE OLDE MILL
INN

DONKEYS

RIVER ELFE

TO
CHELTENHAM
←

ST. A

VILLA

VILLA

ASTONBURY

Chapter One

A Friday afternoon in April

I surreptitiously studied Dave as he stood in front of the mirror adjusting the collar of his starched white shirt. "You know you look quite dashing," I said.

He laughed and turned to me, his eyes twinkling. "Thanks to the fashion-conscious woman who gave me this sweater, right? And insisted I wear it today for my presentation?" He had me there. I'd found the wool crewneck at the Astonbury Tree Lighting in December. Knit by local artisans, the black sweater with four-inch squares subtly outlined in slender white lines set off his black hair and brown eyes.

It had been my Christmas gift to him. I'd visited him in New York City at Thanksgiving, and after spending Christmas in Connecticut with his mother and his sister's family, he'd flown to England to spend ten days with me. We'd split our time between my cottage in the Cotswolds and a stay at the Dukes Hotel in London.

This afternoon's event at the Chipping Camden Literary

arked Dave's first speaking engagement in the UK. ...ce he'd written his October article about the discovery of a previously unknown J.M. Barrie book, he'd given several talks in the States, but none here. With most of the literary festivals in the Cotswolds held in the spring and fall and speakers already booked, I had a feeling that this April appearance would put him in high demand for next year's events. After all, the book had been found in the Cotswolds village of Astonbury, at Sunshine Cottage, home to my retired English teacher friend Wendy and her mum Belle.

Belle's mother had been befriended by playwright J.M. Barrie, and he'd become Uncle Jim to Belle. She'd kept the book in a trunk with childhood keepsakes and had no idea it was unusual or valuable. I kept thinking someone would decide to write a book, maybe a screenplay, about the enchanting tale. *What a treat it would be to see the story on the big screen.* This was a big event for both Belle and Dave.

"Right. I want to be sure I'm with the best-dressed speaker. And Dickens needs to look his best too. While I finish getting ready, can you put Dickens's bowtie on him, please?"

As Dave chuckled, Dickens barked and pranced over to the dresser. My handsome white dog liked dressing up as much as I did. He knew to bow his head so Dave could hook the bowtie, and he strutted into the bathroom where I was putting the finishing touches on my hair.

He sat and looked up at me. "I look grand, don't I? Hurry, Leta. We don't want to be late."

As though he understood Dickens, Dave chimed in, "Your hair looks perfect, and we need to get a move on. You know I want to be early so I can calm my nerves."

Wouldn't it be something if I've found a man who could understand my four-legged friends? I'd never known anyone else with my strange talent, and I worked hard to keep it under wraps lest my friends think I was delusional. For the most part, I was quite content to be the only human who could converse with Dickens and his feline sister Christie.

It was my turn to chuckle as I stepped into my black long-sleeved jumpsuit. With a wide silver accented black belt and a silver choker, it was an elegant yet casual look—and best of all, comfy. "Voila," I said as I spritzed Shalimar above my head and slid into my heels. "Ready!"

Luckily, the walk from the Cotswolds House Hotel & Spa to the library where Dave was speaking was a short one. High heels and walking could be a recipe for disaster, which was why I let Dave hold Dickens's leash. People stopped us along the way to greet Dickens—intrigued that he looked like a Great Pyrenees but was so small. He was a miniature replica of those gentle giants, forty pounds to their typical 120-140 because he was a dwarf Great Pyrenees. Before Dickens, I had a full-size Pyr, but I was past handling such a large dog, and considered myself fortunate to have stumbled across Dickens online.

As we entered the library, we were greeted by a small crowd of our friends. Belle was accompanied by her twins Wendy and Peter, and our friend Ellie—the Dowager Countess of Stow—had joined them for the evening. Gavin Taylor was there with his daughter Gemma, but his wife Libby had stayed behind to handle the guests at the Olde Mill Inn. I was glad the couple had worked it out so Gavin could attend, since he was the book lover in the family and a regular at our book club meetings at the village bookshop.

Astonbury's High Street business owners were well represented too, and it made me smile to think they'd managed to take a busy Friday afternoon off to hear Dave's presentation. Rhiannon had canceled her classes at Let it Be Yoga Studio.

om was in good hands with barista Jill in charge,
knew Beatrix had asked her niece Trixie to handle the
Book Nook Friday through Sunday so she could hear several of
the speakers.

Dave excused himself to take his flash drive to the
computer set up at the front of the room. He planned to share
photos of Belle's book plus a few teasers about his latest
project.

Beatrix hugged me. "I can't wait for Teddy to hear Dave's
talk. He thought Gilbert Ward's Sherlock Holmes presentation last night at our book club meeting was well done, and
I've promised him Dave's will be even better. I told you Teddy
owns Bluebird Books, the bookshop here in Chipping
Camden, right? And that he fancies himself a collector. He has
a typewriter and fountain pen allegedly used by J.M. Barrie
plus an assortment of letters written by various authors who
visited the Cotswolds."

"He told us when we met him last night, and he also
invited us to visit him at his home in the morning."

"Oh, you're in for a treat. I'm meeting him there for dinner
tonight, and I'm looking forward to seeing what he's added
since I last visited. Before he opened his bookshop here, he
was a regular customer at the Book Nook, and a few of his
prized possessions are items I found at the flea market in
Manchester."

Just then, Teddy Byrd came in, accompanied by a gangly
young man. He leaned heavily on his cane and held on to his
companion's arm. "There he is," exclaimed Beatrix. "And that
must be Albert. He drives him from time to time and does odd
jobs at the shop."

Beatrix went to greet them, and Teddy took her arm as
Albert departed. Pointing toward the conference room,

Beatrix invited me to follow them inside, where we slowly made our way to the front row. Once seated, Teddy motioned to Dave. "Are you and Leta still up for a midmorning visit tomorrow?"

Dave grinned and looked at me. "Leta and I are looking forward to it."

I agreed. "I don't know why, but I'm especially eager to see the typewriter."

It was a toss-up as to who was more eager for the Saturday visit, Dave to see the collection or Teddy to show it off. It was close to five as the crowd began to take their seats. Across the aisle on the front row, Wendy had saved me a seat with Belle and Peter. I leaned in and kissed Belle on the cheek as Dickens tucked himself between our chairs. "Are you ready for your appearance, Mrs. Davies?"

She shook her head of soft white curls. "Since all I have to do is turn around and give a royal wave, I'll be fine. Heaven forbid I'd be asked to say anything."

The announcer shushed the crowd and introduced Dave as the man whose writing had enabled modern readers to see J.M. Barrie as more than the author of *Peter Pan*. He'd introduced them to Barrie's wit and generosity and brought his outsized personality to life, and Barrie's friendship with Arthur Conan Doyle was also part of that story. He invited the group to settle in to hear a discussion of *Barrie and Friends*.

Dave opened by explaining that he'd come to the Cotswolds last year in search of tales of Arthur Conan Doyle for an article he was writing for the *Strand Magazine*. "Little did I know I'd meet the characters from Peter Pan. Let me introduce Belle Davies, named for Tinker Bell." Belle stood, turned to the crowd and waved. She remained standing, as she and Dave had planned. "And to complete the cast, please meet her twins Peter and Wendy, named for you know who." When the whole family was standing, a round of applause ensued.

With that, the Davies clan sat and Dave launched into a brief explanation of how Barrie's book had been discovered and how that find had engendered in him a desire to write a book about Barrie and his literary friends. "Did you know that among those who summered at Stanway House with Barrie were not only Arthur Conan Doyle, but also P.G. Wodehouse, A.A. Milne, and Jerome K. Jerome? Imagine all that talent packed into one Manor House. Then picture them playing cricket in Stanway and nearby Broadway on a team formed by Barrie.

"Not that the team, the Allahakbarries, was particularly good. As the story goes, Doyle was a decent cricketer who even played in some professional matches, but the rest of the authors were more talented at writing than they were at playing cricket. One even appeared in his pajamas for a match. To paraphrase Arthur Conan Doyle, they cared very little about cricket but 'a good deal about a jolly time and pleasant scenery.' Fortunately for us, they also cared a good deal about their writing, and generations have continued to enjoy the antics of Winnie-the-Pooh, Peter Pan, Sherlock Holmes, and Jeeves & Wooster."

Though I'd already heard many of the intriguing tidbits Dave was sharing, I continued to be amazed at how little I knew about Barrie and Doyle—their writing and their friendship. The most surprising to me was that the two men had collaborated on an operetta, *Jane Annie*. When Barrie started it and got stuck, Doyle came to his rescue and helped him finish. It was not, however, successful. The critics hated it, and playwright George Bernard Shaw panned it.

After a plug for the *Strand Magazine* and the *New York Book*

Review, the two publications he most often wrote for, Dave took questions from the audience. Turning to scan the enthusiastic crowd, I saw Albert come in and stand at the back of the room. *How wonderful for Teddy that he has someone to help him get around,* I thought.

The questions from the audience were varied, from which authors Dave planned to include in his book to how he'd gotten his start writing literary articles. They were curious as to how much research could be accomplished via online sources versus in-person visits to museums, libraries, and family homes.

One gentleman was interested in Barrie's cricket team. "How about other authors. Did Rudyard Kipling or H.G. Wells play too?"

"Kipling did, but there's conflicting information as to Wells. I can quote one source as saying, 'Wells was famously uninterested in cricket, and they never could get him to play.' And yet, there was another that said both Kipling and Wells played on the team."

Teddy posed the last question. "Excuse me, Dave, do you know whether Bram Stoker played cricket with the author group?"

Dave paused. "Good question. Though he was friends with Arthur Conan Doyle, who not only played on Barrie's team but formed a team of his own, I've never seen mention of Stoker playing. Perhaps his job managing the Lyceum Theatre kept him too busy."

The announcer approached the front as Dave wrapped up. He thanked Dave, who got a nice round of applause, and reminded the audience that Bluebird Books in Chipping Camden was well stocked with books by and about Barrie and Doyle and many of the other authors Dave had mentioned.

The next speaker would come on in thirty minutes to discuss his book on military history—not a topic that held any interest for me.

What did interest me was meeting our friends in the bar at the Cotswolds Hotel. As I went to say goodbye to Teddy, I paused. A young woman dressed in jeans and a baby blue smock was leaning over him and pointing to the back of the room where Albert was standing.

He called to me. "Leta, come meet Fiona. Couldn't do without this young lady."

Looking a bit harried, the blonde pony-tailed Fiona held out her hand. "Nice to meet you. Teddy couldn't stop talking about you last night when he got back from Astonbury. Sorry to rush off, but I've come to get Albert. A little girl climbed up on a display table at Bluebird Books, and it crashed to the floor. We desperately need him to fix it, or at least move it." She helped Teddy to his feet. "We'll make a stop by the shop, and then Albert can take you home."

"Don't rush me, young lady. I want to say hello to Gilbert."

Our friend approached as Fiona helped Teddy to his feet. "I say, Teddy, Dave's talk was informative, wasn't it?"

"Yes, Gilbert. You and he are a wealth of information. I must thank you for your question about that letter this morning. I plan to look through my notes to see when I acquired the document. There was a time I haunted estate sales and flea markets with my wife and came home with treasures like that. Not any longer, though. It's not the same without her by my side, plus nowadays, it's too difficult for me to get around. I'm fortunate that Albert's started doing a bit of book scouting and brings me items to consider from time to time."

We left the pair chatting and made our way to the door, stopping along the way for Dave to shake hands and answer additional questions. A tall, slim, silver-haired man in the back row stepped forward and introduced himself as Alastair Porter. *So many characters here*, I thought as I took in his waistcoat with a pocket watch chain peeking from it. Unlike Gilbert, who sported a bowtie with his waistcoat, this gentleman wore a cravat.

"Your presentation was not only entertaining but informative. If you have any spare time while you're in the area, I think you'd enjoy a visit to my stall at the Bolton Flea Market in Manchester, Alastair's Archives. We carry a large selection of memorabilia and books related to the Cotswolds authors you mentioned, and we're open every weekend."

Dave looked at me. "I'm not sure about our schedule this weekend, but we might be able to make it next week. What do you think, Leta?"

I agreed it might work out, and we accepted his proffered business card. I watched him walk to the front row and speak to Teddy next.

Just then, Gilbert caught up to us. "Almost missed your session, but I made it and found one of the last seats in the back. What an interesting presentation. Well done, old chap." In keeping with his turn of phrase, he clapped Dave on the back and shook his hand. *I can see him now in a tux and a monocle.*

As we continued to the outside door, the gentleman in the cravat approached Gilbert and engaged him in conversation. I leaned in to whisper to Dave, "Look at those two. They could compete for the best costume award."

Dave and I strolled arm in arm down the street. Looking up at him, I smiled. "You know you did a lovely job, right?"

"I hope I did. I felt good, and I didn't see anyone nod off— good signs I think. I trust you'll give me some constructive feedback later." He grinned. "I'd rather you didn't take the edge off my high right now."

"I really don't have anything to say in that regard. I enjoyed every bit, and I think you managed to combine humorous anecdotes and literary gems without drifting into arcane trivia only college professors could appreciate. You made an over-whelming abundance of information entertaining."

Dave stopped and spoke to Dickens. "Do you think she's pulling my leg, boy? Is she buttering me up for something?"

Dickens had a difficult time with idioms. He cocked his head and barked, "I didn't see her touch your leg—not sure about the butter."

Laughing at Dave, I asked him what Dickens thought.

"He's not sure, but I'm taking you at your word."

After a quick stop by our room for me to drop off my purse and reapply my lipstick, we three made our way to the bar. Peter and Wendy were already seated at a large table, and Peter stood and shook Dave's hand. "Jolly good show! Isn't that what you expect us Brits to say? But seriously, you were a hit."

Wendy hugged Dave. "We've ordered some champers and nibbles for the table. I expect the others to be here soon."

I grinned at my friend. "You know, I've seen the word 'champers' in books, but I've never heard anyone use it. Makes me think of Dorothy Sayers's Peter Wimsey or Margery Allingham's Albert Campion. And after hearing Gilbert say old chap several times, I'm beginning to feel as though I've trav-eled back in time."

"You are *such* a word nerd, Leta. I'm not sure when the term got its start. Did you read those books or only watch the BBC programs?"

"I read every single Sayers book and wished there had been more. As for Albert Campion, I've only seen the television series. Maybe I should get Beatrix to order me the books. We could do a few months of Golden Age authors—Sayers, Allingham, Christie, Patricia Wentworth, Josephine Tey—what do you think?"

Peter turned to Dave. "And they're off! Between Mum's affection for Agatha Christie and these two and their books, we seldom discuss anything else."

It was appropriate that Belle and Ellie appeared at that moment. Ellie was a member of our book club too, and we might have embarked on an evening of book talk if Toby, Gavin, Gemma, and Rhiannon hadn't been close on their heels. Everyone congratulated Dave as they joined us. Beatrix arrived as the bottles of champagne and accompanying flutes were delivered. Soon, we were all holding full glasses, and Toby stood. He'd given toasts at two of my parties, and it seemed he'd come prepared to do the same tonight.

"Dave, to paraphrase Hercule Poirot—my favorite character, by the way—your remarks were, 'as always, apt, sound, and to the point.' Cheers!"

As we lifted our glasses, several of us suggested that Toby should have worn his Poirot mustache—or better yet, he should grow one. He'd dressed as the funny little Belgian for my costume party in the fall and acted the part to perfection. *What fun-loving friends I have.*

Several of us were spending the night, but those who were driving back to Astonbury wanted to order an early dinner. Only Beatrix declined to order an entrée, as she was eating with Teddy that evening. She explained they were longtime friends who'd bonded over their love of books. A decade ago when Teddy decided Chipping Camden needed a bookstore, he'd relied heavily on Beatrix's expertise in stocking and managing the Book Nook, her shop in Astonbury. Until a year ago, he'd owned *and* managed Bluebird Books, but his declining health had changed that.

He still oversaw ordering and the scheduling of book signings but left the day-to-day management to Priscilla Price, who'd been his full-time clerk until he promoted her. These days, Priscilla and Fiona and two part-time students manned the shop, so Teddy's physical presence wasn't needed.

As Dave and Beatrix discussed what to expect in Teddy's collection, I leaned across the table to ask Wendy about Brian Burton. We'd met him in December as the Detective Chief Inspector on a local case, and he and Wendy had been dating ever since. They were leaving tomorrow for a week in Cornwall. Though they went out most weekends, this would be their first trip together. "What time are you and Brian heading out?"

Wendy rolled her eyes. "That will depend on how well he's done today putting his caseload in order. We'd hoped for an early start, but in his last text, he mentioned going into the station in the morning for an hour or two. Sounds as though I could have spent the night here instead of rushing home."

Gemma overheard us, and she patted Wendy on the shoulder. "The lot of a copper, as I well know. I hope his caseload's in order, or I may be one of the people who gets pulled in to help out. My plate's pretty full as it is."

That exchange prompted Gemma's dad Gavin to clear his throat and speak up. "Seems a good time to make your announcement, doesn't it?" he asked.

Blushing, Gemma said, "Go ahead, Dad. I can tell you're dying to do it."

Gavin stood and we looked at him expectantly. "Please join me in congratulating Gemma on her promotion to Detective Inspector."

We burst into applause, and Peter called for another bottle of champagne before turning to Gemma. "You're not leaving us, are you? Please tell us your promotion doesn't call for a transfer."

Gemma smiled. "No. I'm happy to say I'll continue at the station in Stow-on-the-Wold and get to stay in my cottage at the Olde Mill Inn in Astonbury. Mum and Dad will have me around for a while yet."

I was happy for her. She'd taken a leadership course in December and had hoped it would aid her chances of a promotion. That plus her hard work in solving several high-profile cases had paid off. Gemma and I weren't friends in the same way Wendy and I were. I'd call our relationship one that could be congenial one moment and uneasy the next.

The difficulty arose when I got involved in what Gemma called snooping. I—along with Wendy and Belle—had somehow gotten tangled up in a few murder investigations, mostly because I had a knack for keen observation. Even Gemma agreed that my presence at a murder scene was invaluable because I saw things others might miss—or, better said, the details at a scene prompted questions for me that others might not ask.

Then there was my tendency to go off on my own and ask those questions. Could I help it if people found it easier to open up to me than to the police? Wendy and Belle said it was because I was a good listener— something about the way I nodded and encouraged people to speak. I was pretty sure Gemma saw it more as me being a busybody. Whatever it was, the three of us had jokingly dubbed ourselves the Little Old Ladies' Detective Agency. At times, Gemma grudgingly invited our help. At others, she was furious with us for interfering.

It was Belle who proposed a toast this time. "To Gemma,

our very own Detective Inspector. May murder and mayhem take a break as you bask in the glory of your well-earned promotion."

The group broke up after that, with those who were staying the night heading to the elevators—or lifts, as my friends would say—and the rest of the gang moving to their cars. Beatrix, Ellie, Belle, Dave, Dickens, and I all squeezed into one. As the door opened on Beatrix's floor, she waved goodbye and said she'd catch up with us sometime tomorrow after her evening at Teddy's.

The first thing I did when we entered our hotel room was kick off my shoes and stand in front of the dresser to remove my jewelry. That prompted two reactions. Dave wrapped his arms around me and nuzzled my neck, and Dickens barked.

"Uh-uh. None of that until you take me out! Did you forget?"

Dave dropped his arms and stepped back. "Why didn't you say something earlier, little fella?"

Dickens barked louder. "I shouldn't have to say anything. Leta knows our bedtime routine."

I couldn't help laughing. "My fault. I wasn't thinking. Let me get my shoes on, and I'll run him downstairs."

One of the things I loved about Dave was how easygoing he was. "Nah. I'll take him while you get ready for bed." He gave a slow smile. "That's our next stop, right?"

A perfect ending to a perfect day. A girl could get used to this treatment.

Chapter Two

The sun streaming in the window woke me, and when I glanced at the bedside clock, I was surprised to see it was almost nine. I stretched and smiled as I rolled over to find I was by myself in bed. I rolled the other way to say good morning to Dickens, but he was missing too. Dave must have taken him for a walk.

Not that I didn't love my furry friends, but it was nice to sleep in without Christie walking on my chest and meowing for her morning milk or Dickens letting me know it was time for his visit to the garden. I was washing my face when Dave and Dickens came in the door.

"Ah, Tuppence, you're awake! Are you ready for your coffee and muffin?" Dave had called me Tuppence ever since my costume party when I'd dressed as the petite Agatha Christie character, and he'd come as her partner, Tommy. I hugged him. "You really are spoiling me, and I love it!"

As I sat in the easy chair and sipped coffee, Dickens licked my free hand. "We saw lots of dogs on our walk, no donkeys, but plenty of dogs. And the lady at the coffee shop gave me a biscuit to eat while Dave read the paper." Most days, Dickens and I walked to see Martha and Dylan, the donkeys in the pasture near my cottage, and Christie, his feline sister, often accompanied us in my backpack.

Dave pulled his sweater off. "I'm going to take a quick shower. If we want to walk to Teddy's cottage, we'll need to leave shortly after ten. Are you good with that? And we'll take Dickens, of course."

"Sure. As soon as you're out of the shower, I'll swing into action."

The shops were beginning to open, and the festival-goers were wandering the High Street. As we left the central part of the village, the pedestrian traffic thinned and we found ourselves on a peaceful lane. Here and there, we saw residents sweeping their walkways or watering plants on this sunny morning.

Set back from the street, Teddy's cottage had a gravel drive and a stone wall on the left with a gate leading to what I took to be his garden. Parked in the drive was an ancient dark green Rolls Royce. We approached the front door and knocked.

When no one answered, Dave tried again to no avail. "Should we try around back? Maybe he hasn't heard us," he said.

Dickens barked and ran to the gate in front of the Rolls. "Don't you hear the cat meowing? It's coming from the garden."

I listened for a moment. Dickens was right. Hearing the cat prompted me to suggest that Dave and Dickens try the garden for another door, while I stayed out front in case Teddy was slowly making his way.

Dickens soon returned to tell me the cat was tucked into a corner beneath the shrubs. "He won't come out, Leta."

"Could he be afraid of dogs? Let's see what's going on with him." I followed Dickens into the garden and put my hand out to the tabby cat.

He didn't blink his green eyes, but he nudged my hand and gave a low growl. "Teddy hasn't let me in this morning. Something's not right."

I checked his nametag and saw that, like my animals, he had a literary moniker—Watson. Looking towards the French doors that were cracked open, I assumed Dave had gone inside. *Maybe Teddy was in the back of the cottage and didn't hear us.* It wasn't long before Dave appeared in the doorway—his face ashen.

He came into the garden and pulled me to him before explaining, "Leta, I think . . . I think Teddy's dead."

"Dead?" I whispered. "How can that be? Where is he?"

"He's in bed. Can you come in with me? And I guess we should call 999."

I accompanied him into the kitchen and to the hallway. Turning to the left, I glimpsed a library through the first door to the right. The next door opened into a large bedroom. Teddy was lying in bed, the covers neatly folded midway up his chest. His left arm lay atop his stomach on a book, the right by his side. I didn't think there was any doubt he was dead, but I checked for a pulse anyway.

"I already did that, Leta, but I know you want to be sure. He's cold to the touch, and it's *cold* in here."

I took in the items on the oval bedside table. A slender lamp with a large shade was closest to the bed. Like most of us, I was sure he positioned it nearby so he could easily turn it

17

off when he was ready to go to sleep. Beneath the lamp stood a cordless phone in its cradle and a carafe of water. Beside it was a small glass.

Dave stood with his hand on the mantel, staring into the fireplace. "The fire's gone out."

Funny, the things one notices at times like this. I nodded and pulled out my phone. I didn't call 999. I called Gemma. As I waited for her to answer, Dickens and Watson came into the room. The cat jumped on the bed, meowing plaintively, and Dickens came to my side.

It was the first time I'd heard Gemma answer the phone using her new title, DI Taylor. "Gemma," I stuttered, "I . . . I need you. Dave and I found Teddy Byrd . . . dead . . . in his cottage."

"Did I hear you right? Someone's dead?"

I explained who Teddy was and what we were doing at his home, and I added that it looked as though he'd died in his sleep. We both knew I had no way of knowing for sure. Gemma told me to go back out the way I'd come in and to wait for her, that she and Constable James would be right there. And, of course, she admonished me not to touch anything. As if I would.

I told Dave what Gemma said about not touching anything. "I feel like I should make a pot of tea, but I'm afraid I could be disturbing evidence . . . Surely he died from natural causes. He looks like he fell asleep and didn't wake up, don't you think?"

Dave shook his head. "I don't know, Leta. I know he's in his eighties, but I don't know much more than that. I mean, he needed help getting around, but I don't know about his overall health. I can't believe we found him like this. I feel so helpless. Is this how it feels when you find a dead body?"

I shuddered at the memories. In nearby Stanway, I'd been out for a walk with Dickens when I'd found the body of a friend, and I'd twice been at the scene of accidents where someone died.

"Yes. It doesn't seem to matter how many times I encounter a scene like this. It's awful." I began to shake, and tears streamed down my face. "I'm beginning to feel as though I should never leave my cottage. Here we are attending a literary festival, for goodness' sake, and we find a new friend dead. We barely knew him, but that doesn't make it any easier to take."

I needed to sit down, and I was sure Dave did too, but Gemma had said to go outside. I'd watched too many BBC mysteries where the position of a chair or a robe draped over the foot of a bed helped explain how someone died, so I understood. "Let's go to the garden and sit on the steps until Gemma gets here."

As we walked past the library, I glanced in. It looked well-lived in. Continuing through the kitchen to the garden door, I took note of the clean dishes in the dishrack and the teapot on the counter with the sugar dish beside it. Everything in here looked pristine.

We sat on the top step, and Dave put his arm around me. I leaned in and buried my face in his chest and tried to calm my breathing. "I can't believe this is happening again. Please let it be that Teddy passed away peacefully in his sleep."

Dave kissed the top of my head and murmured, "Shh, Leta. Hopefully, that's what happened. Gemma will be here soon, and she'll figure it out."

Dickens was sniffing around the flower bed. "I'm checking for other pets, but I don't smell any. I'd ask Watson, but he's kind of upset right now."

His comment reminded me that Beatrix had been here last night, and I lifted my head to gaze at Dave. "I wonder what time Beatrix left. Maybe she sensed he was unwell. Did you notice how spic and span the kitchen is? I bet Beatrix washed up after dinner. Gemma will want to speak with her about how she left everything."

Dave looked at me—I wasn't sure if it was it in amazement or consternation. "Is this how it starts? You find a dead body, and your brain goes into overdrive? Do Belle and Wendy react the same way?"

Oh no. Are we going to argue about this again? "Now that you mention it, I'm the only one of us who's ever seen a dead body —well, except maybe Belle when she was a nurse. But that aside, yes, we three can't seem to help ourselves. Whatever the circumstances, our brains buzz with questions. Maybe it's all the mysteries we read or the shows we watch on TV."

Dave's silence set off alarm bells for me. *Is he horrified or is there a chance he's truly trying to understand?* Despite the tragic circumstances, I thought I detected the beginning of a smile when he finally spoke. "Does me calling you Tuppence encourage this behavior?"

He'd been staying at the Olde Mill Inn when I became involved in my first murder investigation and helped to uncover the identity of the killer, but he'd heard about my role in the next two only from a distance. He'd never witnessed me trying to puzzle things out.

"Only a little," I said. "You know, Gemma calls me Tuppence too. I expect she'll invite me to go back inside with her so she can compare her observations to mine. She says I ask good questions—questions that make her see things in a different light.

We've had such a marvelous week except for our argument about just this kind of situation. Does his playful question mean he's not put off by my curiosity? Or will seeing me in action—up close and personal —lead to another argument?

Chapter Three

The previous Saturday

I awoke to a black cat patting my face. "Christie," I whispered, "Are you trying to tell me something?"

In response, she stretched out on my chest, her pink nose nuzzling my chin. For a moment, I smiled as I thought about my plans for the day—brunch with Ellie in Broadway followed by a shopping foray for a new outfit for Friday night. For a moment, that is, until I remembered that today was the second anniversary of my husband's death.

Henry had been a Vietnam veteran. If I still lived in Atlanta, Dickens and I would drive to the Canton Veterans Cemetery to place flowers on the grave. The year before, I purchased an arrangement in the shape of a bicycle to commemorate not only Henry's favorite leisure activity but also the tragic accident that ended his life. *If he had to leave me, I'm glad he died doing something he loved.*

Dickens may not have known what I was thinking, but he sensed my mood. "Smile, Leta. Why so glum?" he barked as he placed his nose on the bed. "Let's go see the donkeys. They always cheer you up."

I scratched his ears and stared into space picturing the red Mercedes convertible that ran Henry off the road on that Saturday bicycle ride. *Enough of that. Time to reflect on the good times.* That thought propelled me from the bed, and we three headed downstairs to the kitchen, Christie leading the way and Dickens bringing up the rear.

Hitting the on button for the coffee, I let Dickens out to the garden and poured Christie a tiny puddle of milk. The thermometer outside the window registering just above 0° Celsius, or a bit over 32° Fahrenheit, this April morning told me Dickens would enjoy staying outside in the crisp morning air. I took my mug of coffee to the sitting room and got the fire going before settling on the couch with a blanket and my tablet. As I perused the newspaper online, I glimpsed Dickens sniffing his way around the garden.

Christie curled up in my lap and stretched one paw beyond the blanket to the pajama top peeking from my fleece robe.

"What do you think of this plan?" I asked. "I shake off my sad thoughts, enjoy my outing with Ellie, and this afternoon, we look through photos of happy times with Henry."

Sassy comments were standard from Christie, but this morning, she was unusually sweet. "That works. Are there plenty of pictures of me in Henry's lap? You know, he had a comfier lap than you. Funny, he used to say 'Christie loves me best,' and I let him believe that. The truth is I loved his lap *best*."

"So, who did you love best, little girl?"

She purred, "I loved you two equally, but that Dave guy is a different matter." At least she'd made me chuckle. Christie tolerated Dave, but Dickens adored him.

"Yes, well, you'll have to adjust. You know Dave flies in Monday and will be here off and on for several weeks." He was arriving from New York City, another reason I needed to shake off sad thoughts of Henry. I hadn't seen Dave since his ten-day visit in late December. We'd met here in the Cotwolds in September when he was researching Arthur Conan Doyle for an article. Discovering that Doyle and other authors had summered in the nearby village of Stanway had led him to book a stay at the Olde Mill Inn, owned by my friends Libby and Gavin.

A phone call from my friend Peter Davies interrupted my reverie. "How's my biking partner this morning? Are you still up for a ride to Stow tomorrow morning?"

"Yes, looking forward to it. Today, I'm dressing up for an outing with Ellie—food plus shopping—and tomorrow will be my day for a good workout. Will we have time for breakfast at Huffkin's?"

We made it a point to visit the popular brunch spot on our rides. When we first began cycling together, it was our turn-around point, but to increase our mileage, we now cycled beyond Stow to the more rural village of Longborough before turning back for our meal.

"Oh yes, not another thing on my schedule tomorrow, unless someone shows up with an emergency repair. So, you're going from a day with the Dowager Countess to a day with the garage mechanic—quite a contrast." Peter owned the only garage in Astonbury, and the villagers relied on him and also directed visitors his way.

"Ha! Can't imagine you dress shopping nor the countess cycling, so I've chosen my friends well." We agreed I'd meet him at his garage for an 8:30 start, and I promised to text when I was on my way.

A quick shower, makeup, and a blow-dry, and I was almost ready for Ellie's arrival. I chose a purple heather sweater dress, black tights, and flats for my ensemble to make it easier to try on clothes. I was adding jewelry when my phone rang.

It was Ellie. "Good morning, dear. I'm leaving and will be there shortly. Is there any chance you can put on a pot of tea so we can chat before we depart?" That seemed an odd request, but I told her it was no problem. Astonbury Manor wasn't far—just up Schoolhouse Lane between my cottage and the High Street—so she'd be here in no time.

The rumble of a truck pulling into my driveway surprised me, and I was even more taken aback when I saw Brian Peters climb out of the cab. *Now, what's he doing here?* I'd been threatening to hire our local landscaper for months but hadn't gotten around to it. When he went to the passenger side, I wondered who was with him. *Curiouser and curiouser*, I thought when I saw Ellie come around the back of the truck. I knew she had something up her sleeve.

"Ellie," I called as I approached the truck, "what are you up to?"

Dickens ran to greet her, and it took her a moment to answer my question. "Oh, just a little something. You admired my copse of goat willows, and I thought it was time you had one for your garden. Brian obliged by picking up a sapling."

I was touched. "What a lovely surprise. You shouldn't have . . . but I'm glad you did. We call them pussy willows in the States, but I'd never seen them growing until I visited your estate. I've seen them in flower arrangements, but I'm not sure where I thought they came from."

Brian tipped his hat, unloaded the tree, and asked where I wanted him to plant it. I knew just the place. There was a bare spot in the center of the garden near the back wall. Maybe there'd been a shrub or tree in the past, but it was empty when I moved in. He and Ellie agreed it would be perfect and give the goat willow room to grow.

As he dug the hole, Ellie motioned me to the bed of the truck and pointed to a canvas-wrapped object. "I've one more surprise. It's heavy, so Brian will move it, but you can unwrap it and take a look."

Tugging at the canvas, I uncovered a 12" x 12" stone in the gold color the Cotswolds were renowned for. Affixed to it was a bronze plaque inscribed "In Memory of Henry Parker." I was speechless.

Ellie gave a sad smile and hugged me. "Two little birdies named Belle and Libby filled me in. My Nigel dying when he was in his nineties isn't the same as you losing Henry in the prime of his life, but I think the pain is similar. Since Henry's grave is in the States, I wanted you to have a small remembrance here to honor his place in your life. Now, what do you say to a cup of tea before Brian places the marker?"

Blinking back the tears brought on by Ellie's thoughtful gift, I thought, how fortunate I was to have made so many good friends here in Astonbury.

My usual partner in crime for serious shopping was Wendy, but Ellie had called last week to ask if I planned to buy a new outfit for the literary festival. She and I had grown close in December when I'd helped with the Astonbury Tree Lighting and assisted with the investigation into a tragic accident. Since then, we'd had lunch several times, and continued to see each other at the monthly book club meetings.

Her asking about a new outfit told me she knew me very well. I didn't shop as often as I had during my banking career, but old habits die hard. Now, instead of suits and dresses, my wardrobe leaned more toward jeans, leggings, long sweaters, and flowing tops—with the requisite selection of dressier ensembles for parties and events like the literary festival. *This should be fun. I've never been shopping with a countess before!*

When Brian knocked on the door to say he was ready to put the marker in place, we followed him outside. Ellie had a good eye. We quickly chose the perfect spot—not too far out from the base of the tree, but far enough that it wouldn't be hidden as the tree grew. I smiled and looked skyward. "See Henry, now you have a place in my garden as well as my heart."

Ellie's gift had succeeded in clearing the clouds from what could have been a difficult day. My heart felt lighter, and I was ready to make the most of an outing with my friend.

Ellie often drove, but she got a kick out of riding in my refurbished London taxi. It was a sunny day, perfect for taking in the views of honey-colored stone cottages and fences. I was getting used to the weather being cooler here in the Cotswolds than it was in Atlanta this time of year. The hedges and trees were showing new growth, and the landscape was dotted with lily of the valley and tulips. At home, the azaleas would be bursting into bloom and perhaps even the dogwoods. In the Cotswolds, the experts, whoever they are, say the best months for garden tours are June, July, and September; but in my book, every season has its charm.

We lunched at The Wickham Brasserie, a restaurant I hadn't visited before. They called themselves a pub, but it was light and airy, unlike many of the pubs I'd been in. As we perused the menu, a tune sprang to mind. "Ellie, have you heard the song 'The Ladies Who Lunch?' Most famously sung by Elaine Stritch?"

Ellie answered immediately. "How could I forget it? Nigel and I heard Pattie Lupone sing it here in London, and I've seen Elaine Stritch do it on the telly. Absolutely fabulous."

I had an image of the record player I'd owned before the advent of CDs. "I first heard it on Barbara Streisand's *Broadway* album and fell in love with it. Whenever I have a leisurely lunch out, it pops into my head." We chatted about favorite show tunes and then got down to business. For an appetizer, we ordered the Duck Liver & Port Parfait—a fancy name for pâté—and then a salad each for the main course. Keeping it light was a must, as I find it difficult to enjoy trying on clothes when I'm stuffed to the gills.

As we wandered down the wide main street of Broadway, I remarked as to how easily I'd fallen into a routine of yoga classes, morning walks, visits to Toby's Tearoom and the Book Nook, and lunches out. "You know how they say retirees fall into two camps—those who are bored and those who are busier than they've ever been? Color me happily busy."

It was in the second shop that I found the perfect outfit, a black long-sleeved jumpsuit. I was glad they were back in style, or maybe they never went out. I had one in my closet from Chico's that I'd had for years, but it had short cap sleeves, not right for April in the Cotswolds.

I could think of several girlfriends who would say "Not another black outfit." Wendy had pointed out that I had an amazing number of black slacks and skirts. What could I say? They were all just slightly different. My favorite colors were black, white, red, purple, and more recently silver grey. The late addition to the list came about because my brunette bob was greying—or silvering, as Wendy called it.

When Ellie found a new scarf, we declared the day a success. She glanced at me and smiled. "Don't you think we need to celebrate? As in a glass of prosecco at the Broadway Hotel on the Green? I do adore the mullioned windows in their bar."

"A woman after my own heart. Dessert before shopping makes me uncomfortable and cocktails cloud my judgment, but afterward? Perfect. And we can make a quick stop by the chocolate shop after that. I think chocolate truffles will make an ideal dessert for Monday evening when Dave is here."

It had been a full day, and after dropping Ellie at the Manor House, I was ready for a nap—another habit I'd incorporated into retired life. My four-legged friends each greeted me in their own way. Dickens barked hello and wanted a walk. Christie wanted food. I took care of Christie and changed into leggings and a comfy sweatshirt, so I'd be warm enough to sit in the garden and admire the new goat willow and marker. "Dickens, let's sit outside for a bit and then nap. We can visit Martha and Dylan before dinner, okay?"

"Yes, yes, yes," he barked. "I need to inspect the new tree."

I invited Christie to come out with us. They both sniffed the freshly dug soil beneath the tree and inspected the memorial stone before going their separate ways—Dickens to snuffle around the wall bordering the garden and Christie to walk along the top of it.

Christie hopped down and came to my chair. "Are we going to look at pictures now? Or do you *have* to take a nap?"

I reached down to stroke her nose. "Pictures later. You slept the whole time I was gone, didn't you?"

Dickens had a ready answer to that question. "You know she did. That's all she does."

"Right!" Christie meowed. "Like you were awake."

Living with these two was like having children. I'd never had any of the two-legged variety, so I wasn't sure. Henry was in his late forties when we married, and after much back and forth, we agreed that having children wasn't in the cards. It wasn't a decision we'd ever regretted.

Christie may have preferred to look at pictures, but she lost no time curling into a ball on my chest when I laid down on the couch. Dickens lay in front of the fire, snoring softly. The sound of the phone woke me, and I groped for it above my head on the end table. I tried not to yawn as I said hello.

"Hi, sweetheart. Is that a sleepy voice I detect?" asked Dave.

"Yes. You caught me in a nap, but I need to get up. I promised Dickens we'd visit Martha and Dylan." Somehow, it didn't seem appropriate to tell Dave what I'd promised Christie, even though I knew he understood my feelings for Henry would always be part of my life.

"Did you and Ellie have a successful shopping trip?"

"Oh yes! I have a new outfit for Friday night, and I found two new places we can try for dinner in Broadway. What have you been up to today?"

"My usual morning routine. A visit to the gym, and a bagel and coffee before coming home to work. I put the finishing touches on my presentation for next week, I think. You know how it goes. I think I'm done and then I have an idea for a better way to say something."

I laughed and agreed. I wrote weekly columns for two small papers in the States, and I found that until the moment I sent them off to my editors, I couldn't keep from tweaking my words. "Have you finished reading *The Sherlockian*?"

"Not quite. I plan to do that on the plane. I'm enjoying its focus on Arthur Conan Doyle's missing diary, and I'm eager to see how it turns out."

"I knew you'd like it, and hearing what your friend Gilbert Ward has to say about it will be a treat. Good job thinking to invite him as the speaker for our Thursday night meeting."

"I was glad to do it. He's quite a character and should have plenty of anecdotes to share." Dave had met Gilbert last year while working on an Arthur Conan Doyle article for the *Strand Magazine*, and they'd stayed in touch as Dave's idea for a book took shape.

My brain had shifted gears to plans for Dave's visit. "I'll cook dinner at home Monday night, since you're sure to be jet-lagged. Any special requests?"

"You know whatever you choose will be fine. A few quiet days with you are all I need to get the week off to a good start. Will we get to see the gang later in the week or only Thursday at the Book Nook for the book club meeting?"

Dickens had been studying me as I talked. "Can we go to the pub and see Peter and Gavin?"

"Your biggest admirer just barked that we should have lunch at the pub and see Peter, maybe Gavin, and a few of the others too. We sometimes meet up on Wednesdays. That means you'll see at least some folks before Thursday night, plus they're all planning to be at your talk Friday. Maybe we'll lay low Monday and Tuesday and begin socializing midweek."

"You know as long as I'm with you, I'll enjoy myself. Hold on. Just got a text about another article, so I've got to run. I love you, Leta Parker, and I can't wait to see you."

I sat and smiled until Christie nudged my hand. "Hey, aren't you forgetting something? Enough with Dave. What about pictures?"

Dickens barked, "No. A walk first."

"We'll walk first before it gets pitch dark, and we'll take you too, Christie." It appeared she agreed with that plan because she ran to the backpack I kept in the mudroom. A backpack she could ride in had been a big hit with my girl. Dickens and I didn't take her every time we walked, especially in the colder months, but it was warmer today.

I laid out the backpack, and Christie crawled in and turned around to poke her head out. With a leash for Dickens, carrots for the donkeys, and lightweight gloves and a canvas cloche for myself, I was ready. It was true that a hat kept the warmth in, plus I liked hats. Perhaps *liked* wasn't a strong enough word. I wore them every chance I got.

At a leisurely pace, we reached the pasture in twenty minutes. Martha and Dylan could be counted on to come running when they saw us, eager for their carrots. Dickens barked, Christie meowed, and I rubbed donkey noses.

We picked up the pace going home. I had things to do, but only after our trip down memory lane. In my office, I pulled two photo albums from the bookshelf. We'd start with these, from the early days of my twenty-year marriage to Henry, and then move to the computer where the bulk of our photos were stored. Funny how we'd shifted from albums of sticky pages to Shutterfly albums created online to photos stored on the computer, nothing physical to hold—no pages to flip.

Goodness. Was I ever really that young? With no silver in my hair? Except for that change, I tried to tell myself I looked much the same. All those years of bicycling with Henry coupled with yoga and working out at the gym had kept me relatively fit. I loved to eat and enjoyed my wine, so exercise was a necessity if I didn't want to have the well-padded hips and thunder thighs we Greek girls tended to develop in midlife.

Perched in my lap with her paws on the desk, Christie was quiet through the first book of photos, but when I moved to book two, she piped up. "Enough already. Where am I? Who are these other cats? And who is that giant dog?"

"Little girl, this was before your time. Baggins and Moocher are in kitty heaven now." Henry had named both cats, one for the character in *The Hobbit* and the other for a song—"Minnie the Moocher."

Dickens craned his head up and barked. "But the dog. Who's the dog? He looks like Basil at Astonbury Manor."

"This is Banjo, the Pyr we had before you. He's the reason I chose you, Dickens. He had the same personality you have, easy-going and happy-go-lucky—unlike someone else I could name."

That got a screech from Christie. "I heard that, and I know you're talking about me! I have opinions, and there's nothing wrong with that."

"Uh-huh," I said. "What does being snippy and demanding have to do with opinions?"

She moved from my lap to the desktop, turned around, and stuck her nose in my face. "I am direct and assertive. Why should I make you guess what I think? I bet you didn't have a successful career because you were mealy-mouthed, Leta Petkas Parker!"

My feisty cat had me there. Being assertive wasn't a trait I came by naturally, and she had no idea how hard I worked to develop it. Fortunately, I had several outstanding bosses who pushed me along.

"You know, Christie, Henry used to accuse me of being 'short' with him, so maybe we're similar in that regard. Of course, I told him that since I was only 5' 2", I came by that tendency naturally."

Dickens cocked his head. "You can't help being short, Leta, can you? Like I can't help being on the small side?"

Dickens's take on the word made me chuckle. His interpretations never failed to make me think how difficult it must be for non-English speakers to make sense of what we Americans said.

Moving Christie out of the way, I worked my way through photos on the computer. Lots of vacation pics, plenty of them taken on cycling trips in France and Greece. *Will I ever have a partner to do that with again?* Dave wasn't a cyclist, though he was fit enough. Oh well. Time would tell.

I marveled at how Henry hadn't seemed to change through the years, other than his hair turning grey. *His was a life well-lived, and I was fortunate to live part of it with him.*

With that thought, I shifted to checking emails. My sisters Sophia and Anna, plus my friend Bev, had written to say they were thinking of me, knowing what day it was. Both Anna and Bev had sent pictures of their pets to cheer me up. Crunch and Munch, Anna's cats, were snoozing in a large flower pot in her sunroom, one on either side of the trunk of the ficus tree. Bev shared a photo of her latest foster dog, a lab mix named Jumpin' Jack, and explained he was aptly named.

"Christie," I exclaimed when I opened an email from the Jacquie Lawson ecard site. "Belle, Wendy, and Tigger sent a card with cats in it." It was an animated card with cats delivering flowers, sent to let me know they were thinking of me. "Do you think Tigger picked it out?"

"Don't be silly, Leta. Tigger may be a handsome cat, but he's not that bright."

Yup. She's opinionated. "You've only seen pictures of Tigger on my phone, so how do you know whether he's smart or not?"

No answer was forthcoming. Finished with my email, I turned my attention to straightening, dusting, and vacuuming in preparation for Dave's arrival in two days. Before I knew it, Monday would be here—Dave would be here.

In my head, I suddenly heard Louis Armstrong singing "What a Wonderful World," and I smiled. *A wonderful life in a wonderful world. What a lucky gal I am.*

Chapter Four

Does everyone sleep fitfully the night before a big event? I can't be the only one. All through Sunday night and the wee hours of Monday, I rolled over to look at the alarm clock. It wasn't that I needed to be up early or was in any danger of missing the buzzing of my alarm. Dave wouldn't arrive at the Moreton-in-Marsh train station until noon at the earliest, and he'd promised to call when he boarded the train at Heathrow. I grinned. *I'm excited. That's all.*

And with good reason. I hadn't seen Dave since early January. Three long months with nothing but phone calls and emails, and I'd no one to blame but myself. I had an open invitation to visit him in New York City but kept making excuses.

After lengthy discussions with Wendy and my Atlanta friend Bev, I figured out I was afraid things had moved too quickly over Thanksgiving and Christmas. I was afraid the holiday season had artificially amplified our feelings, like the sparkling lights on a tree or a pretty package waiting to be unwrapped—afraid the romance was too good to be true.

When did I turn into such a wimp? I thought. Finally, I

decided it was Henry's fault. I'd given up hope of finding true love, hadn't even dated for over two years before I met my husband. And, bam, I was head over heels. I wasn't convinced lightning could strike twice, nor was I sure I was ready for it.

Looking back, I could see I'd buried my feelings so I didn't have to acknowledge them. By the time I dug deep enough to uncover them, two months had passed. The odd thing was Dave understood what was going on long before I did. He didn't have any doubts about the strength of our feelings for each other. When I used the dreaded words, "We need to talk," it turned out he was relieved—not irritated or anxious.

"Life is too short," I said. "I may have moved to the Cotswolds on a whim, but deep down, I'm not a *carpe diem* kind of girl. I've worried myself sick over our relationship, and it isn't fair to you that I haven't shared my concerns."

A soft chuckle came across the line before he spoke. "And, what are your concerns, Leta?"

I drew a deep breath and launched into my lightning strikes twice analogy. "I've realized this isn't a fling for me."

"And you think maybe it is for me?" His tone was calm but I sensed a hint of surprise, perhaps worry.

"I don't know what I think. Maybe I'm afraid of being hurt. I . . . I . . . oh hell, I love you!"

He made me wait for it. "You know, if we were having this conversation in person, I'd gather you up in my arms, maybe even lift you off your feet and kiss you." He paused. "But since I'm not there, I'll just say . . . I love you too, Leta Parker."

And that was that. He hadn't let up teasing me about my unromantic declaration of love, and I'd been signing my emails to him with "O-H, I love you!" ever since.

As I stretched and rolled out of bed, I realized how stiff my legs were after Sunday's cycling trip with Peter. It was the

longest ride I'd taken since getting up the gumption to climb
back on my bicycle after Henry's accident, and I was proud of
my accomplishment.

"Leta, can't you move any faster?" meowed Christie as she
flew past me on the stairs. "I need my milk." She was such a
demanding little thing. Dickens, on the other hand, pranced
by the door but didn't chastise me. I let him out and turned to
Christie.

"Here you go. Now, let me start the coffee." I wondered
whether I had time to squeeze in a yoga class. That would
loosen up my achy muscles. *Let's see. If I shower before the 9 am
class, I can stop for tea at Toby's Tearoom afterward and still have time
to spare.*

I'd left the door cracked open for Dickens, and he ran in
and checked Christie's dish before barking his question. "Am I
going with you to get Dave? I like Dave."

Christie stopped licking her paws long enough to
complain. "Pfftt. Is it going to be this way the whole time he's
here? He's nothing special, you know."

Dickens nudged her. "You sure thought his lap was special
when he was here before." And so it went, the ongoing
debate between my furry friends as to Dave's merits or lack
thereof.

"Yes, Dickens," I said, "you're riding with me to the train
station. Christie, you can stay here and sulk."

I ate an apple before taking a quick shower. Yoga class
didn't require makeup, but on the off chance I wound up
running late, I wanted to be prepared to dash home, pick up
Dickens, and head to the train station. By 8:45, I was ready to
attack the day.

Rhiannon was setting out bolsters and blocks when I
walked in the door, and Wendy was already seated cross-legged

on her mat. My retired English teacher friend greeted me. "Today's the big day. Are you ready?"

"Yup. Everything's done except for making the pastitsio. I decided on that and a Greek salad for dinner. That's all easily thrown together later this afternoon while Dave is resting. He's bound to be tired after his trip."

"Have you asked him about dinner out with me and Brian Tuesday or Wednesday night? I know Brian would like to see him. If that doesn't work out, we can do it after Dave gets back from Scotland." He planned to spend three to four days at the University of Edinburgh Library researching J.M. Barrie and several other authors for the book he was working on. Most documents were scanned and available online, but when he could, he preferred to conduct his research in person.

"Not yet, but I'll check with him. Maybe we can try one of the restaurants I found in Broadway when I was there with Ellie. And you? Are you ready for your trip to Cornwall?"

"Yes! I'm so excited. I've been wanting to climb to Tintagel Castle, and I'm hoping the weather will cooperate. I haven't been in years, and I understand there's so much more to see now. The experts can debate whether King Arthur existed or not. I choose to believe he did. Who can resist believing in Camelot?"

Wendy and I were of the same mind when it came to King Arthur. We'd read *The Once and Future King*, *The Mists of Avalon*, *Morte D'Arthur*, and more, and seen most of the movies. We agreed one of those books needed to be a book club selection soon.

Several other students arrived, and Rhiannon shushed us and began class. Today's session focused on standing poses, and my tired legs cramped up a few times, but the stretches at the end took care of that. People who think yoga is easy have no idea. I was more than ready for a muffin and a cup of coffee by then. Rhiannon often accompanied me and Wendy to Toby's, but today she had a private session immediately after our class.

As we walked up the High Street, I showed Wendy the text that had come in from Dave saying he'd caught the train at 9:30. Toby greeted us with a wave, and we found a table near the window. Wendy and I split a lemon muffin. Something else we two had in common besides our love of shopping and books was that we were vigilant about what we ate.

Wendy stretched her legs out and sighed. "Do you think we'll ever get to the point where we eat what we want and stop worrying about getting plump?"

I almost choked. "Are you a mind reader? I was thinking much the same thing. Every year, it's a bigger struggle to lose my winter weight. As short as we both are, a few pounds this year, another few the next, and we'd be little butterballs in no time. Thank goodness we walk and take yoga. And thank goodness for your brother Peter getting me out on my bicycle."

Wendy frowned. "I jokingly said something to Brian about having to skip dessert, and he said I could try skipping the wine. I was flabbergasted."

Uh-oh. This is tricky territory. "And what did you say to that suggestion?"

"I sat up tall—well, as tall as I can—and shot back, 'If you think I drink too much, please just say so.' That set him back on his heels. He hemmed and hawed and said that wasn't what he meant. Still, I was none too happy about his comment."

I found Brian Burton to be overbearing and had to work darned hard not to let on to Wendy that I didn't much care for him. Peter had expressed similar misgivings to me, but we were both smart enough not to say any of that to Wendy. She had to figure it out for herself . . . or not.

DCI Burton had transferred to the Gloucestershire Police force in December and was Gemma's new boss. Wendy, Belle, and I met him during a murder investigation, and he and I had gotten off to a rocky start when he chewed me out for interfering. Though he subsequently apologized, his arrogance and his display of temper made me wary.

Wendy had hit it off right away with the man she described as a silver fox, and I had to admit he was good looking. Until now, I hadn't heard any hint of discord in their relationship. I tried to lighten the mood. "Perhaps a woman with a mind of her own is a new experience for him. Don't you need a strong, handsome man to take care of you?" I paused before I added, "Little lady?"

Wendy spluttered and began to cough. "Good thing you're my best friend. Them's fighting words!" I was always taken aback when she came out with sayings like that and had to remind myself that she'd been born in Astonbury but had lived in North Carolina most of her adult life.

"Seriously, though, that's not the first time he's been critical of something I did or said. I nip it in the bud every time, but if he doesn't take the hint soon, a heart to heart will be next. I'm not even sure he realizes he does it."

"Poor man. Is he going to hear those dreaded words, 'We need to talk?'" I doubted Brian would enjoy his *need to talk* discussion as much as Dave had enjoyed his.

We were both giggling by now, and I realized I'd almost lost track of the time. "Listen, I've got to pick up Dickens before I go to Moreton-in-Marsh, so I'd best run. I'll let you know about dinner this week, okay?"

Dickens was inspecting the grassy area bordering the parking lot at the train station when I heard Dave call my name. "Look, Dickens. He's here."

He barked a greeting. "Dave, here we come." I pulled up hard on the leash to remind my boy who was in charge. He wasn't as large or as strong as full-size Pyr, but it was hard to keep his forty pounds from jerking me off balance.

Dave had a computer bag over his shoulder and a duffel bag in each hand, but he dropped the duffels and held his arms wide as I approached. "You're a sight for sore eyes, you and Dickens both."

Moving into his embrace, I put my lips to his ear and whispered, "Oh hell, I love you."

He looked down at me and laughed.

Dickens, meanwhile, pranced around doing his best to tangle us in his leash. "Dickens, settle down. Let Dave breathe."

At the car, I secured Dickens's harness and Dave tossed his bags in the trunk before pulling me into another hug. "I love you, Leta Parker. I know, I know, now you're worried it's all about absence making the heart grow fonder. What if it does? I still love you!"

What could I do but grin? "How do you feel about lunch at The Hive in Stow-on-the-Wold? You must be starving."

"Isn't that the place where we shared the charcuterie board last time? That plus a pint will make a new man of me."

"Or one ready for a nap! Look at Dickens. He's already drooling at the thought of getting a handout from you." I glanced in the back seat. Dickens looked beyond excited. Dave plus a restaurant were a perfect combination.

Though I regularly updated him about Astonbury happenings and my activities with my friends, Dave inquired about everyone as we enjoyed our lunch. He'd hit it off especially well with Peter, perhaps because they were both single. Neither of them had ever been married, though unlike Peter, Dave had at least been in a long-term relationship once. Peter briefly had an Astonbury girlfriend, but it hadn't ended well.

I asked about an evening with Wendy and her DCI, as I thought of Brian Burton. "I'd like for us to spend more time in Broadway this trip, maybe climb Broadway Tower too. It's filled with World War Two history, and it has a view to die for. If we have dinner with Wendy and Brian at one of the restaurants, we can go early and explore the village."

"Whatever you want to do is fine by me, Leta. I'm all yours until the festival. I want to take full advantage of the speakers Saturday and Sunday after I've given my presentation on Friday. Naturally, I'm looking forward to hearing Gilbert's take on *The Sherlockian* Thursday at the Book Nook and then his talk at the festival about the various Sherlock societies and collections. Have you read much Graham Greene? He lived in Chipping Camden briefly, and one of his biographers is speaking Sunday. I'd love to squeeze that in too."

I thought for a moment. "I'm pretty sure one of his novels was required reading when I was an undergraduate, but I can't recall what it was. I saw some of the movies made from his books like *The Third Man* with Orson Welles and *The Quiet American*. I wonder if the talk will cover what brought him to Chipping Camden. Could be interesting."

Probably because I was ignoring him nudging my leg, Dickens moved to Dave. It had been at least five minutes since Dave had offered him a strip of meat. "See, Leta," he said, "what's not to like about Dave? Christie's crazy."

Dave chuckled. "He just said I was a great guy, right? He's such a pushover."

"Right! And I can't wait to see how long it takes Christie to choose your lap over mine. You look like you're having a sinking spell. Are you ready to head to my cottage so you can put your feet up, maybe take a nap?"

He thought that was a good plan. Apparently, Dickens did too, because both of them were sound asleep before I pulled out of the parking lot. Neither one stirred until I turned off the ignition in the driveway. We left Dickens in the garden, and Dave carried his bags upstairs, saying he was going to take a quick shower and be right down. As I put the kettle on the stovetop for tea and lit the fire in the sitting room, I wondered where Christie was.

Dickens came to the door and barked. I'd forgotten he was outside. "Sorry, boy. Did we forget you?"

"I think you did. Where's Dave? Where's Christie? Can I have a snack?"

"One thing at a time. Dave should be down soon, and Christie hasn't put in an appearance yet. As for a snack, you know better. Two meals a day, and anything you can sneak from your sister's dish. That's all you get—that and the hand-outs you get from all my friends."

He seemed torn between following me to the sitting room with my cup of tea and going in search of Dave. When I sat down on the couch, I realized I was tuckered out. It had been a busy morning, and I'd slept fitfully the night before. *A nap wouldn't be half bad.* I was just about asleep when Christie leaped into my lap.

"And where have you been, Miss Priss?" I asked her. "Beneath my bed, in a basket, on Dickens's dog bed in the office? Which spot have you been in?"

"Never you mind. How about some food?" *Why is it my animals are always starving?*

I moved her out of my lap and went to the kitchen to open a new can of food for the princess. Per our routine, I put a small dab in her dish. She took a few bites, sat back, and looked at me. I moved the food into the center of the dish, and she took another taste. Another look, another stir, and another bite. Today, I was quick enough on the uptake that she didn't have to utter indignant demands.

Realizing it was only me and Christie in the kitchen, I assumed Dickens had wandered upstairs to see Dave. *Either Dave's checking his emails or he's fallen asleep,* I thought. I climbed the stairs and found Dickens lying in front of my nightstand and Dave sound asleep on the bed. He didn't stir when I brushed his hair off his forehead. *I could make the pastitsio or I could take a nap.* It was an easy decision. I lay down beside Dave and snuggled against him, pulling a fleece throw over the both of us before draping my arm over his back. I smiled when his hand found mine.

When I awoke thirty minutes later, he hadn't stirred. I quietly rolled over and got out of bed. Downstairs, I started the pastitsio, sauteeing onions and garlic and browning the ground beef before mixing in the cinnamon. After adding the tomato sauce, I let the ingredients simmer while I grated the romano cheese and boiled the pasta. Next, I prepared the bechamel sauce. When everything was ready, I layered it all in the casserole dish. All I had to do was pop it in the oven an hour before we were ready to eat.

The aroma of the meat sauce must have wafted upstairs, because a yawning man soon appeared in the kitchen with a dog at his heels. "You shouldn't have let me sleep that long. I'll never get to sleep tonight."

"Maybe a walk after dinner will help, or we could go now. The sun won't set until around 8:15, and Martha and Dylan will be happy to see us any time."

Dickens ran to the door. "Now. I want to go now."

Dave stretched his arms overhead. "Hmmm. I think Dickens is ready to go. Let me grab my jacket."

I covered the casserole in foil before going to the mudroom—or boot room, as the Brits call it—for my coat and a hat. The temperature had only reached the fifties today and was already dropping, though sometimes in April, it could be warmer. *Now, which hat will it be?* I chose the new black cloche I'd gotten to replace the one I'd lost in the River Elfe in December.

Christie appeared in the mudroom as I was grabbing Dickens's leash. "I want to go. And I want to ride on Dave's back."

Now, that surprised me. I often put Christie in my backpack for our walks, but her wanting to ride with Dave was a first. "My, my. What brought that on?"

"Think about it, Leta. He's taller than you and his back is broader. I bet I'll be able to see more and have a comfier ride." Whatever the reason, this was a move in the right direction. Maybe she liked Dave better than she let on. I placed her backpack on the floor so she could crawl in and position herself.

When Dave walked in, I explained that Christie had requested he be the official cat carrier. Like everyone else, he thought I was joking whenever I said 'Christie or Dickens said.' I helped him with the backpack, attached Dickens's leash, grabbed some carrots, and we were off.

We agreed it felt good to take a brisk walk. Martha and Dylan trotted to the fence when they saw us coming. It was hard to tell who had trained whom, but we had our routine down pat. Dickens stood on his hind legs and the donkeys leaned their heads down in greeting.

I laughed as Christie meowed and placed her front paws on Dave's shoulders. "Me, me. Come see me."

"Dave, remember how I turn my back to the donkeys so Christie can get closer?"

"Sure, let me try that." I grabbed my phone to get a picture. He turned and leaned in, and I snapped a shot of Christie touching a donkey nose.

"Look," I said as I showed him the shot. "This will be perfect to use in a "Parker's Pen" column about the donkeys. I haven't written about them in a while, and my readers seem to love hearing about them."

I contemplated going the additional mile to the Olde Mill Inn to see Gavin and Libby, but a four-mile round trip seemed too much after a busy day. I wrapped my arm around Dave's. "What do you say to a roaring fire and a glass of red wine?"

"Perfect. Can I help with dinner after I get the fire going?"

"You can open the wine, but that's all that needs doing. I'll pop the pastitsio in the oven and prepare the salad right before I take it out. I picked up chocolate truffles in Broadway, so dessert will be easy. We'll have a relaxing evening."

"Sounds great. And I forgot I have something for you. I'll be right back to open the wine." I wondered what it could be as he moved toward the staircase.

He handed me a brown paper bag when he returned. "This is a practical gift, so no fancy wrapping paper."

"Practical? What on earth . . . canisters, key chains. What are these?"

Dave explained that since pepper spray wasn't legal in the UK, he'd researched personal protection devices. "Seeing as how you're prone to putting yourself in dangerous situations, I did a bit of research and found this stuff. The spray will at least blind someone temporarily, though it isn't pepper spray, and it will mark them with one of your favorite colors—purple. It stays visible for forty-eight hours, so there's a chance the police can find them."

"And you got me two? And what are these other things?"

"I got two sprays, thinking you could put one on your keychain or in a pocket when you walk and another in the car. The others are alarms. Stand back and I'll show you." He pressed a button and the tiny gizmo emitted an ear-piercing sound, sending Dickens and Christie running from the room. "I got you five of these."

"Five?"

"I wasn't taking any chances. You can hook them to the zippers on your raincoat, your parka, your windbreaker, your purse, wherever. Plus put one on your keychain and in your bicycle bag. If you want more, I'll go online and order them while I'm here."

I was flabbergasted and touched. "You put a lot of thought into this. Thank you." I wrapped my arms around him and hugged him tight. He kissed the top of my head and murmured something about how precious I was to him.

Funny how a practical gift can sometimes say "I love you" more powerfully than chocolates or a bouquet. I smiled as I handed him the corkscrew and pointed to the glass-fronted cabinet holding the wine glasses.

I rang Wendy as he poured. "What do you say to Tuesday in Broadway for dinner? Depending on how our morning goes, Dave and I may climb the Tower and explore the village before we meet you and Brian."

"Oh! I'm so glad it's worked out. Let's do the Broadway Hotel, say seven? I'll make reservations."

That decided, I accepted the glass of wine Dave handed me, and we clinked a quiet toast. Earlier, I'd loaded the CD player with George Winston CDs, and his piano music played softly in the background. I lit the candles on the mantel and smiled. The setting for a quiet, romantic evening was complete. When Dave patted the cushion next to him and stretched his arm across the top of the couch, I settled into his embrace. *Did Tommy and Tuppence ever have it this good?*

Chapter Five

U p before Dave, I padded downstairs and followed my routine with Christie's milk and Dickens's morning visit to the garden. I took my cup of coffee and my tablet to the sitting room and caught up on emails and games of Words with Friends. My sister Anna was trouncing me despite my having played a 50-point word the day before. She'd also sent an email asking how the reunion with Dave had gone.

I wrote a brief response and copied my sister Sophia and my friend Bev, letting them know all was well—more than well. *Expect limited correspondence from me*, I typed, *until Dave leaves for Edinburgh next week*. He and I had discussed my joining him but decided it would be better for us to visit together another time when he wouldn't be tucked away studying the J.M. Barrie collection at the university. That and the abundance of Arthur Conan Doyle material would keep him too busy to enjoy the city with me.

After that, I poured a second cup of coffee and started breakfast. I'd learned during Dave's December visit that the best way to alleviate his jet lag was for me to cook for him. Just as the aroma of pastitsio had brought him downstairs the day before, the smell of bacon frying did the trick this morning. Once again, a yawning man appeared in my kitchen. I hadn't realized that both Christie and Dickens had returned upstairs until they appeared behind him. *So much for Christie not liking Dave.*

"Bacon! You do know the way to a man's heart."

Not wanting to be left out, Dickens chimed in. "Me too. Do I get bacon?"

I laughed at both of them. "I think Dickens agrees with you. Now, how'd you sleep?"

"Amazingly well given my jet lag. Breakfast and a walk may get me completely on track." He bent to touch his toes. "Tell me more about climbing the Broadway Tower. Knowing you, you've got the day's agenda all planned."

He knew me too well. I liked to have a plan, but Broadway was close enough we could return another day to see any sights we missed. "Not exactly. We have options. I think climbing the Tower and doing a bit of the Cotswold Way while we're there could be a good replacement for your daily gym routine. It could be we choose to come back by here before dinner instead of exploring the village. We can play it by ear."

His head cocked, Dickens was listening attentively. "The Cotswold Way? You're taking me, right?"

Reaching down to scratch Dickens's ears, Dave asked, "Does he want to go out?"

Christie meowed the answer. "Silly man, he wants to go on your adventure."

By now I was grinning. "No. He heard Cotswold Way and wants to go. We've been on parts of the footpath, and the ramblers with their dogs plus the sheep here and there—let's just say it's heaven for him."

"Sound like a plan is taking shape. Breakfast, the Tower, a walk on the trail, and then we'll see about lunch. And I like the idea of coming back by here before dinner."

The bacon, scrambled eggs, and cheese grits I served got us off to a good start. I'd introduced Dave to grits on his last visit, and he was hooked. Two showers, comfy clothes and shoes, and we were on our way. If we were lucky, the day would remain clear and sunny so Dave would have the best views from the top of the Tower.

As I drove, I gave him the short version of the history of Broadway Tower. "Each level of the tower has plaques and displays with lots of detail, but here's some of what I can recall. It was built as a folly in 1798, I think it was, for the Earl of Coventry." I chuckled. "That seems such a uniquely British thing to me. I wonder how many follies dot the landscape across the country. Could make for an entertaining research project, but I digress."

"But you *never* digress! I see your musings as a way to keep your audience on its toes."

"Ha! Wendy says most of my digressions stem from my word nerd tendencies. I hear a word, my brain wanders off, and sometimes, I need help finding my way back. Anyway, to continue the tale, the story goes that the Countess of Coventry wanted to know if their estate was visible from some other estate in Worcestershire. Can you imagine that as a reason to build what's known as the Highest Little Castle in the Cotswolds?"

"Seems like a centuries-old example of 'more money than sense,' if you ask me."

"I'd have to agree, though I get a kick out of the turrets, the balconies, and the gargoyles. I wonder whether the Countess enjoyed it as much as today's visitors do. One of the bits of history I find most intriguing is that a baronet acquired the Tower in the 1800s and installed a printing press and a collection of manuscripts and printed books—over sixty thousand—if you can believe it. I can't recall his name."

Dave turned to me. "Wouldn't it be fascinating to know what he collected? I mean, was it something in particular or was he simply interested in preserving a variety of documents? Let's be sure to find out his name while we're there so I can look him up."

"You know, ever since I read *The Bookman's Tale* for Beatrix's book club last year, I've been intrigued by what makes someone become a collector. The book was fiction, but the author collected copies of *Alice in Wonderland*. I learned some folks are like him, chasing rare copies of a single work. Others collect anything by a given author, and some collect anything rare."

Dave mused aloud. "And lo and behold, a rare book was discovered in the tiny village of Astonbury. Funny how things turn out, isn't it? And now, look at me. I'll never be a collector of letters or books. I see myself as a collector of facts and anecdotes that can be turned into an engaging tale—an article or, hopefully before long, a book. That those tales of late have focused on J.M. Barrie has been an interesting turn of events for me."

I tilted my head and cut my eyes his way. "And aren't I lucky that your passion for collecting keeps bringing you this way?"

Leaning over to give me a peck on the cheek, Dave replied, "Don't fool yourself. It's my passion for Dickens . . . and his owner."

I slugged him in the chest. "Ha! You silver-tongued devil. Wait 'til I tell Christie it's not her you're interested in."

Hearing Dave's comment and mine, Dickens barked. "Don't know why he'd want to see the silly cat. If he only knew the way she talks about him, he wouldn't have anything to do with her." I caught his eye in the rearview mirror and nodded in agreement.

As we pulled into the parking lot, I told Dave he'd have to learn the rest of the story on the tour. The wind was picking up as we approached the Tower, and I was glad I'd grabbed my fleece headband. It would be cold up top.

Stopping on each level to read the history, I jotted down notes as Dave studied the displays. *This is another good topic for a column, maybe two.* I was hard-pressed to drag Dave away from the level that detailed the Tower's part in the two World Wars. It was put to use during both as a lookout tower for the Royal Observers Corp, and, in 1943, a British bomber had crashed into Beacon Hill, less than a quarter-mile from the Tower.

At the top, we gazed in awe at the green countryside. With the sun shining, it was a better view than I'd had on any of my previous visits. I was pretty sure Dickens thought it was his best visit ever because the wind was blowing so hard. He held his nose up, taking in the scents coming his way, and barked in delight.

Dave made a great windscreen as I stood with my back against him. He leaned down and said, "Thanks for this, Leta. It's right up my alley."

I suggested on the way down that we lunch at Morris & Brown, the shop and café located in a converted stone barn in the park, before setting out to walk the Cotswold Way. Over lunch, Dave looked up the name of the collector who'd housed his books in the tower—Sir Thomas Phillips—and it was difficult to pull him away from his phone. When I finally got his attention, we discussed how far to walk on the footpath and decided seven miles to Broadway was too much. Snowshill was said to be halfway, so we could stop there for a coffee and return to the car.

Dickens served as our tour guide along the way. "Red deer! Look at the red deer! Sheep, Leta, sheep. I want to meet that little brown dog."

Dave enjoyed Dickens's interactions with the dogs along the way. "He's a very sociable dog. Some of these others are kind of standoffish, but not Dickens."

"What is it they say about people like him? He never meets a stranger. That's my boy. He gives everyone—dogs, cats, and people—the benefit of the doubt. You'd have to *really* rub him the wrong way for him to dislike you. Okay, here's an example of my wandering brain. It occurs to me that I'm the same way. But boy, when you *do* rub me the wrong way, there's often no coming back from it."

"Thanks for the warning! Why is that, do you think?"

I knew why but had to think how to phrase it. "I tend to believe the best about people and to take them at their word. Too many times, that's come back to bite me. My sister Anna says I've always been naïve and too trusting, and she's probably right. I was certainly that way about a few of the men I dated before I married."

Dave gave me a sideways glance. "On the other hand . . . you went to the other extreme about me and saw me as a villain, if only briefly."

I blushed. Thinking about how badly I'd misjudged him never failed to embarrass me, and Dave liked to tease me about it. "As they say on TV, I formed an opinion based on circumstantial evidence. My bad." That earned me a grin.

Dave motioned to a bench on the side of the footpath, and we sat with Dickens at our feet. "On a serious note, Leta, would you agree your trusting nature has gotten you in trouble in these investigations you've been involved in? You and the Little Old Ladies' Detective Agency?"

Hmm. That's a good question, but where *is he going with this?* "Well, yes and no. Yes, I was guilty of ignoring my misgivings in the first two cases. This last time, though, I was right to give the benefit of the doubt to the person who was arrested. And I was right about who the murderer was, only I was almost too late."

Taking my hands in his, Dave sighed. "Leta, I worry about you. I worry that you take too many chances, too many risks. You joke about the Little Old Ladies, but I worry that one of you—most likely you—is going to get seriously hurt. I mean, you've *already* been seriously hurt—in my opinion—and I don't think you can disagree with that."

I was speechless.

"Maybe it's not my place, maybe you'll think I'm out of line, but may I ask that you think twice before getting involved again in something like a murder case? Hopefully, it's a moot point. Hopefully, there'll be nothing to tempt you, but when I think about losing you . . . it's . . . it's too much to bear."

Tears came to my eyes as different emotions washed over me. I was indignant at the suggestion my poor judgment had gotten me in trouble, and I had to bite my tongue to keep from defending myself. But then his next sentence, his worry about losing me . . . that took my breath away.

He was right that I'd been hurt. I'd been taken to the

emergency room in October and threatened with a return trip in December.

He used his thumb to brush the tears from my face. "Why are you crying? Have I hurt your feelings? Are you angry with me?"

Why am I crying? How can I explain it? "This will sound corny, but I'm overwhelmed by how much you care about me. I know you love me. I don't *doubt* you love me, but I had no idea how much you worried about me. This kind of takes things to a whole new level."

"That tells me I haven't done a good enough job of getting through to you, of explaining how much you mean to me. Dang it! That's the problem with being on different continents."

I smiled through the tears. "Perhaps deep down, I already knew. Perhaps I was scared to believe it in case I was wrong. I mean, the whole 'I love you' thing is pretty recent."

"Uh-huh, but what about the other part, what about you placing yourself in harm's way?"

"Okay, you'll have to bear with me. This isn't going to be particularly articulate because you're making me think, and I'm feeling my way. Why have I gotten involved, not once, but three times? I think it may be that I like to help, to feel needed, and these situations allow me to use the tools in my tool chest—my attention to detail and my listening skills. Maybe retiring early left a hole in my life, and I've found something more fulfilling than helping with the Fall Fête or filling voile bags for the Astonbury Tree Trimming. I'm not sure.

"Yes, calling ourselves the Little Old Ladies' Detective Agency was a bit of a joke, but I think we're darned good at ferreting out information. And I sincerely hope there's no need for us going forward, but . . . but if there is, I want to feel free to step in." I could feel my face growing hot. "Why do I feel as though you're expecting me to ask permission?"

Dave drew back and stood up. "That's not what I said at all. I just want you to consider how dangerous your pastime has turned out to be."

I sprung from the bench. "Pastime? Pastime? Like a hobby?"

He blew out his breath and walked a few paces. When he returned, he said, "Look, if you rode motorcycles and had accident after accident, I'd say the same thing. If you were a runner and insisted on running country roads after dark, I'd worry every time you went out. And, no I don't expect you to ask permission. I wouldn't ask you to give up something that means so much to you, but until just now, did you even know how important it was to you? I sure didn't."

I plopped down and rummaged in my pocket for a tissue. I blew my nose and looked up at him as he waited for an answer. "No, I guess I didn't. Even in December, when Wendy suggested we get involved, I pushed back, but then Gemma asked for our help, and I dove in. I haven't given much if any thought to *why* I get involved, but now that I have, I think it's because I enjoy solving the puzzle and I'm good at it. I don't know . . . I'm rambling. Why are we arguing about this?"

It was his turn to plop down. "I'm not sure. This is new territory for us, and this is our first argument. I sure didn't plan it this way. I didn't plan it at all. I mean, I wanted you to know my concerns and how much I worry, and I tried to think how best to broach the topic, but argue? Not what I intended."

"I'm sorry. It just hit all my hot buttons. I love you, and I love that you love me enough to worry about me. Boy, that was eloquent." I looked down at Dickens, who, sensing my distress, had his head in my lap. "Truce?"

Dave tilted my chin up. "Truce. Good to have that first argument behind us, isn't it?"

I nodded, except I wasn't sure it was behind us.

Chapter Six

"Wow. You two had a full day. You climbed Broadway Tower *and* did a seven-mile walk. Are you sore?" exclaimed Wendy. We were studying our menus and sipping prosecco at The Broadway Hotel.

Dave grimaced. "I certainly used different muscles than I use at the gym, and I walk everywhere in New York, but not all at once. If we keep this up, I may have to try regular walks in Central Park when I get home."

"I'm not sore yet. I think the longer walks I take with Dickens and the biking I do with your brother are paying off. Brian, I know Wendy's climbed the Tower. Have you done that yet since you moved to the Cotswolds?" Brian had transferred from his station in Birmingham to be closer to his elderly mother in the village of Coleford and now worked out of the Stroud station.

"Not yet. You know I'm a runner, so I'd do it more for the history than the exercise. Maybe Wendy and I can tackle it one day after we get back from our trip to Cornwall."

I laughed. "Well, you'll get your exercise climbing to

Tintagel. It'll be easier for you than for Wendy, only because some of the steps are so high. Honestly, Wendy, it was all I could do to get my short legs up a few of them. And you're shorter than I am."

My friend was only five feet tall, but every inch was packed with energy and enthusiasm. I'd commented more than once that she was the poster child for *perky* with her short, spiky, platinum blonde hair and petite frame.

Brian added. "She may be right, love. It may be more than you should tackle."

My eyes widened at that statement, and I felt Dave put his hand on my leg. I wasn't going to leap across the table and choke Brian, but I was tempted. No worries, though. Wendy was perfectly capable of taking care of herself.

"More than I should tackle?! What on earth are you going on about? Of course I'm climbing to the ruins, and I'll be doing it under my own steam, thank you very much!" I could tell she was exasperated, and I wondered, not for the first time, how often he talked down to her.

Brian murmured something about not wanting her to overdo it, and Dave tactfully changed the subject. "So Wendy, is Belle excited about Friday night at the literary festival? Is she ready for a bit of the limelight?"

"Oh, yes. She had to have a new dress for the occasion, in her favorite cornflower blue."

Like her twins, Belle had blue eyes, and I smiled at the memory of the pale blue wool hat she'd bought when we visited Dartmouth in October. "A blue dress with her white hair and blue eyes—she'll look smashing."

Our server approached to see if we were ready to order. Wendy and I went for seafood, and our dates chose the char-grilled beef fillets. When I suggested to Wendy that we share a bottle of sauvignon blanc, I half expected Brian to say something snarky. Wendy winked at me and eagerly agreed. As the designated driver of my taxi, Dave ordered a single glass of red. Brian stuck with water after finishing his glass of prosecco.

My fish was cooked to perfection. "You know, this meal along with details about the shops and Broadway's history could make for a great column. Wendy, I may need your help to do a bit more research."

She chuckled. "It will be a burden, but we can plan a day of lunch and shopping if you insist."

Dave used a stage whisper. "Are you in the market for a second research assistant? One to study the history of the village while you two tour it?"

Brian offered to take the lead on investigating the chocolate shop, and our conversation continued in that light-hearted vein. Overall, it turned out to be a more pleasant evening than I'd anticipated. *I need to try harder with Brian,* I thought, *but he sure doesn't make it easy.*

Wednesday, Dave and I agreed we'd have a light breakfast in anticipation of a big lunch at the Ploughman. He and Dickens were playing fetch in the garden when I called him in for cheese grits. Dickens was the first one in the door.

"Hey, Dickens," Dave called, "save some for me."

When he'd finished licking Christie's bowl, Dickens looked at Dave. "Now, I'm ready for grits."

Everyone got fed, including Christie. She strolled in looking for more cat food despite having left her earlier portion behind for her brother. She meowed plaintively as though I'd neglected her. "Why is my dish empty?"

"Whoa. Didn't you just feed her?" asked Dave.

"Ha! You think that matters? If the princess had her way, I'd stand here adding dabs of wet food to her dish, fluffing it nonstop until she deigned to finish it. And even then, she might walk away or sit back snootily."

Dickens put his paws on Dave's lap and barked. "I like it when she walks away. More for me."

It didn't bother Dickens at all that Dave interpreted his bark as a request to lick his grits bowl. My boy got to clean both our bowls, and then Dave washed them for good measure. We carried our mugs of coffee to the sitting room and settled in to read our emails.

"Leta, I've got an email from Gilbert, inviting us for drinks after the book club meeting tomorrow night. He's thinking of the Ploughman. Will that work?"

"Sure. We may even have a late evening snack, since I'm planning a light meal for our dinner." I was looking forward to Gilbert's talk at the Book Nook. I didn't know what direction his presentation would take, but anything about the world of Arthur Conan Doyle and Sherlock Holmes was sure to be an entertaining addition to our discussion of *The Sherlockian*.

Christie sauntered the length of the couch and leaped onto the arm next to Dave. She gave him the once-over, studying his face, before zeroing in on his lap. Apparently he passed muster, because she slowly descended from the arm of the couch onto his legs. She lay in his lap, stretching her paws toward his face. Soon, she was kneading and purring.

From his position in front of the fireplace, Dickens barked. "Will you look at her? She makes out she doesn't like him, but she has no problem hanging all over him. Cats!"

Dave grinned. "She slept by my knees last night. Does this mean she likes me?"

"For the moment. Sometimes, I feel as though I serve at her pleasure and could be replaced in a heartbeat—particularly when I fail to feed her fast enough. Her attention to you could be part of an elaborate plot to put me in my place."

"Aw, come on. Look at her sweet face. How can you say that?" He looked down at her and stroked her head. "Tell her, Christie, you like me, right?"

Christie meowed, "Oh, puh-leeze, get over yourself. You just have a comfy lap, roomier than Leta's."

We continued our intermittent banter as Dave caught up on the news and I played Words with Friends. I'd overtaken Anna in our game but didn't expect my lead to last. I was much more evenly matched with my other opponents.

My phone rang, and I saw it was Wendy. "Good morning, Leta. Have you checked today's post on the Astonbury Aha!, with the photo of Dave and Mum? There's a lovely article about Dave speaking in Chipping Camden this Friday."

"Oh! Thanks for the alert. I'll have to find it and show him. Will you and Belle be at the Ploughman for lunch?"

"Yes, Mum wouldn't miss it. She claims she's miffed Dave's been here since Monday and hasn't come to see her. Her sense of humor is priceless, you know."

Dave was tickled he'd made the local online news and said he'd be sure to make a fuss over Belle at lunch. The two of them had become great friends since the fall.

"If we're going to walk to the pub for lunch rather than drive, we need to finish up here and get dressed. It's three miles. Are you up for it after yesterday?"

"Sounds like a plan, but who's going to hold Christie? Is this when she decides she's peeved with me? The moment I move her from my lap?"

I chuckled. "You're beginning to understand. She may or may not forgive you."

Armed with carrots, we set out on our walk, allowing plenty of time to visit with the donkeys on the way. It wasn't as windy today, but the sky was overcast. We'd been lucky to have clear skies for our visit to the Broadway Tower the day before.

We arrived at the pub a few minutes past noon, and I spied Belle's head of white hair at a table in the middle of the room. Her twins were seated on either side of her, with a chair left empty between Wendy and her mum. Dickens jogged to Belle's side, and she leaned down to kiss his head. Both my animals adored Belle.

Wendy sprang up and pointed to the empty seat. "Dave, this is for you. Mum insists."

After the men shook hands, Dave knelt to hug Belle and give her a peck on the cheek. "Miss me, sweetie? And are you ready for your star turn Friday?"

Belle patted him on the cheek. "I feel as though I have my very own agent. Have you booked us any more engagements? Perhaps in London?"

With their heads together, the two caught up. I sat on the other side of Peter, and we were soon joined by Beatrix and Rhiannon. They explained Toby couldn't make it this week, but we'd see him Friday. When Libby and Gavin arrived, our favorite server Barb was on their heels.

Several of us ordered Astonbury Ale, a product of our local brewery, and I reminded Dave how much he'd liked it when he was here last. When Barb shared the day's specials, I was tempted by the lamb burger but knowing we'd be finishing the leftover pastitsio tonight, I opted for the crab salad. I laughed as Peter ordered the bacon and beef burger. The man was a burger-eating machine.

Dickens moved to lie at Peter's feet. "Can't wait for my bit of burger." Peter was incorrigible when it came to sneaking food to Dickens, no matter my attempts to convince him to stop.

Orders placed, our usual lively conversation ensued. Gavin brought us up to date on the Cotswolds Lions across the river from the inn. Matthew Coates, the Earl of Stow, had added another fifty head of the distinctive sheep to his herd at the estate and had just hired a stockwoman to oversee them. Lambing had started in January, and the last set of youngsters had been born in late March. The sweater I'd given Dave for Christmas was knit from wool from the herd.

Beatrix was sitting on my left side, and I asked if she was ready for the book club meeting Thursday. Typically, a club member volunteered to lead our discussion, but for the April meeting, Beatrix had chosen to take that role. With the Chipping Camden Literary Festival kicking off tonight and stretching through Sunday afternoon, she'd invited a few festival visitors to attend, and was excited that Dave had arranged for Gilbert Ward to present. It would be good PR for the Book Nook.

"I'm only disappointed my friend Teddy Byrd can't make it," she said. "A young man who does odd jobs for his bookshop often functions as his driver because of his mobility issues, but everyone at the shop is swamped this week. I wish I could think of some way to get him here."

I thought his name sounded familiar. "Is this your friend who owns Bluebird Books? In Chipping Camden?"

"Yes, and he's eager to hear our book club discussion. He

drives some, but he's had such difficulty walking this last year, even with his cane, he has to be selective about where he goes. Finding a place to park in Astonbury and walking to the Book Nook would wear him out."

Having overheard our conversation, Peter offered a suggestion. "If someone could get him to Astonbury, I could take him home. Mum doesn't usually go to your meetings, but she wants to attend this one to hear this Gilbert fella speak. Since Wendy has plans with Brian afterward, she asked me to pick Mum up when it's over. Mum and I could easily run your friend home, Beatrix. And you know, I'll pull right up front to get Mum, since she has the same difficulty with walking very far."

Beatrix clapped her hands to her chest. "Oh, Peter, that's so kind. It would mean the world to me *and* to Teddy. He plans to sit in on Gilbert's session at the festival but was looking forward to hearing this one too. So now I just need someone to fetch him."

Peter looked across the table at Gavin. "Mate, can you help us out here? Would you mind running to Chipping Camden tomorrow before the book club meeting? To pick up Beatrix's fellow bookshop owner?"

"Not a bit. You know, if he's the owner of Bluebird Books, I think I've met him. On the heavy side with a cane?"

Beatrix beamed. "Yes, that's him. Delightful, isn't he?"

"Oh yes. We had quite a chat about books on Churchill, and he recommended I read the Michael Dobbs trilogy—the fictionalized account of Churchill's life. Loved those books."

The plan had come together in minutes, as things so often did when this group of friends got together.

Lunch was never a long affair midweek because folks like Beatrix and Peter had to get back to their businesses, but it gave us all an opportunity to catch up. Often, Gavin and Libby threw a spur-of-the-moment cocktail party at the inn when they felt they had a congenial group of guests, so that was another way we stayed connected. It was at one of those affairs I'd met Dave.

As we strolled back to Schoolhouse Cottage, as the locals referred to my home, Dave and I reminisced about our chance meeting. I'd found him attractive but thought he was interested in Wendy. Dickens had known from the get-go it was me Dave was attracted to. Strange how perceptive my canine companion was, and Dave had proved him right when he asked me to dinner. It was the first date I'd had since Henry had died eighteen months prior, and I wasn't convinced it was a date at all, but when he asked me out a second time, I had to admit it was.

Dave ticked off the things we had in common. "Think about it. We're both writers. We love to read and gravitate to mysteries first. You enjoy learning about authors, and I write about them. We're both pretty active—me with my gym membership, you with yoga and cycling. And, we're both a bit introverted, not shy necessarily, but we enjoy our quiet time."

I smiled up at him. "And yet, we could have had all those things in common and not hit it off. Funny how things work out."

Dickens barked. "Coulda told ya!"

At home, I gave Christie a dab of food and offered to make tea, a habit I'd picked up from my British friends, but Dave declined. "The rest of the day is free, right?" he asked.

"Yes. Did you have something in mind? Would you like to visit Bourton or Stow?"

"No, I was thinking more in terms of a nap—a leisurely nap." *A man after my own heart.*

I bolted upright when I heard the bell. *What time is it? What is that?* When I got my wits about me, I realized it was my neighbor Timmy ringing the bell that hung beside my front door. It was the original schoolhouse bell with a rope pull. Little Timmy liked nothing better than to climb on the stone bench beneath the bell and tug on the rope.

I scrambled from the bed and ran downstairs to stop him before he disturbed all the neighbors. Dickens dashed out when I opened the door, and he and Timmy rolled on the grass. "Dickens, where's your ball? Let's play fetch."

"I hope you didn't want to see Christie, Timmy. You know she won't come out for hours now that you've rung the bell."

"Nope, I came to see Dickens. Christie's not much for playing ball."

I yawned and told him to meet me in the garden, and I'd bring some balls. Not my preferred way to come out of a sound sleep, but I enjoyed my young neighbor. I dug a few balls from the basket in the mudroom and tossed them outside. Leaving the two companions playing, I started a pot of tea and sat at the kitchen table. I knew Deborah Watson would soon appear at my door to check on her son and share a cup with me.

Grinning, Deborah let herself in. "Uh-oh. You have sleepy eyes. Did Timmy wake you from a nap? Sorry."

"No worries. It was time I got up. Grab a cup and we'll sit out back and watch the fun." We chatted about Timmy's school, Deborah's volunteer activities, and her husband John's dental practice. The family was constantly on the go.

It wasn't long before Dave joined us outside. He yawned and mumbled something about waking the dead before greeting Timmy. "Can I play too?"

They played keep-away with Dickens before relenting and

letting him catch the ball. Timmy wandered to the goat willow and read the plaque on the stone. "In memory of Henry Parker. Who's Henry Parker?"

Dave knelt beside Timmy and explained. "Henry was Leta's husband. He died before she moved here with Dickens and Christie, and this stone helps her remember the happy times they had together." I had wondered whether Dave would feel uncomfortable about the marker in the garden, but he had taken it in stride and commented about how thoughtful Ellie was.

Timmy studied Dave, and then looked back toward his mother. Deborah nodded and added. "Timmy, do you remember we went to the funeral for Nicholas last year? Like Leta's husband, he died in an accident." Nicholas, the previous Earl of Stow, had perished when his car ran off the road. Timmy nodded and seemed unfazed, which I supposed was a good thing. Dickens ran up with a ball and playtime resumed.

When my neighbors said goodbye, I took the leftover pastitsio from the refrigerator and stuck my head in the sitting room where Dave was stoking the fire. "Is it too early for a glass of wine?"

"Not at all. How 'bout I put some music on and we put our feet up. Any chance we'll see Christie before tomorrow?"

I raised my hands in the who-knows gesture. "She may come out after dinner, but no guarantees." I returned to the kitchen where I prepared a plate of grapes, hummus, and pita chips, and I smiled as Billy Joel's "Shades of Grey" played in the background. It was a song about being mature enough to realize that not everything in life is black and white.

Dave wandered into the kitchen to see if he could help. "That Billy Joel album is one of my favorites," he said. "Have you ever seen him in concert?"

"No. I wish I could. I've seen Paul McCartney twice, and that was a treat."

"Well, Billy Joel plays pretty regularly at Madison Square Garden. Let's say we try to see him there soon."

I beamed. "I would *love* that!" Dave uncorked a bottle of red wine and filled two glasses. We carried the wine and hors d'oeuvres to the sitting room and made ourselves comfortable. When I heard a Van Morrison tune come on, I was confused. "Aren't we listening to CDs?"

"Yes."

"But I don't have a Van Morrison CD."

With a grin, Dave turned to me. "You do now. I thought my brown-eyed girl needed one."

It was my turn to grin as I thanked him. "So, the evening is complete. Good food, good music, and good wine. What more could we ask for?"

"A good woman? I'm pretty sure I've found one."

I slugged him. "Only pretty sure? Ye of little faith."

How is it I've found a man who's so easy to be with? "Moon-dance" was the next song, and the lyrics echoed my thoughts. *It* is *a marvelous night.*

Chapter Seven

Thursday evening was crisp and cool, and Dave and I decided to walk to the Book Nook. Turning right out of the driveway, we strolled up Schoolhouse Lane past the gates to Astonbury Manor, and I commented we'd get to see Ellie tonight.

I noted the parking spaces on the High Street were filled—all the way down to the Village Green and the lot in front of the Village Hall. We had a big crowd tonight. Trixie, Beatrix's niece, greeted us when we entered the bookshop. "Good evening. Can you believe how many people are here tonight? Good thing Aunt Beatrix brought in extra chairs."

I waved at Belle, seated with Ellie in the front row. They pointed to the three empty seats beside them, and I took that to mean they'd saved two for me and Dave. Wendy must be parking the car. I spied Gavin speaking with a portly blonde man who sported a bow tie and Harris tweed vest—or waist-coat, as the Brits called it. He was on the short side, perhaps 5' 7", with a blonde mustache and long sideburns. This had to be Gilbert Ward, our guest speaker. Dave had told me Gilbert spoke like someone out of the pages of an Agatha Christie novel, and his attire seemed a nod to that affectation.

Gilbert motioned to Dave so we made our way through the crowd. "Hello, Gilbert. Let me introduce Leta Parker, my . . . my girlfriend." I could tell he found the word awkward. I felt the same way about *boyfriend. They seem such odd terms for couples our age. I never imagined I'd have a* boyfriend *in my 50s.*

Gavin smoothed the awkward moment. "And quite a girl she is. Leta is our resident American, a Greek cook, and on occasion, a regular Nancy Drew."

Gilbert looked amused. "You don't say? Then I imagine you quite enjoyed *The Sherlockian*, with an amateur detective as the main character."

I glanced at Dave, hoping this joking reference to my sleuthing wouldn't put a damper on our evening. I answered Gilbert truthfully. "I was much more intrigued by the tale that came to life in the fictional diary—Doyle's friendship with Bram Stoker, the fact he wrote a story that Stoker produced as a play—all of that is fascinating. Will you be shedding light on the facts behind the fiction?"

"To the extent that's possible, young lady. You know the missing diary has never been found, which means I can only piece together disparate facts to arrive at a probable explanation."

As I was chuckling at Gilbert's manner, someone tapped me on the shoulder. It was Beatrix, accompanied by an elderly gentleman whom I assumed must be the owner of the Chipping Camden bookshop. "May we interrupt, Leta? I'd like to introduce you all to my friend Teddy Byrd."

She made the introductions and thanked Gavin for delivering Teddy safely to her door. Teddy must have been an imposing figure in his prime. Even stooped over his cane, he was taller than Dave and Gavin, and he dwarfed Gilbert. With his bald pate, surrounded by fuzzy white hair, his wire-rimmed spectacles, and his rotund figure, he could have been a character from an Agatha Christie novel—I could imagine him as the vicar of Miss Marple's church in St. Mary Mead.

What ensued was a lively conversation among Gilbert, Teddy, and Dave about Doyle, Stoker, J.M. Barrie, and Robert Louis Stevenson. Gavin and I exchanged glances and smiled. It was like being a fly on the wall at a gathering of Victorian and Edwardian literary scholars. Tonight's book discussion coupled with Gilbert's presentation promised to be entertaining.

Beatrix quieted the guests and told us to take our seats, so I grabbed glasses of wine for Dave and me and sat next to Wendy. Beatrix started with facts about author Graham Moore. We all found it amazing he'd been only twenty-eight when he published this debut novel in 2010. Beatrix further surprised us with the fact that Moore had also written the screenplay for *The Imitation Game*, the 2014 movie about Alan Turing, the genius behind cracking the German's Engima code during WWII, and that he'd won an Academy Award for that effort.

As for the book, Sherlock Holmes lovers would enjoy it for its nod to real-life Sherlock scholars and societies, and Anglophiles were sure to get a kick from the many well-known authors, actors, and playwrights it featured. I appreciated it for both reasons. While I'd learned of the friendship between J.M. Barrie and Arthur Conan Doyle when Dave had written his article on Barrie's lost manuscript, I'd been unaware of Doyle's friendship with Bram Stoker. I was eager to hear what Gilbert would add to that part of the story.

He kicked off with questions for the audience. "Who's read any of the original Sherlock Holmes stories?"

Several of us raised our hands, and a few said we'd mostly watched the old black and white Basil Rathbone movies followed by the movies with Robert Downey, Jr. and the BBC Benedict Cumberbatch series.

Ellie interjected, "I adored *The House of Silk* by Anthony Horowitz, and you know he wrote *Foyle's War*, right? I adored that series too."

Gilbert was enjoying the audience's obvious love of the subject. "How about Bram Stoker's *Dracula*? How many of you have read it?"

I was interested to see I wasn't alone in only having seen the movies. I'd never read the book but recalled watching the black and white Bela Lugosi versions with my father on lazy weekend afternoons. As an adult, I'd enjoyed the version with Gary Oldman and Winona Ryder and, of course, the campy *Love at First Bite* with George Hamilton.

"It's not unusual for readers to be surprised Stoker wrote twelve novels, *Dracula* being the fifth. Fact: He *was* close friends with Doyle. Fact: He attended Doyle's second wedding in 1907. Fact: He produced a play based on a Doyle short story. Fiction: He helped Doyle solve the mystery of the letter bombing. Fact: Doyle *did* receive a letter bomb, just not in 1900."

Gilbert was an engaging speaker, and he had the full attention of the audience. I found the Q&A as fascinating as the book. One attendee asked about Doyle's trips to the States and American authors he might have met while there. Another questioned why Oscar Wilde didn't figure more prominently in the story.

Gilbert prefaced his answers with a caveat. "I'm an avid Arthur Conan Doyle and Sherlock Holmes fan, but I am by no means an expert. I can tell you he made a trip from New York to Boston especially to meet Oliver Wendell Holmes, but unfortunately, Holmes died shortly before he arrived. As for Oscar Wilde, the two knew each other well and respected each other's writing. We'd have to ask Graham Moore why Wilde doesn't have a larger part in his tale."

He ended his presentation with a reminder that he was speaking at the Chipping Camden Literary Festival Saturday afternoon and that his friend Dave Prentiss was leading a session Friday.

After a robust round of applause, the audience descended on the table displaying Sherlock Holmes books, calendars, and notecards in addition to Conan Doyle biographies. A line quickly formed at the checkout counter.

Teddy remained in his seat and waved Dave, Gilbert, and me over. "Gentleman, let me extend an invitation to you both, and to you too, young lady, I believe you'd enjoy viewing the collection of literary memorabilia I have in my library. It's somewhat eclectic, but it *does* include letters and newspaper articles written by Doyle, Barrie, Wodehouse, and others. I'm especially proud of the humorous Barrie article about the personality of his typewriter. Would early afternoon tomorrow work, or perhaps mid-morning Saturday?"

I could tell Gilbert and Dave were intrigued, but when they compared schedules, a joint visit didn't seem to be in the cards. Gilbert liked Friday, but Dave wanted plenty of prep time before his presentation that afternoon. He preferred Saturday, but Gilbert had the same issue about reviewing his notes for his two pm Sherlock presentation. The only pressing engagement I had beyond the two presentations was a Saturday afternoon massage appointment in the hotel spa.

I looked at them. "Teddy, would it be too inconvenient for

you if Gilbert came on Friday and Dave and I made it Saturday morning?"

Teddy smiled. "It would be a terrible imposition for me to have to brag on my collection more than once, but if I must, I must. Actually, it will be three times in two days, as Beatrix will be joining me for dinner Friday evening. She's seen my collection many times, and it's a game for her to pick out the recent additions. Consider it done—Gilbert on Friday and Leta and Dave Saturday."

Peter had arrived to pick up Teddy and Belle, so we told Gilbert we'd meet him at the Ploughman and left him to chat with other members of the audience. At my cottage, we let Dickens out. He made a quick trip to the garden and barked. "A walk? Are we taking a walk?"

Dave glanced at me. "Let's take him with us."

Dickens thought that was a grand idea and clambered in when I opened the rear door. The parking lot of the pub was surprisingly full for a Thursday evening, and Barb had her hands full inside. "What on earth?" she said as she greeted us. "Where did this crowd come from?"

I surveyed the tables. "Looks like spillover from the Book Nook. Who knew book lovers could be so thirsty? Hope you have a table for three. We're expecting one more."

Barb found us a table in a corner and took our drink orders while Dickens squirmed beneath the table. When we saw Gilbert in the doorway, Dave stood and waved. Several people greeted Gilbert as he made his way through the crowded room. He'd added a pipe to his ensemble since we'd seen him at the bookshop. I saw it as another affectation, since smoking of any kind wasn't allowed in the pub.

"Goodness, this is quite the reception. It's not often I enter a room where I'm this well-known. And who's this?"

Dickens stuck his head out for a pat. "I'm Dickens, and I'm pretty well known too."

Barb arrived with three glasses, a pitcher, and three shot glasses filled with an amber liquid. "Astonbury Ale and shots of Cotswolds Single Malt, compliments of that large table across the room." Gilbert grinned and waved an acknowledgment in their direction.

"Okay, Barb," I said, "I'm not a whiskey drinker, and I had no idea there was a Cotswolds brand. Where does this come from?"

"You've at least got to sip it, Leta. It's from the Cotswolds Distillery in Shipston-on-Stour. The distillery tour could make for a nice day trip for you and Dave."

"A sip is all it will be. I might have a mixed drink from time to time—but shots? Not happening!"

Barb shook her head. "Right, then, how 'bout food? Is food happening tonight?"

We ordered several appetizers before Dave and Gilbert dove into a discussion of Doyle, Barrie, and Bram Stoker. Gilbert wondered whether Barrie and Stoker had known each other well. He'd not run across references to a friendship between them, but as Doyle was friends with both men, it was likely their paths had crossed.

As Gilbert packed his pipe with tobacco, Dave pulled a small notepad from his coat pocket. "I'll have to see what I can find in Edinburgh in the Barrie collection. I've never seen anything on it either. Teddy may have an idea, though he strikes me more as a collector than a scholar. Still, you can pick up lots of information from memorabilia."

"As I should know," said Gilbert. "I can assure you, my compatriots in the Sherlock Holmes Society of London consider me neither a serious collector nor scholar. Compared to many of them, I merely dabble. My extensive dabbling, though, provides me opportunities like tonight's engagement and the invitation to speak at the literary festival Saturday—quite an enjoyable way to spend my time."

When the food arrived, Gilbert called for another round of shots, but Dave and I quickly declined and requested two more pints. I wondered about Gilbert driving back to Chipping Camden, but kept that thought to myself.

I chuckled when Gilbert said, "I say, old chap, you may want to find yourself a copy of *Arthur Conan Doyle: A Life in Letters*. Could trigger some ideas for your book on friends. I seem to recall letters to H.G. Wells and Robert Louis Stevenson as well as Barrie." *The man sounds like Albert Campion*, I thought as Dave jotted the title down. *He's quite a character*.

By ten, I was stifling a yawn and Dave took note. "Have to get my date home before she turns into a pumpkin. I'm surprised she's lasted this long. Hope to see you tomorrow, Gilbert."

"Count on it, my dear friend," Gilbert said as he pulled out a pocket watch. "It's time I returned to my bed and breakfast." He chuckled as he checked the time and held the watch up for us to see more closely. "You know, I purchased this at a stall in the Jubilee Market in Covent Garden. The proprietor claimed it was like the one owned by Dr. Watson, and it amuses me to imagine how many he's sold to unsuspecting tourists who believe Dr. Watson to be a real person."

As we traveled the short distance home, we laughed over Gilbert's mannerisms and attire. We wondered if he stayed in character twenty-fours a day or whether he turned it on and off. No matter, we agreed it was amusing—in small doses.

Dave wanted to check his email and research the book Gilbert had mentioned, so he suggested I go on to bed.

Knowing how easily I could tumble down the rabbit hole when I sat down with my laptop, I suspected the same would happen to him, and I didn't hesitate.

A good night's sleep before the full day we had ahead of us Friday was a must. Chipping Camden was only a thirty-minute drive, but we had lunch reservations and had requested an early check-in at our hotel.

I left Dave dealing with Christie's demands—he was getting the hang of moving her food around her dish until she was satisfied. As I climbed the stairs, I heard, "Not there, you silly man, move it to the middle. Oh for goodness' sake, fluff it." *Perhaps I was hasty in my assessment.*

Chapter Eight

Midmorning Saturday in the garden at Teddy Byrd's cottage

As Dave and I waited for Gemma, we sat quietly, with our separate thoughts. Dickens continued his garden inspection, but we hadn't seen Watson since we left the bedroom. I heard a car pull up, and soon after, I heard my name.

Constable James opened the gate, and Gemma walked through. "Leta? Dave? Oh, here you are. I'm so sorry you had to be the ones to find him. I know you've checked, and I trust you, but Constable James will stay here with you, while I double-check to be sure we *really* do have a death on our hands."

Dickens barked a greeting and rolled over at Constable James's feet.

"Good way to lighten the mood, fella," said the young constable as he knelt to give my boy a belly rub.

Dave told Gemma the bedroom was down the hall to the left, and she quickly entered the cottage. When she returned, she looked grim. She scanned the garden as she stood on the steps. "I'm afraid you're right. The man is dead. I remember him now from the festival. Sat on the front row, didn't he?"

Nodding, Dave replied, "Yes, he did. We first met him Thursday night at the Book Nook. That's when he invited us to visit."

"And this is the door you went in? What made you come around back?"

After Dave explained about not getting an answer to our knock, I told her about the cat. "It was Watson's crying that got our attention."

I could tell she was half-listening as she scanned the garden. "Right," she said. "So, Dave, this door was unlocked? Was it open?"

Dave walked her through his entry. He'd gotten no answer to his knocking back here either. When he tried the door, he found it was unlocked, so he went into the kitchen, calling Teddy's name. "I first took a few steps down the hall to the right and glanced in the sitting room and then went in the other direction past the library to the bedroom. I checked his pulse and then came to find Leta."

"Odd the door was unlocked. I'd best get the Scene of Crime officers here before we proceed, just to be sure there's nothing else off about the situation." She moved to the rear of the garden to place the call and came back to us when she was done.

"Leta, did you notice anything amiss?"

"To be honest, Gemma, once I heard the words, 'I think Teddy's dead,' I didn't see a thing until we got to the bedroom." I closed my eyes. "I can see the covers neatly folded, the book beneath his hand. There must not have been anything obvious, or I would have noticed. Oh! I didn't see his spectacles, but they must have been on the nightstand or the bed somewhere. I don't think he could read without them."

Dave was looking from me to Gemma, his mouth open.

Gemma shook her head. "Dave," she said, "I'd hoped never to see your girlfriend at another scene like this, but since she's here . . . I'd like to take advantage of her attention to detail."

Constable James interjected, "She's brilliant, you know. You can't believe the things she sees right off that others tend to miss."

Gemma frowned at her constable. "Are you *through*? You're right about her powers of observation, and if she'd stop there, we wouldn't have a problem. Now's not the time to get into that, though. Leta, shall we retrace your steps and see what catches your eye?"

When I nodded, she turned and handed Dave and me plastic gloves. "Hopefully, your friend died of natural causes, but on the off chance that's not the case, let's be careful."

I noted again that the kitchen was pristine and told Gemma I assumed the dishes in the drain were from the dinner Beatrix and Teddy had shared. That got her attention. "Beatrix was here?"

I gave Gemma the little bit of information I had about Teddy and Beatrix's relationship. "She was looking forward to spending time with him and seeing his collection. Oh my! Will you tell her about his death, or shall I?"

"Let's finish this walkthrough and then discuss that. I see the teacups are clean, maybe set out for your visit?"

Dave looked puzzled. "Except wouldn't he have had tea and a bite when he got up, and only clean the counter and set out the cups for us after that?" *Hmmm. I'll have to point out to him later that he was thinking like I did.*

"You make a good point, Dave," replied Gemma. "Unless he usually used a mug or had a coffee most days. Hard to say." She proceeded down the hallway and into the bedroom. Dave and I hung back in the doorway as she moved deeper into the room.

Taking a deep breath, I studied the room. I imagined Teddy sitting up reading in the library before going to bed with his book and his newspapers. Watson was curled up on top of the papers spread on the bed, and I wondered if that was how the two spent most evenings. I studied the bedside table. "Goodness, he has lots of medicine, doesn't he?" In addition to the bottles of pills, there was one of those plastic containers that held pills by the day.

"Uh-huh. Not all that surprising for someone his age, in my experience. Did one of you turn off the bedside light when you were in here before?"

I looked at Dave. "Did you? It was off when you brought me back here, wasn't it?"

Dave shook his head. "No, I didn't touch it. I checked his pulse, but that was it."

Why would his book still be on his chest if he had turned the light off? I pointed at the book. "That's kind of odd, isn't it? I do sometimes put a book or a magazine on the other side of my bed rather on my side table, but I certainly don't turn out the light with a book in my hand."

Dave shook his head no. "I do. Sometimes I nod off with my book propped on my chest, and I hardly stir when I reach over to switch the light off. It's when I roll over and knock the book off the bed that I wake myself."

"Leta, you must be rubbing off on Dave. He's pretty observant too. You say he wore spectacles? I wonder whether they're in this pile of papers the cat's on?" Watson jumped off the bed as Gemma carefully sifted through the newspapers. "No, not here. Wouldn't they be close to hand?"

Dave answered for me. "Having seen him twice, I can't imagine him going to bed without them nearby, but maybe he's like my mom and had cataract surgery and doesn't need them all the time. But, wait, what are we doing? We're acting as though there's something fishy going on when what we have is an elderly man who died in his sleep. I mean, that's what happened, right?"

Gemma sighed. "I'd like to think that's what we have, Dave. But when there are anomalies at the scene, we have to account for them. I'm hopeful it will turn out to be a peaceful natural death, but I've got to check everything out to make an informed decision. The evidence gathered by the SOCOs when they arrive will help plus whatever the coroner tells us. I'm not overly concerned about the bedside light, but the missing spectacles puzzle me. Hopefully, there's a logical explanation like the one you suggested."

"DI Taylor, Constable James said you were in the bedroom. Oh, here you are." Dressed in a white plastic jumpsuit, the middle-aged man who entered the room looked surprised to see three of us in the room. "And who are these two?"

Gemma rolled her eyes, one of her more annoying habits. "Ah, well, these two found the body, and since they've already been in here, I'm taking them through their actions to be sure they didn't inadvertently disturb anything."

He looked annoyed as he cleared his throat. "I trust they haven't touched anything?"

"No, no. Well, only before I got here. They checked to see if he had a pulse. Then they called me. Since then, they've been confined to the entry to the room. The body is all yours."

We three left the bedroom, and Gemma whispered, "Leta,

I know you've never been here before, but I'd like your take on the library." *Funny how she so often invites my input, even if we don't always see eye to eye.* "And, Dave, your observations could be helpful too. Just don't move anything."

I could tell Dave was surprised, but he went with the flow. In the library, a young woman dressed in a white jumpsuit looked up as we entered. Flashing her badge, Gemma moved into the room followed by Dave, but I stayed in the doorway. I preferred to observe the overall scene before focusing on smaller details.

I saw a desk centered on the far wall in front of a window. I'd gotten a general impression of a cozy room earlier but hadn't taken in the layout. On the left wall, there was a built-in bookcase, then a fireplace, and last, another bookcase. Two wingback chairs with a table between them faced the fireplace. The wall opposite the fireplace held more bookshelves and a display case centered between them, mirroring the arrangement on the other side of the room. "Look, Dave, that must be the typewriter we heard about, the one that belonged to J.M. Barrie."

Dave tentatively approached the display. "Gemma, is it okay for me to touch it?"

"No!"

I almost laughed as his head whipped around, but he took it in stride. "Oh my. And to think, Teddy wanted to show me an article Barrie wrote about his typewriter. I wonder where the papers are. Some collectors keep them in three-ring notebooks in protective plastic pages." When Gemma gave him a stern look, he continued, "I know, I know, If I find any documents, I won't touch them, much as I'd like to. I would have loved sitting with him to go through his memorabilia."

He stood staring at the typewriter and suddenly stooped.

"Um, Gemma, the typewriter is sitting on top of this glass case that's filled with knickknacks. Could the fact that the door on its front has a brass key in it and is hanging open be one of those anomalies you mentioned?"

Simultaneously, Gemma and I joined Dave by the case. "Look," I said. "There's a notebook faceup in the middle with children's figurines behind it. The brass plate affixed to the cover reads 'Teddy's Treasures, Bless the Children,' so the figurines make sense. I wonder whether there are other notebooks—with letters and newspaper clippings and such."

Gemma knelt to get a better look. "What are these? Characters from children's books? These aren't valuable, are they? Pooh, Piglet, Tigger, Peter Pan, Wendy, the Cheshire Cat, Alice—you can find these in most gift shops, can't you? But you're right. There's a good bit of space. If there were more notebooks, I wonder where they've gotten to."

Peering between them, I commented, "I bet Beatrix knows. After all, she was here last night for dinner and to see the collection again."

"Depending on what else we find, I may need to speak with her sooner rather than later," said Gemma.

She moved to inspect the area around the desk, checking the trash can and opening drawers. I stood in front of the first bookcase to the left of the fireplace. Teddy had an extensive collection of old books, though I had no idea which, if any, might be collector's items.

One shelf was filled with books by Graham Greene. I imagined Teddy collected them because Greene had briefly lived in Chipping Camden. Another was devoted to the mysteries of Ngaio Marsh, who was a New Zealand author. It appeared Teddy was as much a mystery lover as I was, and his choices weren't confined to British authors. He'd been correct when he said his collection was eclectic.

Beyond mysteries, he had one shelf devoted to King Arthur books—the classics like *Morte d'Arthur* but also more modern takes on the beloved tale, like Mary Stewart's *The Crystal Cave* and Rosemary Sutcliff's *King Arthur Trilogy* for children.

I realized I was becoming so engrossed in Teddy's books, I'd lost sight of why Gemma had invited me into the room. As I moved to the right, I almost tripped over Gemma kneeling in front of the fireplace. "Just checking to be sure there's nothing of interest here."

Kneeling beside her, I studied the ashes. "You mean like in the movies when someone's burned something odd in the fireplace and it's a vital clue?" She nodded and stood, indicating there was nothing to see.

I turned and surveyed the room again. I'd overlooked a binder on the table between the chairs. "Here's another binder. Perhaps he and Beatrix were looking at it, here beside the fire last night." When I leaned over, I saw it was labeled "Teddy's Treasures, Miscellany."

I moved to the bookshelves beyond the fireplace. The shelves from the middle on up were arranged much like those on the other side, by author. The ones closer to the bottom looked more like those of any avid reader, a hodgepodge of genres and authors. Beyond telling us about Teddy's reading taste, I couldn't discern anything particularly enlightening.

"DI Taylor, may I see you a moment?" came a voice from the hallway. It was the SOCO we'd left in the bedroom. I could tell he was none too pleased to encounter Dave and me again, this time in the library. "Excuse me, are these two on the payroll, or what?"

Once again, Gemma rolled her eyes. "Ah, well, I'm taking advantage of their knowledge of books and literary memorabilia to see if any details leap out at them." *That's a stretch. But, I guess she had to offer some plausible explanation to the man.*

He looked annoyed as he cleared his throat. "I trust they haven't touched anything?"

Gemma assured him we were following the rules as the two returned to the bedroom. I wondered whether he had something significant to show her.

Though Gemma had checked the desk area, I studied it too. It was a mess, but perhaps that's the way Teddy kept it. I couldn't speak, given that mine stayed cluttered with papers, notebooks, and newspaper clippings except when Christie cleared it with a swipe or two of her paws. I could see another binder peeking out from the papers, but until and unless Gemma gave me permission to sort through the desktop, I knew not to touch it.

She returned and pulled me aside to whisper I should take Dave and return to the garden. I pointed to the edge of the binder, and she cleared the papers from it. "Teddy's Treasures, Author Letters," she read aloud.

I shrugged my shoulders and went to Dave. He was standing by the display case, looking dazed. "Let's go," I murmured to him.

We joined Constable James in the garden. He was standing at attention by the garden gate, and Dickens was stretched out in a shady spot on the stone patio. Dave and I sat on the steps as we'd done earlier.

Grabbing my hand, Dave asked, "What next? Are we free to go?"

"I think we need to wait for Gemma to tell us." It was close to 12:30, and we'd arrived around 10:30. It seemed as though we'd been here much longer than two hours. *I wonder whether we'll make Gilbert's 2 p.m. session.*

"I'd like to have time to change before we go to the literary festival," I said. "Oh my! I can't believe I said that. That should be the last thing on my mind. Heck, is it even appropriate for us to be there? Do we still want to go? There's no guide for manners following the discovery of a dead body." I looked at Dave. "I'm babbling!"

"Yes, you are, but you're echoing the random thoughts running through my mind. I mean, do we stroll in as though nothing's happened? Do we tell Beatrix and Gilbert, the only two people I'd feel a need to tell? Are we sworn to secrecy?"

I had more questions. "I wonder whether Albert is scheduled to drive Teddy today? He could show up any minute if he is. Or maybe he'd arranged for someone else to take him. Maybe Albert's doing odd jobs at Bluebird Books. And, I hate to say this, but I'm starving."

The last line produced a smile from Dave. "Now that you mention it, I am too. That carb-laden breakfast we had didn't last long."

Overhearing our conversation, Constable James offered to check with Gemma as to what she wanted us to do. It wasn't long before he came back with her in tow.

She frowned. "I know you two must have plans today, and Dave, I have no further need of you right now. I can take a formal statement from you later today or tomorrow. Leta, technically, I don't need you either, but I'd sure like to get your take on the library once the SOCOs have gone over it. If you want to go with Dave, maybe we can arrange to meet back here at another time."

I know what I want to do, but there's no way I'm ditching Dave to stay here with Gemma. "I'm going with Dave. We want to see a presentation at 2, I have an appointment at 4, and we have dinner reservations . . . "

"Right. Why don't you text me later, and we'll talk. I assume you'll be seeing Beatrix shortly?"

"Yes."

"Would you feel comfortable breaking the news to her? If she were the next of kin, I'd feel compelled to do it, but in this case, it doesn't have to be me or Constable James. By the way, do you know who the next of kin is?"

I blinked. "I have no idea. Beatrix might know, or Fiona, or the manager at Teddy's bookshop. Can't recall her name."

It was then Albert walked through the gate. "What's going on? Where's Teddy?"

Gemma flashed her identification. "And you are?"

He stepped back. "Albert Porter. I work for Teddy. Why are the police here?"

Putting her hand on his arm, Gemma pulled him aside. I couldn't hear her words, but the gasp and the shocked expression on Albert's face told the story. Seeing him again, I realized he was older than I'd taken him for on Friday—perhaps in his thirties. *It was probably that shaggy brown hair curling around his collar that gave me the impression of youth.*

They moved closer to us. "Now, Albert, why are you here?" asked Gemma.

"Most days, either Fiona or I come by for one reason or another. If I'm not taking him to the grocer, Fiona's bringing him a bite to eat or delivering books. Some days, Pris comes by if she needs to chat with Teddy about the bookshop, but usually it's me or Fiona. And today, I'm supposed to run Teddy to the school to hear one of the literary festival sessions."

"And Pris is . . . ?"

"Um. Pris manages Bluebird Books."

Constable James and Gemma exchanged a glance. An unspoken message must have passed between them because the constable went to Albert's side and ushered him to a chair at the garden table. "Would you like a cup of tea? Let me take care of that, and then I'd like to ask you a few questions."

While he attended to him, Dave, Dickens, and I took our leave. "Oh wait, one more thing," I said over my shoulder. "Is it okay for us to tell today's speaker, Gilbert Ward, about this? He was here visiting Teddy only yesterday. It doesn't seem right to keep it from him."

Gemma agreed that was okay, but asked us to try to keep a lid on things beyond that. She'd soon be trying to interview the manager of the shop, and if she could find the names in the cottage, she planned to contact Teddy's doctor and his solicitor. "The coroner will need a report from the doctor, and hopefully, the solicitor can tell me pretty quickly what happens to the bookshop so we don't leave the employees in limbo."

We barely had time to get back to our room and change before it was time to dash to Gilbert's presentation, which was scheduled at the Chipping Camden School. The events for the festival took place at various venues around the village. I'd hoped to catch Beatrix at the hotel, but when I rang her room, there was no answer. She'd probably attended a morning session too, taking advantage of the opportunity to hear as many speakers as possible.

Dickens barked as he'd been doing intermittently since we'd left the cottage. "We need to talk. Don't you want to know what Watson had to say?"

As I reattached his leash, I whispered, "Yes, but not now. I can't do it in front of Dave."

Still starving, Dave and I grabbed apples from the front desk and set out for the school. I saw Beatrix inside the Great Hall at the refreshment table. "Dave, should I tell her now or wait until after we hear Gilbert? She can't do anything about it no matter when I tell her, and she won't be able to concentrate on 'Happenings on the Holmes Front' if she's got Teddy on her mind."

Dave didn't hesitate. "I'm not sure I'll be able to focus *my* mind, so I say let's not spoil it for her. Another hour won't make any difference."

When Beatrix greeted us with, "Oh, how was your visit with Teddy?", I almost told her. I'm sure the expression on my face was a strange one, and I was momentarily speechless.

Taking her elbow, Dave came to the rescue. "More on that later. They've sounded the gong indicating Gilbert's about to start, and I don't want to miss anything."

I was surprised that I was able to take in most of what Gilbert had to say. It was a testament to him that his entertaining talk distracted me from the morning's events, though when he spoke of Sherlock's study of ash, my mind momentarily drifted to the fireplace in the library. Sherlock was best known for being able to identify myriad types of tobacco ash —not that from wood or paper. *Bet the great detective would be helpful if we found a pipe.*

When the presentation was over and the applause had tapered off, I turned to Beatrix. "Why don't we wait until the audience is mostly done approaching Gilbert, and then see if we can speak with him?"

"Okay. I'm not in any rush. The next session I'm attending

is at the library—the one on R.F. Delderfeld and his historical novels."

"Funny, I don't recall seeing that on the schedule. How did I overlook a talk on Delderfeld? I read some of his books when I was in my twenties and thoroughly enjoyed them. It was a phase, though. I read historical novels for years and then shifted to mysteries and never looked back."

Dave had been sitting quietly while we chatted, and as the crowd around Gilbert evaporated, Dave motioned him over.

Gilbert was all smiles. "Well, hello again. Glad you could make it. I trust the thrust of today's talk was different enough from Thursday night's to hold your attention."

We all assured him it was and I suggested he take a seat. "I have some distressing news to share with you and Beatrix." I explained how we'd gone to Teddy's as planned and discovered he'd died—in his bed.

Probably because Gilbert hardly knew him, he took the news better than Beatrix did. She gasped as her hands flew to her face and she began to cry.

Dickens put his paws on the chair seat and nudged her elbow until she reached to pat his head. Somehow, he'd learned that his presence was a comfort to those in distress.

"What do you mean? He was perfectly fine last night, if a bit tired. We had our usual lively conversation about the role of independent booksellers in today's world, our favorite books of late, the new additions to his collection, and how the festival was going. I can't believe he's gone."

I rubbed her shoulders and murmured we couldn't either, but that he'd looked peaceful when we found him. Dave added how sorry he was he hadn't gotten the opportunity to spend more time with him.

Gilbert shook his head in disbelief. "Dave, I wish you and

Leta could have been with me. He was quite the raconteur, and I enjoyed viewing his collection while he shared stories of how he'd come by the pieces. For some reason, he had doubts about a J.M. Barrie letter he had, but since I'm no expert, I suggested he ask you. I suspect he thought he'd been taken in by a few clever reproductions. Unlike so many collectors who enjoy the hunt and then hardly look at their acquisitions, he was involved with his. By that, I mean he spoke of the documents and memorabilia as though they were his children."

Dabbing at her eyes, Beatrix smiled. "That was Teddy. His treasures were his world. His wife died a few years ago, and they never had children. Books, his bookshop, his assortment of objects, and of course, Watson, his cat—all of that was his life. I guess you noticed the labels on his binders of letters and clippings—'Teddy's Treasures'?"

I nodded. "Beatrix," I asked, "Did you know him well enough to know who his next of kin might be? A sibling, a niece or nephew, perhaps? Gemma needs to know whom to contact."

"I'm not sure, but I honestly don't think there is anyone. If there is, I doubt they were close. Fiona or Priscilla might know."

Gilbert had to leave for an appointment, and we three debated whether we should change our afternoon plans because of Teddy's sudden death. Beatrix wasn't sure she was in any shape to attend the Delderfield talk.

I had a massage appointment and Dave had no concrete plans. "Beatrix," he offered, "how 'bout I join you for the session? I've never read Delderfield's books, but I'm always up for learning about another author."

At least that comment made Beatrix smile. "Aren't we all?

I'll take you up on your offer because I know Teddy would want me to carry on."

When I mentioned I had to grab a bite before my appointment, we walked together to the High Street where we ducked in a bakery for some snacks before going our separate ways. I hugged Beatrix and pecked Dave on the cheek. "See you back in the room around 5:30."

"Being alone with my thoughts could be a big mistake," I said to Dickens as we left Dave and Beatrix.

He stopped and cocked his head. "But you're not alone. You've got me, and I've got lots to tell you."

Chapter Nine

I had some time to spare before my massage, and I'd held Dickens off as long as I could. He was dying to chat. "I like Watson. What's gonna happen with him? We need to be sure he gets fed. If he's like Christie, he's probably screeching right this minute. I can't imagine how I'd feel if something happened to you—"

Leaning against the side of the bed, I sat with Dickens on the floor. "Whoa. Slow down. Nothing's going to happen to me, so don't worry. I haven't thought of who will look after Watson, but I'm sure someone will take him in. Did he tell you anything? Was he home last night or is he one of those wandering cats?"

"He went out when Fiona left, as usual, but got worried when Teddy didn't let him in this morning. I guess Teddy was like you, fixed his tea, and then took care of Watson. He gets milk and then wet food, just like Christie—except he doesn't have a dog to help him with the leftovers."

"When Fiona left? Does that mean she was there—after Beatrix?"

"Um, I didn't know to ask about that, but Watson made it seem like Fiona leaving at night and letting him out was a regular thing. He described sitting in Teddy's lap in the library in front of the fireplace. Oh! And something about Dracula. Who's that? Maybe he was there too."

I stroked Dickens's back as he lay by my side on the floor. "He's a vampire, a character in a book. What else did Watson see?"

"Oh. Lots of things. Every night, he walks along the garden walls up and down the street. He taunts the dog three doors down, chases a few squirrels, visits his girlfriend across the street. He gets around."

"Right, but did he see anyone else?"

Dickens cocked his head. "Not last night. In the morning, he saw your friend who wears the bowties—same as me. And he saw that Albert bloke pick Teddy up and bring him home earlier during the day. Watson likes Albert. Says you can always tell a cat person."

This was a serious subject, but I couldn't help laughing at Dickens. "Albert bloke? You think you're British now? So, you're sure, Watson didn't see anyone or anything unusual at Teddy's cottage?"

"Don't think so, but maybe we need to visit him again. Can we? Can we?"

Nodding, I thought about Gemma wanting me to set up a time to return. I wondered what she'd discovered while I'd been listening to Gilbert's tales of Sherlock Holmes. Maybe by now, she'd determined Teddy had died quietly in his sleep, his book beneath his hand. *I'd be happy to go like that when my time comes.*

Downstairs in the spa, I relaxed facedown beneath the hands of the masseuse. I was plagued by tight shoulders, and she was working wonders on the knots, though not without a few yelps from me. Amazingly, I managed not to dwell on the morning's events, and I felt rested and rejuvenated when my hour was up.

When I opened the door to our room, Dickens lifted his head, but that was it. Dave hadn't returned yet, so I lay on the bed, intending to continue relaxing until he showed up. Our dinner reservation wasn't until eight, meaning I had plenty of time to shower and make myself presentable. No luck on the snoozing front because my phone rang as my head hit the pillow.

It was Gemma. "Are you okay? You sound funny."

I yawned. "I'd be more okay if I could take a nap. Where are you?"

"Believe it or not, I'm back in Chipping Camden, waiting to meet with Fiona and then Priscilla. I'm trying to get a handle on who saw Teddy when on Friday. I'd like to speak with Beatrix, as she was the last person to see Teddy yesterday, but she must have her phone turned off. Did you tell her?"

Uh-oh, how do I tell her that Fiona was the last person to see him when all I have are the words of a cat and a dog? Hopefully, Fiona will tell her, and I won't have to worry about it. "Yes," I told her. "She was torn up, but all in all handled it pretty well. And I bet you're right about her phone, since she's been in and out of presentations all day."

I suggested Gemma leave Beatrix a message at the front desk so she'd get it as soon as she returned to the hotel. "So, are these interviews, or whatever you call them, simply a matter of course, nothing suspicious from your perspective?"

"Yes. Unless the coroner tells me something different, I'm leaning towards natural causes. I won't have the report until

Monday at the earliest as we're not seeing this as a priority. More likely Tuesday.

"If I can speak with Beatrix after I'm done at the book-shop, that should take care of things for today. I was able to find the solicitor's name, and I have a call into him, but I doubt I'll hear from him until next week. He should be able to point me to the next of kin. Beyond hoping Beatrix might have been with you, I was calling to say I don't think I'll need you back at the cottage."

"Okay. That's good to hear. I wasn't keen on telling Dave I had to leave him to meet up with you. I've only discovered this week how concerned he's been about my mishaps these past few months."

I heard a chuckle. "Mishaps? Is that what you call them? One visit to Accident & Emergency and almost a second? Gee, does he think the 'little lady' needs to mind her own business? Maybe stop sticking her nose into police affairs?"

Why is it Gemma never ceases to get under my skin? Little lady? I've used that phrase regarding Brian Burton, but Dave was nothing like him. "He didn't say it that way, and excuse me, wasn't it you who wanted me to apply my observation skills today at the scene? You can't have it both ways, Gemma. Remember that next time you ask for my help."

"Oh, get off your high horse, Leta. I've managed to admit —from time to time—that you're helpful, but, and this is a huge *but*, you put yourself in danger way too often—you're careless in that regard. It's no wonder Dave is worried. What man wouldn't be?"

It's past time to end this conversation. I can feel my feminist hackles rising. "Fine. Doesn't look like it's an issue this time anyway. If I see Beatrix, I'll tell her to call you." And I ended the call. Too bad I didn't have a real phone to slam down for emphasis.

I was still fuming when Dave walked in. He smiled as he handed me three books. "I heard you mention enjoying Delderfeld's books in your younger days, and I thought you might want to revisit his popular trilogy. He wrote the books in the late '60s—*Long Summer's Day*, *Post of Honour*, and *The Green Gauntlet*. Heck, I might even read them, since the saga starts between the Boer War and World War I, moves on through World War II, and into the '60s."

Looking through the first book, I glanced up and smiled. "I loved these books, and I recall friends marveling at how I managed to read one a week, though each was over 600 pages. I couldn't put them down—I had to know what happened to the family through the hardship and heartache of two world wars and rebuilding a life in England. You know, it could have been these books that first made me fall in love with this country."

"You've just sold me. Beatrix was enthralled with the discussion, and she's planning a historical fiction window display at her shop for the summer. Maybe it will be a book club selection. Who knows?"

I stood and hugged him. "Thank you. Thanks for going with Beatrix so her day wasn't awful, and thanks for my thoughtful gift."

After a quick shower for me and forty winks for Dave, we decided to arrive early at the restaurant we'd chosen for dinner—Michael's at Woolmarket House—billed as "A little corner of Cyprus in the heart of the Cotswolds." We planned to have cocktails on their terrace before moving inside to the table we'd reserved near one of the inglenook fireplaces. They might have welcomed Dickens, but we were in the mood for an elegant evening sans the dog, much to his dismay.

I smeared a bit of the fried halloumi cheese on a chunk of pita bread and took a bite. "Oh my goodness. If the main courses are anything like this starter, I'll be in heaven. Actually, I think I'm already there." We agreed on a bottle of Merlot instead of mixed drinks, and it was the perfect accompaniment.

Despite the horrible start to the day, we managed to enjoy ourselves and steer clear of any discussion of the morning's events. Inside, when my lamb shank was placed in front of me, I closed my eyes and took in the enticing aroma. "I've cooked this dish, but not often. It's nice to eat Mediterranean food without having to be the chef."

Dave was equally pleased with his prawns, and since we were on foot, we indulged in a second bottle of wine. Neither of us had room left for dessert, though it was tempting. It wasn't until we were strolling back to our hotel that the morning's events intruded on the evening.

When the phone rang, I fumbled in my purse to locate it, hoping it was one of my sisters, but I had a feeling that wasn't who I'd find on the other end of the line. I was right. It was Gemma, and I knew she wouldn't be calling if she had good news. "Ye-es," I answered hesitantly.

"Sorry to call you this late. Please tell me you've had a lovely evening, and I haven't interrupted your dinner."

"It was heavenly, and we're stuffed. And no, we've finished our meal, so you're not interrupting anything but our walk." I looked at Dave and mouthed "Gemma" as she continued.

"Well, I'm glad for that. Listen, speaking with Priscilla and Fiona spurred me to return to the scene at the cottage, and I'm there now. I've discovered some discrepancies that don't sit well with me. I wouldn't dare ask you to come over now, but could you meet me here in the morning? I have a feeling the SOCO may have been a bit perfunctory in his observations."

Telling her to hold on, I covered the phone and spoke to Dave. "She wants me to go back to the cottage to take a look around in the morning. Do you want to go with me?"

I could tell he was hesitant. This was all new to him. "Teddy is gone, Dave, so we'll just be taking another look at the scene, maybe the books, the memorabilia, you know."

When he said okay, I spoke to Gemma. "I'll come if I can bring Dave and if it's not too early. We've promised ourselves a sit-down breakfast for Sunday morning."

With that settled, I hung up, turned to Dave, and asked, "What are you thinking?"

"My thoughts are a jumble. Naturally, I wonder why Gemma wants to revisit the scene. What's she found out since this morning that makes her want a second look? I heard Constable James say you're 'brilliant', so I guess I know why she wants you there. Still, I have to wonder why the police can't do their job on their own, without you."

I shrugged my shoulders. "I don't have any good answers to your questions. She said it was something she heard when she interviewed Fiona and Priscilla, but she didn't say what. As for wanting me there? I'm not sure I can explain that."

When Dave frowned and shook his head, I elaborated. "Gemma can be kind of inconsistent on that front. She didn't want me involved the first time I discovered a dead body, but when I started asking questions she hadn't thought of, she listened—not willingly, mind you, but she did. The same thing happened when her mom found a dead body on the riverbank. Gemma called me in to take care of her mom, and it went from there."

He still didn't look convinced, so I gave it one more shot. "Let's just say my relationship with Gemma keeps evolving, and it's not easy to explain. Sooo . . . how do you feel about me going back to scan the scene?"

He pulled me closer to his side. "It sounds innocent enough, but I can't help being worried. Is this how it starts? You meet with Gemma, and you're pretty safe. But then you somehow wind up in the middle of things? And before you know it, you're in danger?"

Then he chuckled. "Maybe if I'm your sidekick instead of Wendy or Belle—maybe if I don't let you out of my sight—things will turn out differently. What do you think?"

We laughed together, and I threatened to get him a deer-stalker cap and a magnifying glass. *Maybe it will put his mind at ease to see that my so-called detective work is mostly a matter of observing and brainstorming. He'll be on his way to Edinburgh Monday, so if my involvement progresses beyond that, he can remain blissfully unaware.*

Chapter Ten

After a leisurely breakfast, we took our time walking to Teddy's cottage. Dickens rolled over for belly rubs whenever walkers stopped to admire him, so it was fortunate we were running ahead of schedule. When he spied Watson lying in the sun on the stone walkway, he ran over to greet him. "How are you? Did someone feed you? Where'd you sleep?"

Watson carried on licking a paw. "My, you're an inquisitive bloke, aren't you? I slept inside, which wasn't my first choice, but that lady with the blonde ponytail locked me in last night. She was back first thing to let me out and feed me, so it was okay—if a bit lonely." He nudged Dickens with his nose. "Teddy's not coming back, is he?"

Dickens laid down beside Watson and licked him between the eyes before trying to explain about Teddy. As we'd done Saturday morning, Dave and I opened the garden gate and went to the back patio. We found Gemma sitting at the wrought iron table, flipping pages in a small spiral notebook.

She scowled as she looked up. "Either I'm losing my touch

COLLECTORS, CATS & MURDER

or Constable James's scrawl is getting worse. Probably a bit of both."

As she handed me the notebook, I laughed. "I can't speak because my handwriting is abysmal. It was always bad—unsatisfactory marks in grade school—but it's only gotten worse with the advent of computers and email. My mother was so unhappy with me. Anyway, is there something particular you want me to look for?"

"No . . . yes. I don't know. I'm second-guessing myself. Maybe if you and I do a walkthrough, we can compare and contrast what we see. And, Dave, I'm hoping you can look over the bookshelves and collectibles with your literary eye to see if anything looks amiss to you. My conversation with Fiona yesterday got me thinking."

She handed us each a pair of plastic gloves as we entered the kitchen. I was struck a second time by how clean and uncluttered it was. The only thing that had changed was two teacups were now in the dish drain, because, I assumed, Constable James had fixed tea for Albert. "Have you spoken with Beatrix? Did she clean up after dinner? I ask because I find it hard to believe Teddy did such a thorough job."

"Now, wait a minute," said Dave. "We guys can wash dishes and put leftovers away."

"I know that, but I suspect Teddy was tired after his day at the festival and wouldn't have had the energy to do all this."

"Leta, that's part of what I need to tell you. I've spoken with Beatrix. She helped wrap the food and put it in the fridge, and she put dishes in the sink to soak, but that was it. It was Fiona who cleaned this room spic and span."

Phew. She already knows Fiona was here Friday night, so I don't have to find a way to tell her Watson gave Dickens that bit of information. "Oh! What was she doing here?"

"I'll tell you eventually, but I'd rather we do the walk-through first, so your observations aren't clouded by the details of Fiona's visit." With that, we moved to the hall and the bedroom.

In the bedroom, I again noted the lamp and the absence of his spectacles. "Did the SOCOs find Teddy's glasses?"

Gemma shook her head. "No." We all knew that was odd. If they weren't in the bedroom, they should at least have been in the house.

"Okay, ladies, has anyone looked beneath the bed?" Dave looked pleased with his question.

Gemma smiled. "See, Dave, two brains, or in this case, three, are better than one. Would you like to do the honors?"

"Sure." He knelt and then laid flat to scoot farther under the bed. He came out with a pair of wire-rimmed spectacles.

"Bloody hell, I was right to be bothered. I called the SOCO in charge to followup on a few items, and he admitted they hadn't checked for them. He hemmed and hawed about being called away to a fatal car accident near Stow and this being a straightforward scene. Let's just say I'm not best pleased with him. The glasses were something obvious he should have checked for.

"We may still conclude this is a natural death, but allowing hasty assumptions to lead us astray is unacceptable." She stared at the bed where the covers were in disarray, probably wondering what else might have been missed.

I could tell she was irked and couldn't blame her. All the more reason for us to do a thorough job. "Did they take the book away? The one in the bed?"

"Yes. He was reading *Dracula*. Found that out by speaking to Fiona."

So that's where the mention of Dracula came from. I'll have to remember to tell that to Dickens. "Did she help him to bed too? I mean, how'd she know about the book?"

"Yes, but let's move to the library, and after we're done in there, we can sit and I'll share the rest of what I heard from her."

Dave and I followed her down the hall. I went straight to the desk. "These papers are calling me. Are you okay if I look through them and try to sort them into some meaningful stacks? Oh! I see you moved the binder to the edge of the desk."

"Go for it, Leta. Maybe you'll find something more than book orders, bills, and random scribbled notes. I didn't have time to go through it all as well as I'd have liked to."

It was an interesting hodgepodge, and as I moved papers and books aside, I began to discern a pattern. One group of papers in the upper middle of the desk had to do with the bookshop, another to the left had a medical focus—doctors' bills and articles on hip replacement and such. Off to the right were receipts from the local garden center and pages torn from a garden catalog. Mixed in among the somewhat organized piles, I noted two odd items and set them aside. They were yellowed sheets of paper with typing—one by T.S. Eliot and the other by Mark Twain. *Odd. Guess they're reproductions or something, since they're not in a notebook.*

The topmost piece of paper in the bookshop stack was a list titled "Ask B". That had to be Beatrix. The bulleted list made me smile—Book club, window display, used book section, Facebook, Cotswolds authors, Flea markets, Trixie. I was willing to bet he wanted to see if he could carry the handmade notecards and bookmarks made by Beatrix's niece. Since Trixie had come to Astonbury and begun working in the Book Nook, she'd made a name for herself. I'd have to ask Beatrix whether they got around to discussing his questions.

In the desk drawers, I found bank statements rubber-banded together, flyers for estate sales, a colorful map of the Cotswolds, and a list of Charing Cross bookshops. I flashed on the state of my desk drawers. They weren't any less chaotic, but I knew where everything was. One, of course, held only a soft towel. That was Christie's drawer where she curled up whenever she pleased.

I saved the binder for last. My mouth dropped open as I turned page after page of letters written by famous authors . . . many from the 18 and 1900s. *These must be worth a fortune.*

Dave, meanwhile, sat in one of the chairs looking through the binder he'd found in the display case. "What a fascinating collection—probably not much of value, but interesting." He held it up to show me a black and white illustration of Pooh and Piglet. It looked as though it had been torn from a book or a magazine. "I guess this is why the brass plate is titled 'Bless the Children.' It's mostly illustrations and clippings, even a torn paper book cover—all from children's authors from the late 1800s and early 1900s.

"Every item is slipped into an archival protective cover to keep it from being damaged by moisture and fingerprints. Collectors like Teddy put the pages in special collector-grade three-ring binders like this one."

I held up the notebook I'd looked through. "I think this one may be the most valuable because it contains letters."

I went back to studying the desk and its surroundings. Something on the bookshelves to the right caught my eye. As I'd noted the day before, the shelves on the lower half of the bookcase weren't dedicated to particular authors. Instead, they looked to be the books Teddy read. One book was positioned with its front cover facing out instead of its spine. It was *Safe Haven* by Nicholas Sparks. *Odd, I can't imagine Teddy being a Nicholas Sparks fan.*

From my seat behind the desk, I scanned the other books on the shelf. They were mainly thrillers and mysteries by authors like Lee Childs, Quintin Jardine, Robert B. Parker, and Ian Rankin. I stood to take a closer look.

When I went to pull *Safe Haven* from the shelf, I realized two things—one, it was taller and slightly wider than the other books, and two, it wouldn't budge. I pushed and prodded and only by accident moved it—grabbing the right edge and opening it to the left as I would any book. It was a clever reproduction of an actual book cover, heavy cloth-covered cardboard encased in a shiny paper cover.

Behind it was a small safe. *Some detective you are*, I thought. On the inside of the cover was a handwritten inscription—

You found me! Now you must find my key.

"Oh my gosh! Come look at this!" Dave and Gemma looked over my shoulder.

Dave reached over and flipped the cover open and closed. "How clever. 'Must find the key?' This is like a game—like something from an Agatha Christie book. All we need now is Hercule Poirot and his little grey cells."

The expression on Gemma's face was inscrutable, something between a grin and a grimace. "Right. Clever. Just what we need. Why couldn't it be something straightforward?"

I felt around the edges of the safe and then outside the book cover. "Wouldn't it be marvelous if the key were tucked in here somewhere, or would that be too simple?"

By now, Gemma was clearly grimacing. "Simple, I'd like simple. I don't have time for puzzles. Let's leave this for now, and maybe you two can come back to it."

I could tell Dave was trying to stifle a laugh. Like me, he was probably dying to brainstorm ideas on where the key could be hidden, but he shifted topics. "Okay, then. How 'bout you tell us what you learned from Fiona?"

That proposal seemed more to Gemma's liking. She sat in the desk chair, and Dave and I turned the wingback chairs towards her. "Turns out Fiona has known Teddy since before his wife died. They first met when she worked for the NHS—the National Health Service to you Yanks—as home help for his wife. He and his wife took such a liking to the girl, Teddy hired her as a fulltime caretaker and had her move into the spare room. When his wife died some years back, he took Fiona on part-time at Bluebird Books and let her move into the tiny flat above the shop—for a pittance, in my opinion.

"Of course, she couldn't make ends meet with only part-time work, so she also worked a few shifts at a local pub."

"And she also pitches in over here?" I asked. "When does she find time to sleep?"

Gemma continued. "She's given up the work at the pub since Teddy's mobility has decreased, and now she comes over here most evenings after the bookshop closes to help him with whatever needs doing. I get the impression they had almost a father-daughter or grandfather-granddaughter relationship."

I thought about the pill case in the bedroom. "Does she help him with his medications?"

"Yes, and several nights a week, stays here until she knows he's in and out of the shower safely, and then helps him to bed. He liked for her to read to him in here, and she was reading *Dracula* to him Friday evening before tucking him in bed with the book."

Guess her home health care experience has come in handy. "Sounds like a wonderful arrangement for them both. He was lucky to have her. And, just think, there's no way she could have afforded to live in the heart of Chipping Camden without his generosity."

Dave looked thoughtful. "Gemma, what was it in the conversation that prompted you to come back here?"

"The door—the door was unlocked, but Fiona told me she put the cat out and locked the door behind her as she left. She has a key, and that's her routine."

"And when I tried the door, it was unlocked. So who unlocked it?"

It was as though a lightbulb went off in my head. "Someone was here after Fiona left! Someone else must have a key too."

Gemma nodded in agreement. "Exactly. That's what I thought—someone has to have a key, as there's no evidence of a break-in. And they came in after Fiona and failed to lock the door when they left."

Now, Dave looked confused instead of thoughtful. "I get that all this sounds like a mystery novel, but if Teddy died in his sleep, does any of it matter? Do the police need to spend time trying to work out every little detail of the evening or the puzzle of the safe? Or worry about whether notebooks are misplaced or missing?"

Gemma chuckled. "Tuppence, do you want to explain to your partner-in-training why it matters? Sorry, Dave, but Wendy and Belle—the other two members of the Little Old Ladies' Detective Agency—wouldn't have to ask those questions."

I nodded. "Until the coroner does his job, the police won't know for sure whether Teddy died of natural causes. And it's a best practice to piece together evidence as soon as possible after what could be a crime—before clues go stale or disappear.

Even if it's not a murder, it may be a crime scene—if anything was taken."

When Gemma laughed, her blonde ponytail shook. "Spoken like a true amateur sleuth. Wendy and Belle would be proud of you. And they'll be disappointed you didn't call them in."

Dave let the jibes bounce off of him and joked he was insulted. "Okay, you two, I've had enough of being compared to the LOLs and found wanting. Next time you ask for my help, I may be otherwise engaged . . . with a pint . . . in a pub."

As we returned the chairs to their positions facing the fireplace, a leg on my chair snagged on the rug. When I tilted the chair forward to try to unhook it, Dave told me to hold on. He pointed to the chair leg where it had pulled back the rug and knelt to retrieve a piece of paper. "Look at this. It's a page torn from one of those black and white composition notebooks like the kids carry to school."

Gemma held out her hands like she was directing traffic. "Hold still. Let me grab an evidence bag."

He came to her side with the page and watched as she carefully inserted it into the bag. Holding the page, Gemma looked puzzled. "Yeah, but what's special about it? It's a handwritten list—not old or anything."

Detective Dave, as I was beginning to think of him, took the bag from Gemma when she held it out. "Hmm, I think it's a list of where he planned to donate parts of his collection. See how the list is separated into universities and individuals? Oh! And look here, Gilbert's name is scribbled at the bottom, as is mine. Looks as though he wanted to give Gilbert items related to Arthur Conan Doyle, and he's written J.M. Barrie next to my name."

He's getting into the spirit of this detecting thing, I thought.

"Okay, but why is it on the floor? Why isn't it on his desk or in one of his notebooks? We've stumbled across a loose page and there's a key to the safe secreted somewhere. This gets more and more like a treasure hunt by the minute."

Gemma almost cracked a smile, but not quite. "Great. Just what I need! So, do I call in Constable James to help and tell him to bring a copy of *Treasure Island* with him?"

Stifling a giggle, I said, "How 'bout the game of *Clue*?" As I flashed on an image of the board game, I had a sudden more serious thought. "Hold on a sec, I want to check something in the bedroom." *What if Teddy hid something in there?*

I got on my hands and knees and lifted the bed skirt to look beneath the bed. Dust bunnies filled the space near the center, as though whoever regularly vacuumed never got beyond the edges. I sat back on my heels and pulled out my phone, switching the flashlight on.

Dave knelt beside me. "What on earth are you doing, Leta? I didn't see anything else when I retrieved the glasses."

"I'm not sure. I just want to be sure there's not something else that could be important. I saw a movie once where someone stuck a treasure map between the bed slats and the boxsprings, and of course, we should check between the mattress and boxsprings too."

I was as surprised as Dave and Gemma when my hunch paid off. Encased in another of those plastic sleeves was a quote from *Hamlet*, centered in the middle of the page—the word *dreams* in all caps.

> *To sleep, perchance to dream—ay, there's the rub,*
> *For in that sleep of death what DREAMS may come*

Gemma snorted. "Oh, bloody hell. Why on earth would he hide that? It's not like it's valuable. I know this is in poor taste, but it's almost as though he planned to send us on a wild goose chase."

Looking at me, Dave shrugged his shoulders. "To paraphrase Shakespeare—from the same play—'Methinks the lady doth protest too much.' What do you think, Leta?"

I couldn't help laughing at the exasperated expression on Gemma's face as I explained, "*Hamlet*. Both quotes are from *Hamlet*. Though what the heck any of it means is beyond me."

When Gemma's phone rang, she looked relieved. "DI Taylor. Yes, yes, I am. You're willing to see me today? Sure. I can be there at two. Yes, see you then." Before she turned back to us, I took the opportunity to snap a photo of the quote.

She hung up and smiled. "Finally, something straightforward. That was Teddy's solicitor, and he's prepared to meet with me today. As much fun as I'm having with you two, I think I'm ready to leave the treasure hunt behind for some real police work—seeing the victim's will."

Dave patted her on the back. "I understand. It's been an interesting hour, but I don't know that we've gotten anywhere. Do you? I mean, are you any closer to knowing whether or not the poor man died peacefully in his sleep?"

Looking at me, Gemma sighed. "Not exactly. But, as Leta pointed out, we've got to consider everything. When I hear from the coroner, I'll let you know whether all this is moot—beyond perhaps helping the heir or heirs determine if anything was stolen."

We left by the kitchen door and Gemma locked up. Dickens and Watson were lounging beneath a shade tree. They seemed to have become friends.

Gemma," I asked, "who's taking care of Watson?"

"Blast. I forgot all about the darned cat. Any chance you

could take him for a day or two until I talk to the solicitor and possibly the next of kin?"

Dickens barked. "Yes, let's take Watson with us."

Even Dave knew that was iffy. "Um, do you think Christie would accept him? No offense, but she can be kind of uppity and downright cranky."

"Cranky? That's an understatement. She managed to make friends with Paddington at the inn, but I'm not sure she'd welcome him or Watson at our cottage."

Gemma threw up her hands. "Guess there's nothing for it but to take him home to Mum and Dad and hope Paddington takes it in stride. Those two would never forgive me if I called in Animal Control."

Watson wasn't buying it. "Why do I have to leave? Can't Fiona come over?"

Poor guy. This was a lot for him to deal with. Still, I was happy Gemma had a solution, if only a temporary one. If I'd been the last resort, I couldn't have said no. Time for me and Dave and Dickens to head to the Graham Greene session.

Dave came to an abrupt stop as we exited the garden. "The garbage can. We need to check the garbage can."

"What? Why?"

Pulling the lid off, he peered inside. "Who knows? It's just an idea. Look, empty plastic sleeves—two of 'em." That brought Gemma running.

"Blimey. Good call, Dave. If the SOCOs didn't bother to check for the specs beneath the bed, it was a good bet they didn't check the wheelie bins. Here's another pair of gloves. Do you mind reaching inside to grab them off the top? We can leave the rest to the SOCOs. I'm not digging through the rubbish, and I don't expect you to either, but, can you roll the wheelie bin back inside the gate, please? That way, it won't get picked up before we can get to it."

Gemma held up her hand and asked us to wait as she jogged to her car. She returned with more evidence bags. Dave hesitated as he handed the plastic to Gemma. "Look, here's a smashed painting or something—maybe a framed print—but there's only a corner of the page left. How odd." He pulled the frame from the bin and studied it more closely. "There's nothing on this scrap to indicate what it was."

One look at Dave told me he was dying to examine his find more closely and to return to the binders to study them as well. *I may have created a monster.*

"Bloody hell. Even more reason for the SOCOs to get back here. Meanwhile, because the frame and these plastic things weren't in the cottage when they were here, they haven't been dusted for prints. Depending on what I learn at the solicitor's office, I may have time to run these over to Quedgeley to SOCO headquarters. And, before you ask, Dave, I'd love to have you go through the binders Monday or Tuesday to give me your take on their contents."

Crestfallen, Dave looked at us both. "No can do, much as I want to. I leave for Edinburgh tomorrow and expect to be gone all week. Someone like Gilbert or perhaps Beatrix might be able to help." He looked at me. "Leta, I bet you'd have a valuable perspective too. Regardless, I sure hope I'll be able to sit and study them when I return. Teddy knew I'd be interested in them because of the book I'm writing."

All Gemma could offer was to let him know when they might be available, which I thought was very generous of her. No matter that she'd asked for our help in this early stage, all too often, I'd known her to cut me out of the loop as an investigation progressed. It would be interesting to see what happened with this one.

We went our separate ways, and I was more than ready to be distracted by a final session at the literary festival. After that, it would be back to the hotel to pick up our bags for the trip home. With Dave taking off for Edinburgh the next day, I could settle back into my routine of yoga with Rhiannon, lattes at Toby's Tearoom, and walks with Dickens. *Even Nancy Drew needed a break from solving mysteries. Didn't she?*

Chapter Eleven

Monday morning, we were up early. I dropped Dave off in Bourton-on-the-Water to pick up a rental car and drove back to Astonbury for yoga. He planned to be gone most of the week and to adjust his schedule based on what he found at the university.

Christie had made her irritation with us clear when we arrived at my cottage Sunday evening. She wouldn't speak to us or get in either of our laps. Instead, she voiced her complaints to Dickens, nonstop.

"They were gone two nights, for goodness' sake! Why didn't you make them come home? Why should I have to make do with little Timmy from next door while you're off gallivanting? He never gets my wet food quite right."

This morning, after her disdainful looks didn't get the desired results, she finally directed her comments to me. "Pfft. The least you can do is get down here and fluff my food."

"I've done that several times, missy."

"Right! Amazing how quickly you can lose your touch when you're gone. Try again."

I turned my back and sipped my coffee until she was slightly more polite. "Okay already, add another dab—please."

And so it had gone until Dave and I drove off. Now, I tried to calm myself on my purple mat as Rhiannon took us through a restorative class, exactly what I needed after the weekend in Chipping Camden. With Wendy off in Cornwall, there'd been no distracting chatter as I found a spot for my mat. If I'd had to explain to her what had gone on Saturday and Sunday, I would never have succeeded in clearing my mind for class.

Rhiannon approached me as I rolled my mat and pulled my sweatshirt over my head, in preparation for the walk to Toby's. "The grapevine is working overtime about your Saturday morning discovery. Given that experience, it was good to see you focusing on your breathing. I only noticed your brain racing a few times. I wish I could go with you to the Tearoom, but I have another class this morning. If you'd like to have a late lunch, give me a call." Leave it to my yoga instructor to allude to the weekend's happenings without prying.

"Thanks, but I've left the day open for puttering around my cottage, catching up on emails, and writing a column about the literary festival. I may have enough information for two columns. Perhaps we can do lunch another day."

I didn't linger at Toby's. After Jenny handed me my vanilla latte and a bag with a lemon scone, I strolled to my car, still feeling pretty relaxed. I'd no sooner unlocked my front door when Christie accosted me. "You owe me a walk. Let's go see Martha and Dylan." That was the good thing about having nothing concrete on my schedule. I could take a walk with my furry friends.

I laid Christie's backpack out and went upstairs to find my walking shoes. When I returned, she'd already positioned herself with her little face poking out, and Dickens was rubbing noses with her.

He barked at his feline companion. "Okay, I admit I missed you some, but I met a cat with green eyes named Watson. If you'd stopped your grousing long enough for me to get a word in edgewise last night, I'd have told you all about him."

"Just who is Watson? Let's get this show on the road, and then you can fill me in."

I sipped my latte as we walked the mile to the pasture, and I listened with half an ear as Dickens regaled Christie with Watson's story. I'd heard most of this Sunday afternoon but hadn't paid much attention then either. It was difficult to have a conversation with Dickens when Dave was around—or anyone else, for that matter. The good news was, unlike Christie, Dickens took my distraction in stride.

He chattered about how much Watson liked Fiona, how he sat in her lap as often as he sat in Teddy's, how she let him out every night, and how he prowled the neighborhood. *It's too bad he wasn't there when the second visitor put in an appearance,* I thought. *What I wouldn't give to know who that was.*

"Dickens, I'm thinking aloud here. If the last visitor had a key, it had to be someone Teddy knew and gave a key to . . . unless somehow the person had access to Teddy or Fiona's key and made a copy. And, who knows? Maybe that someone asked to look at or borrow Teddy's binders and Teddy said okay. Except he wouldn't let the binders leave the house when he was planning to show them off to Dave the next morning, would he?"

"Don't know, Leta. Watson talked a lot about Fiona, and he mentioned Albert came over to drive Teddy several times a week. Also, someone named Pris visited from time to time."

Christie sniffed. "Well, since I wasn't invited, I don't know any of these people, but couldn't that Fiona girl have given her key to someone?"

Now, that's a thought. Gemma thinks Fiona and Teddy had a granddaughter-grandfather relationship, but what if Gemma's wrong?

Dickens continued as though he hadn't heard Christie. "Beyond that, Watson especially likes the grey-haired lady next door. She sits—or sat—in the garden with Teddy sometimes, and she always brings cat treats."

The last line got Christie's attention. "If Timmy would bring cat treats when he takes care of me, that'd be a different story. Hardly any of your friends bring me treats, Leta."

I reached behind me to rub her nose. "I thought Peter brought treats when he took care of you in December."

She extended her paw and patted my neck. "Silly girl, that was forever ago."

"Here come Martha and Dylan." The two donkeys trotted up and stuck their noses over the wall. I pulled carrots from the side pouch on the backpack and smiled at the familiar chomping sounds. Dickens stood on his hind legs, and Martha leaned down to nuzzle him. Then it was time to turn so Christie could get close. That reminded me that I'd taken a photo of Christie riding on Dave's back and needed to write a column to go with it.

We strolled home as my mind wandered to which column to tackle first. Chewing the remaining chunk of scone, I wondered about emailing my sisters that Dave and I had found a new acquaintance dead in his bed. *Nah, no need. I'll write to Sophia about the festival, especially about Graham Greene. That will be right up her alley. Anna, not so much, since she's more into the fantasy genre these days.*

The phone rang as I rolled out my chair and Dickens scooted beneath the desk. It was Libby, and I barely had a chance to say hello before she started up. "So, you declined to take this handsome cat home? He and Paddington had a standoff last night before they settled down. Remember when you brought Christie here in her backpack, and she all but ran Paddington out of his own home? Last night's meeting was much easier."

Since Libby had gotten the scoop from Gemma, she also wanted to know how I was doing. She'd never met Teddy, but Gavin had described him as jovial and interesting, and he'd been shocked to hear of his death.

I stroked Christie, who was sprawled on my desk. "I know you can appreciate how distressing it was. Not nearly as bad as when you found the dead body on the riverbank, but still awful. If the coroner determines he died of natural causes, it will be much easier to deal with. I don't suppose Gemma's told you anything on that count, has she?"

"Nope. She ran in late yesterday afternoon, handed me the cat, and took off. By the time she and Jonas went to Quedgeley and back, it was late. She did tell me she took Jonas—I mean Constable James—so he could hear her read the riot act to the lead SOCO. She wanted Jonas to understand that the officer in charge—that would be my Gemma—must see to it that everyone does their job properly. Plus the ride over and back allowed her to bring him up to speed and brainstorm with him in person.

"She must have gotten up earlier than usual this morning to take her run because I saw her driving off before I had her basket of scones and fruit ready. With this case and handling some of DCI Burton's caseload, she's been running full-out since you called her Saturday morning."

Gemma was fortunate her mom took such good care of her. Living in the guest cottage at the inn, she could always count on a breakfast basket. We wrapped up and I turned my attention to email and Facebook. I saw my editor had shared my latest column about cycling in the Cotswolds and it had garnered lots of comments. There was nothing urgent in my email—there rarely was since I'd retired last year from my corporate career. I responded to the few chatty emails I'd received from family and friends and thought, *I need to work on my columns.* For some reason, I was procrastinating, and I knew why when my phone rang and it was Gemma. I'd been anticipating her call all morning, without realizing it.

"Hello. Do you have news for me?"

Sometimes I could picture Gemma's smirk in her voice. "Now, now, Tuppence, I have some news I can share and some that will have to wait. You can't be privy to everything I know."

Aaargh. That condescending tone makes me want to strangle her. She only puts me in the know when she needs something from me. I wasn't smirking—I was scowling, and I was sure that came across in my reply. "Fine, then. Tell me what you can."

"First, I met with the solicitor. Nice chap who was eager to help. You don't often find one who wants to speak with you on a Sunday. When I explained there was some question as to how Teddy died, he understood right off that knowing who stood to benefit was important. You know, *cui bono?*"

"Yes, it's Latin for who benefits. Is it some distant relative?"

"I can't tell you yet, but I expect you'll find out through the grapevine soon enough. Now, the other thing—"

I cut her off. "Why would I hear anything through the grapevine? I'm not plugged into Chipping Camden gossip."

Her chuckle irritated me no end. *Why even bother to bring it up if she wasn't going to tell me?* "You'll have to trust me on this.

Now, back to the second thing. Apparently, my *discussion* with the SOCO about his unsatisfactory processing of the scene got back to the coroner and lit a fire under her. When she called, she mentioned wanting to avoid getting on my bad side. Whatever it takes. Anyway, I'm afraid I *do* have a murder on my hands. Mr. Byrd was smothered.

"The coroner said it was fairly obvious—blue lips and purple splotches in his eyes—even before she did the autopsy."

"But he looked so peaceful. With his book beneath his hand. Oh my gosh! Did the killer arrange him that way? How awful!"

"I'm sorry to say, the killer probably did, and I wonder whether he went into the bedroom with the intent to kill. Regardless, Mr. Byrd had to have struggled."

"Was he . . . was he smothered with his pillow?

"We think it was the pillow, yes. Thank goodness I got the SOCOs back over there to go through the bin and do a more thorough walkthrough. Is Dave there? Need to tell him thanks for thinking to look in the wheelie bin."

"He's on his way to Edinburgh, remember? Do you think the killer was looking for something? Or came to kill Teddy for another reason entirely?"

"Hmmm. I haven't figured that out yet. Sure, we found some odd items in the wheelie bin, but Teddy could have put them there. We don't know yet that anything was stolen. That's why I was hoping Dave could look through the binders."

I was puzzled. "What exactly are you hoping Dave will find? I know he'll want to look through them from a curiosity perspective, but I'm not sure what you think he'll see, since he never saw them in their original condition. I bet Beatrix would be more helpful."

"I'm not sure either. I just know Dave found empty plastic sleeves in the wheelie bin, and I was hoping there'd be some rhyme or reason to what might have been in them if he studied the binders. And we know Fiona last saw one of the binders on the bed, but all three were in the library by the time we arrived on the scene."

Then why not ask Beatrix, as I suggested? I don't know why I bother trying to mask my irritation with her. Well, yes I do. I was raised in the South, and we Southern ladies don't do angry and confrontational if we can avoid it.

"Gemma, Dave's a writer, and he's knowledgeable about a few authors like J.M. Barrie and Arthur Conan Doyle because he's written about them, but he's not a scholar. I'm as likely to see anomalies in the flow of the books as he is, if only because I've listened to him talk about his research for months." There, I said it—without biting her head off. *What part of my attention to detail did she not get?*

"Hmmm, didn't think of that." And why not? I wondered. I'd made good suggestions she was choosing to ignore, and Dave and I had already done plenty to move the investigation along. *I found the safe, for goodness' sake.*

I'd hardly known Teddy, so I wasn't invested in solving this case. At least, that's what I told myself. "Well, Gemma, I appreciate the update. I guess I'll let you get back to work, since I don't have a dog in this fight."

She chuckled. "Dog in this fight . . . haven't heard that expression in . . . well, in a dog's age!"

Dickens stirred and looked at me from his position beneath my feet. "Fight? You know I don't fight." Tickling him beneath his chin, I thought about his issue with our funny human language and almost missed Gemma's next comment.

"I think before long you *may* have a dog in this fight, but that's all I can say for now. Seriously, if I could, I'd tell you. I just can't. But, I guess I could use some help with those binders. Have you got time today or Tuesday to go through them?"

Who am I trying to fool? Sitting in Quedgeley going through letters and clippings from famous authors is right up my alley, plus it would be perfectly safe. Nothing for Dave to be worried about. I blew out my breath. "Sure, I'll work it out. Do I need you with me, or can you just set it up for me to go on my own?" She promised to get back to me with an answer, and she requested I contact her when the grapevine news about Teddy's heir reached me.

So much for writing any columns. With a visit to Quedgeley looming and my curiosity piqued as to the grapevine, I wandered into the kitchen and stared into the fridge. I *need to visit the grocery for salad fixings and fruit, maybe ingredients for a pot of soup. I should have Belle and Peter over for dinner too.* Peter and Wendy coordinated their schedules so that when Wendy was away, Peter spent the night at Belle's cottage, and this week, Wendy was vacationing in Cornwall.

I called Belle and Peter and invited them for Wednesday evening. Peter was effusive. "You're a lifesaver. Mum's not much for cooking these days, and my skills are limited to two or three dishes. We'll be down to beans on toast soon unless I get takeaway."

My list started with Greek salad ingredients, as they'd expect one of those no matter what else I served. I flipped through a recipe book and finally decided on simple—as in a Bolognese sauce served with ziti or rigatoni and some freshly grated romano cheese. I rarely followed a recipe, as I'd been making the red sauce since I was a teenager. I varied the ingredients depending on what I could find at the grocery store.

Ground chuck was a must. If I could find ground pork, I'd add that. I'd never gone in for celery and carrots in my sauce, though many chefs did.

I can't go grocery shopping on an empty stomach, I thought. It was slim pickings in the fridge, so I settled on cheese and crackers. Staring out the window as I munched, I wondered how long I'd have to wait to discover who was named in Teddy's will. *I bet if it were a complete stranger, Gemma would have told me the name. So, who can it be?*

When my phone rang and I saw Beatrix's name pop up on the screen, I realized I hadn't checked on her since I'd gotten home, and I hoped she was doing okay. Of all my friends, she was the only one who'd known Teddy more than a few days. "Hi, Beatrix, how are you?"

"Oh my gosh, Leta. Can you come to the shop, *now*? I need you."

"What's wrong? Yes, I can come, but what's wrong? Where's Trixie?"

"She's here. That's not it. He . . . he left me his bookshop. Teddy left me Bluebird Books. What am I going to do?"

At least I knew she and Trixie were okay, but I couldn't tell if she was excited, horrified, or what. I told her I'd be right there and shot out the door, hollering to Dickens and Christie that I'd be back. *Guess I've got the answer to cui bono.*

Chapter Twelve

Trixie looked relieved when I opened the door to the Book Nook. "Thank goodness you're here. Aunt Beatrix is beside herself with worry or grief or both. She's in the back-room, pacing."

Rushing to the back, I grabbed Beatrix in a hug. She wasn't crying, but her eyes were red and she was sniffling. The pacing and the wadded tissue in her hand told me my typically matter-of-fact friend was distraught. I sat her at the table and made tea.

She sipped and moaned. "I can't believe Teddy's dead, and I can't believe I'm in his will—he's left me his bookshop and . . . just about everything else. The solicitor called and said he'd give me more detail in person—that he wouldn't typically have contacted me this soon except he'd spoken to Gemma. Oh my gosh!"

I didn't know how it worked in the UK. When Henry died, I had a copy of our wills in the safe in the bedroom, so there were no surprises. And when I thought back to my mother passing away, I recalled my father had handled everything. Mom had made a list of her jewelry and how to divide it, but that was it. *Guess it's different when the bequest is a surprise.*

"How can I help, Beatrix?"

Her response had nothing to do with my question. "And then Gemma called and said Teddy didn't die quietly in his sleep—he was murdered. It was enough of a shock to hear he passed away in his sleep. To hear someone killed him—It's all more than I can deal with.

"And I . . . I feel I need to see the solicitor today so I can let Pris and the others at Bluebird Books know. Beyond their shock and grief at Teddy's death, I'm sure they're worried about their jobs. I at least need to let them know the shop will go on, though I've no idea how I'll manage that." Her elbows on the table, she put her face in her hands.

"Let's take one thing at a time. How much did Gemma tell you about how Teddy died?"

"He was smothered. I can see this horrible scene in my mind. Someone holding a pillow over his face until he . . . he stopped breathing. How could someone do that? Who could do that?"

I let her murmur about that for a moment, and then I asked about the will. "I take it that wasn't your only shock. The news about the will comes as a complete surprise too?"

She looked up. That topic was easier for her to talk about. "Yes . . . and no. He's been after me to buy the shop for over a year now—ever since he got to the point where he couldn't go in every day. I kept telling him I couldn't handle two shops, even if we could work out an affordable price. And then Trixie arrived." Trixie had moved in with Beatrix in the fall and become a tremendous help to her aunt. She was a natural with the customers, and her handcrafted cards and bookmarks had taken off with the locals and the tourists. "He stepped up his campaign after that."

"And how did you feel then? Did having Trixie here change your mind about taking on another shop?"

"A bit. Teddy and I began to talk more seriously about my purchasing the shop but I wasn't eager to go into debt. Two weeks ago, he proposed I take over managing it for the summer as a way to judge whether I saw it as viable, and over dinner Friday night, we ironed out the details of that arrangement. The rascal! He must have been pretty sure of me if he'd already put me in his will."

"Or at least he was sure you could make a go of it. He knew you were a capable businesswoman. Do you have an appointment with the solicitor to get more information?"

"Yes, at 4:30, and I'm hoping you'll go with me, Leta. It's all so much to absorb, and you've got such a level head—and a background in banking."

"I'm happy to go, Beatrix. I'll take notes and try to ask good questions, but you know I wasn't a banker in the way most people think of one." I laughed. "I worked in leadership training and communications, not anything to do with loans or credit. Heaven forbid they'd let me near the money!" I looked at my watch. It was already two. "Let me run home and change into something more appropriate for a solicitor's office, and I'll be back to pick you up by three." It was about a thirty-minute drive to Chipping Camden, and it wouldn't do to be late.

Dickens greeted me at the door and followed me upstairs, where Christie was curled up on my bed. "Are we going somewhere, Leta? You're putting on nice clothes. Is it a car ride? Can I go?"

No matter how often Dickens peppered me with questions, his rapid-fire barks always entertained me. When I told him I didn't see why he couldn't go, he raced downstairs. Christie rolled and stretched but remained silent. As long as I was back to feed her this evening, she'd be content.

On the drive to Chipping Camden, Beatrix babbled. I suppose it was her way of working through the news she was now the owner of two bookshops and goodness knows what else. She and Teddy had discussed his concerns about the shop Friday evening.

"He'd been worried about Pris's management of the shop for a while, but couldn't put his finger on what the problem was. Was she just a poor manager, an inept recordkeeper, or was she maybe skimming off the top? All he knew was that since he stopped going in, the shop was losing money. It had never been a huge moneymaker, but this was different.

"That was one thing he hoped I'd figure out when I took over for the summer. Pris had been a good sales clerk, but maybe management was more than she could handle. Regardless, she was quite upset when he told her Friday morning I'd be coming in as manager. He planned to continue paying her the same salary, but I guess the idea that there'd be someone else in charge didn't sit well."

I told her about the list I'd seen on Teddy's desk and asked whether they'd had a chance to discuss it.

"Oh yes. In his mind, that was part of the problem. He couldn't do those things himself and kept asking Pris to take them on, but she put him off—told him she had too much to do to start anything new. I bet she didn't have any idea how to create a Facebook page for the shop, and probably wasn't a natural at window displays. You have to be a jack of all trades in this business."

The solicitor's office was close to the High Street. *We should be able to walk to Bluebird Books once we're finished here.* "Why don't you go on in, while I let Dickens walk a bit? I'll be right behind you."

A quick inspection of the ground beneath the rowan tree out front was all Dickens needed. "You know, of all your friends, Beatrix pays me the least attention. I mean she's nice enough, but she never gives me belly rubs or scratches my ears."

"Shush. She's more of a cat person, and you've got plenty of admirers without Beatrix." Inside, the receptionist directed us to the stairs and said she'd be up shortly with tea.

Once introductions were made and tea served, the solicitor quickly got down to business. "Miss Scott, I can understand why you're shocked to discover Mr. Byrd bequeathed almost his entire estate to you. When there's family involved, there's an expectation on their parts that they'll inherit something, but in situations like Mr. Byrd's where there's no family, a bequest can come as quite a surprise. Now, do you understand that, except for the parts of his collection he designated to go to museums and one smaller bequest, you are the recipient of the bulk of his estate?"

There was an audible gulp for Beatrix. "Yes, I haven't quite absorbed it, nor do I know what his entire estate is, but I understand most of it comes to me. I guess that means the cottage, its contents, and Bluebird Books, right?"

"Primarily, yes. Plus the Rolls and the funds in his investment accounts. This is a substantial bequest, and I hope you have a solicitor of your own and a financial advisor to assist you. I, of course, would be happy to take you on as a client, should you so choose."

Dickens was concerned about Watson. "What about the cat? Who gets the cat?"

We all looked at him, and I jumped in with a humorous but

truthful explanation. "My dog is asking why there's no mention of the cat. Gemma took him to her parents, but surely Teddy mentions the cat in his will."

He nodded. "But of course. The cat goes to Miss Scott as well. Watson, as I believe he's called, used to go with Mr. Byrd to the bookshop, so I suppose it's possible he could take up residence there."

Beatrix looked overwhelmed, so I jumped in. "Thank you. As you've mentioned, this is quite a shock to my friend. She brought me along to offer support and to ask questions she might not think of. My most immediate question concerns Teddy's cottage. When will she able to visit?"

"I'm able to give you the keys to both the cottage and the shop, but as the constabulary has informed me the cottage is a crime scene, they will have to grant you permission for access."

Was that why Gemma wanted me to contact her once I knew who the heir was? "Would that be DI Gemma Taylor? Did she give you further instructions in that regard?"

"Yes and no. She said the cottage is off-limits for now. Miss Scott, you may visit the shop, and you may drive the car, but of course, there is paperwork required to finalize the transfer of ownership. I will begin the process for that and notify you when we can meet again. In the meantime, I have a piece of private correspondence Mr. Byrd left for you." He passed a brown envelope to Beatrix.

She fumbled with the clasp and pulled out a single sheet of parchment paper. It was a short letter written in a beautiful script. As she read to herself, her mouth formed an "O." Looking up, she passed the parchment to me.

I read aloud—

Dear Beatrix,
I can think of no better person to care for my beloved

Bluebird Books and my treasured collection. You have been a good friend to me these many years, and I trust you will be a loving custodian.

As one who shares my passion for literature, I hope this little puzzle will remind you of my playful nature and lighten your mood as you take on the task of clearing out the clutter in my cottage.

In my office, you will find a small safe. Start there and follow the clues! Enjoy yourself, dear friend, and remember me fondly.

Love Teddy

"That is so like him." She sobbed and looked across the desk. "But what if I can't solve the puzzle? How will we get into the safe?"

"I have an extra key and instructions to give it to you, should you be unsuccessful. But Mr. Byrd also directed me to ensure you make a good-faith effort to solve the puzzle. I'm not sure how I'll ascertain that, but I'll try." He smiled and shook his head. "He was a rascal, wasn't he?"

Funny, Beatrix had used the same word about Teddy. I was sorry I wouldn't have a chance to get to know him better. *I can't wait to tell this story to Dave. He'll get such a kick out of it.* "Beatrix, we've got a head start because I stumbled across the safe when I was there with Dave. It was disguised as a book! We'll figure it out. And as soon as we leave here, I'll call Gemma to see about access to the cottage, though I don't see us tackling that today."

With the keys and the envelope tucked safely in Beatrix's purse, we stood outside the solicitor's office. The new owner of Bluebird Books seemed dazed, and I suggested she collect her thoughts before we walked to the bookshop.

"Beatrix, let's think of what you have to accomplish in this initial visit. First, I think we need to establish who has keys to what. I know from Gemma that Fiona has a key to the cottage. And did you know that Fiona lives in the flat above the shop? And, oh my goodness, does Albert have a set of keys to the car?"

She nodded. "I know Teddy and Fiona were very close, and he may have mentioned the flat, but I don't recall. Pris must have keys to the shop, and if Fiona opens for her on occasion, she may have keys too. It could be useful to let Fiona keep her set of cottage keys so I have someone here in Chipping Camden to pop by when need be. If Teddy trusted her, that's good enough for me."

"What about Albert and the car?"

"I don't know much about Albert, except he looked vaguely familiar to me when I saw him at the festival. I know he drives for Teddy and does odd jobs at the shop. I think he has a carpentry background. What do you think about the car keys?"

I was trying to decide what I thought when Beatrix said, "But wait a minute. When I had dinner with Teddy Friday night, he told me something that struck me as odd. You were there at the festival when Fiona came to fetch Albert to fix the table in the shop. The three of them left together, and after tending to the table, Albert drove Teddy to the cottage. He helped him inside, as usual, and Teddy went to the loo. When he came out, he found the lad in the library. He expected him to be gone."

"Was Teddy concerned?"

"Not really. Said Albert wanted to confirm the pickup time for Saturday. Teddy said he's turned into quite a reader since starting work at the bookshop. He's always haunted estate sales in search of furniture he can refinish and sell, and nowadays he also scouts for books. From time to time, he brought Teddy the odd item for his opinion about its value, and sometimes Teddy bought the book or old newspaper for his collection. If he wasn't interested, it wound up at the Bolton Flea Market in Manchester. You know, could be that's where I've seen Albert, since I'm there so often stocking up on used books."

"Maybe so. As far as the car keys, though, I think you need to get them back. I can't see you needing a driver, can you?"

Beatrix shook her head no. I wondered aloud what she'd eventually do with the Rolls and suggested she consult Peter. As a garage owner, he could check it out for her and help her decide whether to keep it or sell it and probably help her find a buyer if she didn't want it for herself.

In my head, I shifted gears to what Beatrix should say to her new employees. She needed to express her sorrow about Teddy *and* put them at ease about the immediate future of the shop and their jobs—while being careful about making any long-term commitments. It would take time for her to get her arms around the shop's inventory and finances, not to mention the work ethic and expertise of Pris, Fiona, and whoever else worked there.

"Beatrix, I know you've got a good business head, but this is new territory for you. I suggest you keep it short and sweet. They're sure to fix us tea, so there will be a bit of time to reminisce about Teddy, but let's not spend too much time there. Today's not the day to ask questions beyond what you absolutely must know—like who has keys."

"You're right, Leta. I need to get my arms around the business, but not today."

"Have you visited the shop before? Oh! That's a silly question. Surely you have if you agreed to manage it for the summer."

"Yes, I have, but not as often since Teddy wasn't going in anymore. And, since he hadn't told anyone about our new arrangement until Friday morning, I've not been in recently. I think Pris and Fiona will remember me as Teddy's friend and fellow bookshop owner, and Pris, of course, knows I was set to begin managing Bluebird Books."

The shop closed at six, so our arrival at 5:45 was good timing. Beatrix surprised me by stopping a few doors before the shop to stare in the window of the Chipping Camden Café.

"Beatrix, are you okay?"

"Yes, I just need to calm myself before we walk in."

As Dickens and I moved to her side, a greeting rang out. "Beatrix, is that you?"

I looked around and saw a familiar-looking gentleman crossing the street. *Where do I know him from?* I studied him as he approached. *Oh! It's the man with the cravat, the one we met Friday at the festival.* Today, instead of the cravat, he sported a turtleneck and a tweed jacket.

When he touched Beatrix on the arm and leaned in to kiss her on the cheek, her eyes brimmed with tears. "Alastair," she said, "are you on your way to Bluebird Books?"

"No, no, my dear. I'm popping in to the candy shop to get sweets for my Bonnie. I've spent the afternoon assessing and making an offer on a large personal library. You know, I get calls from time to time when a book lover is forced to downsize to a retirement home. This gentleman has close to 1500 books he'll not be able to take with him." He paused. "I was shocked and saddened to hear about Teddy. I know you two were close."

A tear trickled down Beatrix's cheek, and the two murmured together before she shook herself and looked my way. "Leta, have you met Alastair Porter?"

Stepping up, I offered my hand. "Yes, we met at the Barrie presentation last Friday." We exchanged pleasantries about Dave's talk, and he once again suggested Dave and I visit his flea market stall. With that, he hugged Beatrix and explained he had a three-hour drive to Manchester ahead and needed to get on the road.

The brief interlude seemed to have fortified Beatrix, and we approached Bluebird Books just as Fiona was flipping the sign from Open to Closed. The bell overhead jangled as she opened the door and said, "So sorry ladies, but we're . . ." She stopped in mid-sentence, perhaps because she recognized me or Beatrix or both of us.

When she opened the door wide and stepped back, I dropped Dickens's leash, and as I knew he would, he barked hello. Kneeling to greet him gave Fiona a moment to regain her composure as I introduced myself. "Hi, I met you at the festival Friday afternoon. I'm Leta Parker, and this is Dickens."

She shook my hand and hesitated. "Leta—oh! You're the one who found Teddy!"

Without sharing any details, I explained it had been a shock and expressed my sorrow for her loss. "I understand you'd been with Teddy for several years and also cared for his wife when she was ill. This must be hard for you."

Her eyes shone with tears. "He was like a grandfather to me." She turned to Beatrix. "And I remember you. Teddy loved your shop in Astonbury. He said he learned a lot from you."

We were consoling each other when a grey-haired woman came out of the back room. *This must be Pris.* I introduced myself again, and as Beatrix stepped forward, Pris hugged her.

The two murmured together before Beatrix turned to include Fiona. "I'm in shock, and I know you must be as well. Losing Teddy is a blow for us all. I . . . I'd like to chat with you both. Could we put out the Closed sign and sit down together?" Pris nodded and motioned us to the back as Fiona locked the front door and flipped the sign.

Much like the room at the Book Nook, this one had tall shelves around the walls, a rectangular table in the middle, several chairs, and a counter with tea and coffee fixings. There was a comfy armchair and ottoman in one corner, and I wondered if it had been Teddy's spot. I offered to fix tea, but Pris stepped in to handle it. Dickens looked at her expectantly until I called him. Instead of coming to me, he settled by Fiona's side and nudged her hand until she scratched his ears.

Beatrix cleared her throat. "Pris, I know Teddy told you he'd asked me to come in to manage Bluebird Books this summer. He wanted me to set up a book club like we have at the Book Nook, plus a few other things." She was fudging a bit, probably to spare Pris's feelings. "I'd planned to begin mid-May. Here's the thing. As you are, I was absorbing the shock of Teddy's sudden death. Then, today, his solicitor called me. Leta and I just met with him."

She looked at me, and I nodded in encouragement as she dabbed at her eyes. "I don't know how to say this other than to come right out with it. Teddy has left Bluebird Books to me. It's another shock, and I can't quite wrap my brain around it . . ."

Fiona's mouth dropped open, and Pris turned red and muttered something I couldn't make out. Beatrix paused for a beat allowing Pris a chance to speak up. When nothing was forthcoming, she continued. "Please know that Bluebird Books will go on and remain open as Teddy would have wanted it to. And I hope you will remain too. You know your customers and they know you."

She continued in that vein, and I thought she was doing a good job. Shifting to the topic of keys, she confirmed that both Pris and Fiona had shop keys, but that only Fiona had keys to the cottage. When she asked about car keys, Fiona told her Albert used the ones hanging in the kitchen at the cottage, that he didn't have a set of his own.

Fiona burst into tears when Beatrix asked if she would hold on to the cottage keys so she could drop by if needed. "Yes, yes I will, but . . . but what about my flat?"

Beatrix moved around the table to put her arms around her. "Fiona, please don't worry. Did you think I'd kick you out? As good as you've been to Teddy?" She shushed her, and Fiona's sobs subsided.

Pris had been oddly quiet, and I wondered whether it was grief, surprise, anger, or some combination that was causing her silence. When she finally spoke, her tone was curt. "Will you be taking over the bills? And the ordering? Setting up book signings? Teddy did most of that."

"We'll work that out in good time. Are you okay to leave things as they are for now—at least for a few days? I'll have my hands full sorting through things at the cottage, and I don't want to make any hasty decisions. Let's set a time for next week, Pris, so you can tell me exactly what Teddy was handling, so nothing falls through the cracks. Will that be okay?"

The conversation turned to Teddy's organizational skills or lack thereof, and the reminiscing began. I wandered to the front of the store while they talked about their friend and employer. I liked the inviting arrangement of tabletop displays and the several comfy chairs scattered in corners. Centered on a large oval table was a two-sided sign that read, "Inspired by the Cotswolds." Along with those who had summered at Stanway Manor with J.M. Barrie— A.A. Milne, and P.G. Wodehouse—were others like J.K. Rowling, Beatrix Potter, T.S. Eliot, and Nancy Mitford. A small card about T.S. Eliot noted that he was a regular visitor to Chipping Camden. It was written in beautiful script.

Another table was devoted to Arthur Conan Doyle and Sherlock Holmes. There were several biographies of the author, and I spied the *Russell and Holmes* series by Laurie R. King, Leonard Goldberg's *Daughter of Sherlock Holmes* mysteries, and the *Sherlock Holmes Bookshop* mysteries by Vicki Delaney. Hopefully, after Gilbert's presentation, these books had sold like hotcakes. Several small handwritten cards were scattered around the table with quotes—*Who Dun It? The Game's Afoot. Elementary, my Dear Watson.* I wondered who'd done the calligraphy.

As I moved from the tables to the shelves, I noticed movie posters displayed on the walls around the shop—*Pride and Prejudice, Persuasion, Murder on the Orient Express, Howards End,* and more—all, of course, movies based on books. Beneath the Jane Austen posters was a table of her books. *What a great way to get people interested in reading the classics.*

I was flipping through the E.M. Forster books displayed near the *Howards End* poster when Beatrix emerged from the back room, followed by Dickens. Her eyes were red and she looked exhausted. "Let's go home. I think the day has suddenly caught up with me."

We walked slowly to the solicitor's office, letting Dickens sniff along the street to his heart's content. "I like it when there's no rush, Leta."

In the car, it wasn't long before both my companions were

asleep. *I need to call Gemma about access to the cottage for Beatrix, and I'd like to be there too. And I need to squeeze in a trip to Quedgeley.*

When Beatrix stirred, I asked whether Gemma had mentioned the binders to her.

"I've looked at those notebooks any number of times through the years, and again Friday evening. Does this have something to do with Teddy's death?"

"That's what Gemma is trying to figure out. Can you think of any reason someone would want to kill Teddy? Did Gemma ask you about enemies?"

She'd been staring out the window, and she whipped her head around to look at me. "Enemies? He was a sweet old man, in his eighties. What enemies could he have?"

Being elderly doesn't preclude someone from having enemies. "I don't know, Beatrix, but that's the first question the police ask —that and who benefits. Based on the will, you're the primary beneficiary. There's another person who gets something smaller, and then a few museums. So, the next question is enemies."

I paused. "Unless it started as a robbery and got out of hand. We found empty plastic sleeves in the wheelie bin, so knowing what was in the binders and whether anything is missing from them would be a start on motive. And other things could be missing from the cottage—or nothing at all. Other than you and Fiona, I'm not sure who would know."

Beatrix was looking at me as though I had two heads. "Bloody hell, you're playing detective, aren't you? Should I expect to hear from Wendy next? Or Belle?" She gulped and burst into tears. "I'm sorry. I didn't mean to snipe at you."

My first instinct was to snipe back, but I held my temper. *It must be the stress. She can't have forgotten last October, when*

COLLECTORS, CATS & MURDER

Wendy, Belle, and I went all out to ensure her niece wasn't charged with murder.

"I know, Beatrix. You haven't asked for my assistance beyond today, but couldn't you use some help? Gemma's already asked me to look through the binders, but you and I doing that together would work better. We can bounce questions off each other. The truth is I've been thinking of asking Belle to help too, whenever you're ready. How does that sound?"

She gave a tremulous sigh. "You're right. Of course, you're right. I remember how shocked I was when I heard you three brainstorming motives for the murder at the Fall Fête. The LOLs think of things that would never enter my mind. I don't think my brain's wired that way, no matter the mysteries I read."

"Okay, it's settled then. Let's call Gemma." It was much safer to have Siri place the call so I could focus on staying on the proper side of the road. I just needed to be sure to let Gemma know she was on speakerphone when she answered.

"DI Taylor. Oh, hi, Leta, I was wondering when I'd hear from you. Has the grapevine only now caught up with you?"

"Gemma, not only has it caught up with me, Beatrix is sitting beside me and we're on our way back from seeing her solicitor."

"Well, well. That was quick. How are you doing, Beatrix?"

It took Beatrix a moment to answer. "Okay, I guess. I don't think I could have made it through without Leta, though. She asked good questions and made sure I found out who has keys. It's all too much to think about."

I took over. "Listen, Gemma, I've been thinking—"

"Right! Sounds like trouble's brewing."

Gritting my teeth, I let that remark slide. "You asked me to make time to go to Quedgeley, but Beatrix knows more about the contents of the binders than I do. And two heads are better than one. And while I'm tossing out clichés, let's add 'we could kill two birds with one stone.' What if Beatrix and I go to the cottage tomorrow, open the safe, and see where that gets us. Plus, Beatrix can walk through the rooms to see if anything obvious is out of place—"

"You found the key to the safe?! Bloody hell, Leta, if you've been to the cottage without me, I'll . . . I'll—"

"Stop right there! Of course, I haven't been back to the scene of the crime. I know better than that."

Beatrix closed her eyes and shook her head. "Cut it out, you two. I wish it were that simple. What we have is a treasure hunt."

Gemma hesitated. "Um, Beatrix, you've lost me."

I explained about the letter from Teddy and reminded her about the note we'd found. "So, we're fine to go to the cottage, right? The solicitor said we needed your permission." *She's thinking Beatrix is a suspect but doesn't want to say it.*

Instead, she hedged. "But what about Quedgeley? I think that's more important."

That gave me an idea. "Back to killing two birds . . . could Constable James meet us at the cottage and bring the binders? That way, he'd hear our observations firsthand, and if we're lucky, we'll solve the puzzle of the safe and open it. He'll be there for it all." *That should give Gemma a graceful way out. If he's with us, he can observe Beatrix for suspicious behavior. As though my friend could have had anything to do with smothering Teddy!*

"You know you're pushing it, right Leta? The Gloucester-shire Police don't work for you." *Good, I've gotten under her skin like she so often gets under mine.*

"I don't know any such thing. What I *do* know is you've got a murder to solve." *And should be glad of my help,* I thought. We went back and forth in that vein before she finally acquiesced. I decided there was no need to mention Belle. Gemma would find out soon enough.

I should start making notes so I can explain to Dave how it all starts—how the LOLs get involved in investigations—because it's happened again. As far as I'm concerned, we're now on the case.

Chapter Thirteen

When I called Belle, she was all ears. She knew Teddy had died but had missed the rest of the news. Wendy was her connection to the grapevine via the *Astonbury Aha!*, the online newsletter and bulletin board for our village, and Wendy was off on vacation. Belle was horrified that someone had smothered her new octogenarian friend in his sleep. *Hits too close to home*, I thought.

As I'd anticipated, though, she was excited at the prospect of searching for clues at the cottage in Chipping Camden. "Marvelous. I've had two quiet days since Ellie brought me home Saturday. Peter comes for dinner and spends the night, but he's not anywhere near as lively as you and Wendy. What time are you picking me up?"

"Is this where I say, 'The game's afoot'? I think it is, don't you?" I wasn't sure which one of us was Sherlock, but I knew Belle and I were up for the challenge. For someone near ninety, she was amazingly sharp. Heck, she was sharper than many a forty-year-old.

"Yes! You know Wendy's going to be jealous. Wouldn't it be something if we solved the case without her?"

I chuckled. "The thought *did* cross my mind. Have you heard from her? Is she having a good trip?"

"I think the jury's out on that. When she called Saturday, she grumbled that Brian had been speaking with Gemma about Teddy's death, but last night she said he'd managed to stay off the phone all day. 'Course, they were climbing to Tintagel, so he'd be hard-pressed to look at his phone without falling off a cliff."

"So Sunday was a good day. Let's see how the week goes now that Teddy's death has been declared a murder."

Feet up, I was sipping a glass of red wine in the sitting room when Dave called. His drive to Edinburgh had been uneventful and he was checked into his hotel. He'd chosen the Hotel du Vin for its central location between the university and the National Museum of Scotland. "We'll have to come back and bring Dickens. I've seen several dogs, and the place is charming. The room is comfy with a good view. Of course, right now, my notes are spread out all over the bed—"

"And that's why Dickens and I chose to send you off on your own this time. Once you start your research tomorrow, you won't be able to think of anything else."

Dickens looked up and barked when I said his name. "Who's that? What did they say about me?"

"Put me on speaker so I can talk to the little Dickens. Hi, boy, do you miss me already?"

"Is that Dave? Where are you? When are you coming back? We took a trip today."

I chuckled at the two of them. "You got all that, right? No need for me to tell you about my day?"

"Let me guess. You said you wanted a quiet day, so it was

yoga, the Tearoom, maybe the grocery. Did you see the donkeys too?"

Little did he know. I filled him in starting with the fact that the police had determined his new friend had been murdered. I lightened the mood by teasing him that Gemma had said thanks and was quite interested in *him* looking at the binders. "She seemed *awfully* disappointed when I told her she'd have to make do with me. Could it be she's interested in you for more than your literary expertise? How would a young, blonde detective suit you?"

"Not my type. I go for petite brunettes—beautiful, highly intelligent, petite brunettes."

"Don't forget mature—mature with silver highlights in their hair."

He was as surprised as I'd been that Beatrix had inherited the bulk of Teddy's estate and also intrigued by the letter. "Teddy was quite a character, wasn't he? I wish I could be there to help solve the puzzle with you and Beatrix. Despite the circumstances, I think it could be fun."

When I told him Belle was going with us the next day, silence echoed down the line. *Please don't let things get tense between us again.* I waited. Wendy would say I was working the pregnant pause like I did when we spoke with folks to ferret out clues. Dave needed to say whatever was on his mind, and I wasn't going to prompt him, nor apologize for getting involved.

When he finally responded, my first thought was he'd done a masterful job of tamping down any misgiving he had. "Sounds like a party. You, Beatrix, Belle, and Constable James. Are you taking Dickens too?"

"Of course. There's no telling what he might discover digging in the flower bed. On a serious note, I think determining whether anything's missing from the binders or anywhere else in the cottage will help establish motive. That should give Gemma and Constable James a line of inquiry. If it wasn't theft, I don't know what their next steps will be."

"I'm sure you're right. I can't imagine Teddy had the kind of enemies who would kill him. And bad as it was, what you and I saw makes me think it's more likely a robbery gone bad. Now, dear Tuppence, I expect daily bulletins. I don't want a call from that young, blonde detective telling me anything has happened to my beautiful brunette."

I'm not sure what I'd expected, but I felt the conversation had gone well. Christie sauntered into the room and leaped into my lap. I knew before she spoke what she wanted. "Those loud voices woke me up, but I'm glad. So, you've been off on an adventure without me? You're not thinking of leaving me behind again tomorrow, are you?"

That's exactly what I'd been thinking. It wouldn't do any harm to take her, but I couldn't get her, Belle, Beatrix, and a dog in my taxi. I tried explaining that to her.

"Leave the dog behind! It's his turn. You know I'm better at sniffing out clues than he is."

Dickens had already heard me say he was going, so I couldn't disappoint him now. That explanation didn't go over well.

"Dickens," she meowed, "you're okay to stay home, right? So, I can go? Think about it. First, you and Dave and Leta spent Friday and Saturday night away. Next, you went off without me *again* today. It's only fair you let me take your place."

I watched Dickens. It would be just like him to give in to his pushy feline sister. Fortunately for both of us, we were saved by the bell—the ringing of my phone. It was Beatrix.

"Leta, I can't thank you enough for taking care of me today. It's a load off my mind to have met with the solicitor and delivered the news to the ladies at the bookshop."

"You know I was glad to do it. How are you doing now? You sound perkier."

"I don't know that I'd call it perky, but Trixie fixed dinner, and we shared a bottle of wine. We talked through ideas for Bluebird Books and how to manage two bookshops, and I feel confident it will work out. Now, about tomorrow. I'd like to meet you there maybe around ten a.m., and when we're done, treat you to lunch. Then I plan to take a copy of the will to my solicitor in Stow to talk through my questions. If we have two cars, you won't have to make that stop. How does that sound?"

"All good, and I've spoken with Belle and she's eager to join us. She'll be a great help with the treasure hunt." *And much more, but no need to go into that.*

"That's fine by me. I'll see you then, and thanks again for everything."

Shaking my head, I looked at my four-legged companions. Now I could take them both, and Christie would be happy. A happy cat beat an angry one any day. Dickens? He was happy all the time.

I never did make it to Sainsbury's for groceries, so it looked like another round of cheese and crackers. And I never did work on my columns. There'd be no rest for the weary tonight. I prepared my makeshift dinner, poured another glass of wine, and headed to the office, cranking up my new Van Morrison CD for inspiration. *I should be able to finish at least one column.*

"Thank you, Leta. This is perfect," meowed Christie as I positioned her backpack in the car. Would wonders never cease? She hadn't uttered a single complaint this morning, but the day was young. I didn't have an official car harness for her pack, so I passed the seatbelt through its loops. Then I secured Dickens behind me. Belle would ride shotgun.

When I pulled up to Sunshine Cottage, Belle was waiting outside by the front door. She locked it behind her and made her way to the car. I hopped out to open the passenger door and noticed she was moving more slowly than usual. "Is your arthritis bad today?"

She handed me her cane as she settled herself in the front seat. "Seems so, but I hope these old joints will loosen up as the day goes on. Can't let a few aches and pains stop the LOLs, can we?" Belle had played a big part in naming our detective agency. When Gemma had first referred to the three of us as little old ladies, I was fit to be tied, but Belle loved it. We didn't think of ourselves as an official business, but we had fun with the name, and plenty of the villagers referred to us that way.

I'd had Little Old Ladies' Detective Agency business cards printed to give Wendy and Belle for Christmas. Wendy's were tucked in the pocket of an aqua hoodie embroidered with the phrase, "Your first mistake is thinking I'm just a little old lady." I'd gotten myself an identical one in red. Since Belle would never wear a hoodie, I'd given her a blue canvas bag embroidered with the saying. She carried it everywhere.

"Hold on, Leta. Maybe if I greet Christie and Dickens properly, they'll quiet down." She was right. All she had to do was rub their noses and scratch their chins while cooing how glad she was to see them, and their chatter stopped. Christie, especially, adored Belle, so there was a chance my prissy cat would be on her best behavior today.

I pulled up in front of Teddy's cottage. A police car was parked by the cottage next door, and Beatrix's car was in the driveway behind the Rolls. "Such an elegant car that Rolls. It makes me think of that BBC show we watched, *The Mrs. Bradley Mysteries*, with Diana Rigg. You know I *loved* her hats."

Belle glanced at me and smiled. "Those hats from the 1920s were something, weren't they? A bit much for this day and age, though, when you can hardly get a woman to wear a dress, much less a hat." I was pretty sure Wendy and I rated high in Belle's eyes because we liked to dress well.

I helped her from the car before I unfastened Christie's pack and placed it on my shoulders. Last, I went around to Dickens's side to let him out. As our little entourage proceeded up the walkway, I asked, "Can you ever forgive me for wearing jeans today?"

"Let me see, not just jeans—jeans tucked into boots and topped with a fashionable hip-length sweater? I think so. Much better suited for a treasure hunt than a dress."

Beatrix greeted us at the front door. "Perfect timing. It's eerie being here without Teddy, and I don't know that I could manage it without you two and Constable James—well, you four. Shall I lift Christie out of her pack?"

"Yes, but let's be careful not to let her outside. I don't want her wandering off in a strange place. Where would you like to begin? The library?"

Since Constable James was already in there, that seemed the logical place to start. He jumped up to help Belle to one of the wing chairs and then knelt to talk to Dickens. Christie tucked herself onto the lowest shelf of one of the bookcases and surveyed the room. She would come out in her own time.

Constable James glanced at Christie and shook his head before he stood and pointed to the binders on the desk. "I'm not sure where you ladies want those, but DI Taylor instructed me not to let them out of my sight. And, I've brought plastic gloves for us."

Belle motioned him over. "You know, this will be a first for me—the gloves. Do you think Miss Marple wore them?" Her demure manner cracked us all up.

I suggested to Beatrix we tackle the treasure hunt for the key first. "Who knows what's in the safe? It could be something as mundane as ledger books for the shop or it could be a priceless manuscript, but I'm dying to know. Have you had a chance to find it yet?"

"Since I only just got here, I haven't looked. Let's not waste time with me trying to guess, since you know where it is." I walked past her to the bookshelf near the desk and pointed to *Safe Haven*.

"Just like Teddy." She put her glasses on and read the inscription inside the oversized book cover.

You found me! Now you must find my key.

As I had, she felt around the safe for an obvious spot for the key. Based on the letter the solicitor had given us, I was sure there had to be more clues. "So, ladies, if you were hiding a key and not tucking it right beside the safe, where would you put it?"

Belle thought for a moment. "Could it be in the desk drawer? Or in that little glass bowl with paperclips? That would make it convenient for Teddy, but not much of a treasure hunt." I quickly checked both places. No luck.

Standing in the middle of the room, Constable James turned in a circle. "This room is filled with books. Could it be hidden in a book?"

"That makes sense," I said, "but where do we begin? We could be here all day looking in books."

Beatrix stared at the safe. "Teddy was a bookshop owner and well-read." That description fit her as well as Teddy. "The safe was hidden in a book with the word *safe* in the title. What book titles contain the word *key*?" That seemed like an easy question, but none of us suggested an answer.

It took Constable James pulling out his phone to google book titles with the word key. The first thing he called out was *Key to Rebecca*. "If that's it," he asked, "Where do we look? Is there some logic to the way the books are organized?"

I explained what I'd ascertained on Saturday. "Some shelves are dedicated to one author, others have several all arranged alphabetically. *Key to Rebecca* was written by Ken Follett, and the Fs are here on the left, in this first bookcase." I moved to study the shelves. "He has quite a few by Faulkner, Ferber, Fitzgerald, even Freud, but Ian Fleming takes up the most space. I count fourteen James Bond novels, and look, I'd forgotten he wrote *Chitty-Chitty-Bang-Bang* too."

Belle reminded me of the task at hand. "Leta, dear, what about Ken Follett?"

"Oh, right! No Follett here. Beatrix, look on the shelves near the safe. The layout seems to go from collectibles to more modern books read for pure pleasure. You know—the Spenser and Bosch novels and Inspector Lynley. Maybe Follett is among those."

"He is. Teddy seemed partial to his thrillers—*Lie Down with Lions*, *The Eye of the Needle*, and *Key to Rebecca*. And tucked in *Key to Rebecca* is another sheet of paper." Again, she read aloud.

Now, now, did you think it would be that easy?
Perhaps you need to sleep on it.

"Seriously? Is he suggesting we come back another day? Or . . . is he sending us to the bedroom to nap?" Belle asked.

Taking the page from Beatrix, I stared at it. "If we follow the same logic about him being a bookshop owner and reader, maybe it's another book."

Constable James had his phone out in a heartbeat, but before he could say anything, I spotted Raymond Chandler's *The Big Sleep* on a shelf beneath the safe. It was tucked next to a copy of *In Cold Blood* by Truman Capote. It was my turn to search for a piece of paper. And there it was. I grinned, unfolded it, and read.

I can see why you'd look here, but this is just a book You can't sleep in it.

Belle shook her head. "I bet *now* he's sending us to the bedroom. Are there books in there?"

I explained that the book *Dracula* had been beneath his hand, but I hadn't noticed whether there were any others. Beatrix theorized he'd been interested in it because we discussed the author Thursday night at the book club. "Doesn't that seem an age ago?" she asked.

"Yes to you, and yes to Belle. Maybe he *is* sending us to the bedroom. I bet the library, the bedroom, and the kitchen are the rooms he spent most of his time in, so maybe the clues are in those rooms."

Belle said she'd stay where she was, and the rest of us went down the hall. There were no books in sight, none on the mantle nor the nightstand. I looked in the closet, thinking there could be a book tucked in with the extra blankets. Nope.

Beatrix pulled open the drawer to the nightstand. "Here's a book, *The Lost Book of the Holy Grail*, by Charlie Lovett. This better not be an indication that our search will be as fruitless as that one."

"Keys, sleep, it must have to do with sleep, right?" I murmured. And, then it hit me. *What was it I found beneath the bed the other day?* "Hold on, I completely forgot—look at this," I said as I pulled my phone from my pocket.

Constable James looked over my shoulder and did the reading this time.

To sleep, perchance to dream—ay, there's the rub,
For in that sleep of death what DREAMS may come

"Oh! I've got that with me. It was in a separate evidence bag, and I brought it with the binders."

I'm sure I looked rather pleased with myself. "I found it between the bed slats and the boxspring on Saturday."

Beatrix blinked. "And what were you doing under the bed?"

I explained about my random brainstorm and that reminded me of the list we'd found on the floor in the library. Turning to Constable James, I asked, "Did you bring the other piece of paper we found?"

He had it with him, and Beatrix and I huddled over it when he pulled it from his briefcase. She shook her head. "Some of this is probably in the will, but Teddy couldn't have made the updates about Dave and Gilbert. I'll be sure they get the items he's mentioned."

Returning to the library, we found Belle looking at an umbrella stand filled with walking canes. Christie had taken over her seat, and Dickens was at her side.

She held out a cane. "It's a shame these are all too tall for me. You know your canes have to be proportioned properly. I'd forgotten, by the way, that Teddy and Peter had a conversation about antique canes on the way home Thursday night. The one he had with him that evening was an antique sword cane supposedly identical to the one Dr. Watson carried, and he had to demonstrate it for us."

One with colorful playing cards painted on it caught my eye. "Look at this. I've seen canes with brass heads or carved ivory knobs, but these are amazing. Oh my gosh, this one unscrews and has four shot glasses stowed in it. I never even noticed these on Saturday."

Belle asked if we'd found anything useful in the bedroom, and I showed her the photo to see what she'd make of it. She looked puzzled. "So, if there's only one book in there and it doesn't have anything to do with sleep or death or dreams, does that mean we're back to searching in here? Oh! The quote is from Shakespeare's *Hamlet*. Maybe we're looking for *A Midsummer Night's Dream*? That would cover sleep and dreams."

That search took a bit more time. We had to look through six editions of Shakespeare's plays, but none held the next clue. *Where did I see the word dream today?* "Wait, on the shelf with Fleming and Ferber—Freud's *The Interpretation of Dreams*. Nothing says it has to be a work of fiction, does it?"

Constable James was closest to the bookcase and quickly found Freud's most well-known work. I nodded encouragement when he pulled another piece of folded parchment from the book. He had a perplexed expression as he read.

No need to interpret my dreams.
Instead, consider my passions.

Beatrix chuckled. "Finally, something that's easy. Look around you. The man was passionate about books."

Now, Constable James looked dismayed. "Doesn't sound easy, not if you mean we have to look in every one of these."

Returning to her chair, Belle placed Christie in her lap. "If he was passionate about books, perhaps we're looking for one that has *that word* in the title—book!"

"Right!" I exclaimed. Two books immediately popped to mind. "Could it be *The Book Thief* or *How to Find Love in a Book-*

shop? Those aren't collectibles, per se, so if he has them, they should be on the bookcase near the desk—but I can't recall the authors."

Of course, Beatrix knew. "Marcus Zusak wrote *The Book Thief* and Veronica Henry wrote the one about finding love in a bookshop. It hasn't happened to me yet, but I guess there's always hope." She opened Zusak's book. "Nothing here. Fingers crossed . . . blast, nothing in the other one either."

Books, books, what others had the word in the title? "Okay, maybe I'm reaching. It doesn't have the word book in the title, but it's about the love of books—*The Readers of Broken Wheel Recommend.* Could that be it?"

Of course, as the owner of a bookshop, Beatrix knew right away who the author was—Katarina Bivald. *I'd have never come up with that.* But that book wasn't on any of the shelves.

"Leta," said Constable James, "if we think something may have been stolen, is it possible that book was here but taken?"

"I suppose it is. But I can't imagine why anyone would bother to steal it. I loved it and got a kick out of all the books that were mentioned in it, but you can get it at any bookstore. I think it's much more likely they stole a few of Teddy's collectible books like the older Ian Flemings and Graham Greenes. But where does that leave us?"

It was Belle who had the brainstorm. "You know, Wendy had me read a nonfiction book—not my usual cup of tea—but I enjoyed it. It was *The Diary of a Bookseller.*"

"Oh my goodness, I loved that book," said Beatrix. "Here it is, by Shaun Bythell, and here's another clue!"

Ah, yes, I do feel a kinship with this author, but I have one other passion.

Guess right, and you will find the key.

"Have you noticed," said Belle, "that you've found most of

COLLECTORS, CATS & MURDER

the clues in the bookcase by the desk? Don't know that it's significant, but maybe we'll solve this last bit more quickly if you stay over there. So, Beatrix, what was his other passion?"

She plopped down in the desk chair and twirled it around. "Books, isn't it everything to do with books?"

I looked up and down the shelves. "It must be. I mean, look around. This room is filled with books and book memorabilia. He even has a typewriter that belonged to J.M. Barrie and figurines of characters from children's books and book covers and clippings. Wait, that's it!"

All eyes were on me. I could tell they had no clue what I meant. "It's not only books. It's everything *to do* with books. He's passionate about his *collection*. That's why he invited Dave and me to visit him. That's why he invited Gilbert over. To show off his collection."

Pulling out his phone again, Constable James started searching. "Collecting," he muttered. "Good grief, there must be a million books about collecting. Stamps, china, knives— what am I looking for?"

My face lit up as I glanced at Belle. "You noticed most of the books had been on this one set of shelves." I pointed to the bookcase by the desk as I walked to the safe. Next to the Ken Follett book was one by John Fowles, *The Collector*. "This has to be it." This time, the piece of folded paper was in an envelope—with the key.

You've found the answer and the key! I'm passionate about collecting.

The brass key had a dainty bronze-colored tassel attached to it. *This is straight out of an Agatha Christie movie,* I thought, as I handed the key to Beatrix. *Cue the suspenseful music.*

Chapter Fourteen

I set my phone to video so I could tape the big scene. Beatrix inserted the key into the lock with her right hand and placed her left on the tiny brass knob above the keyhole. Like a book, the door opened to the left. We collectively held our breath.

Inside were two grey archival storage boxes, standing upright. There was something beneath them, but I couldn't quite see what it was. Beatrix removed one box from the safe. Her movements were almost reverential as she examined her find. "It doesn't have a lid," she murmured. "It has an insert."

She gasped when she slid the insert out to reveal its contents. "It's volumes one and two of Edgar Allan Poe's complete works—and they're quite old. I know there was a four-volume set published in the UK. Could this be one of those?" She handed me the insert holding the two books and removed the second box. It contained volumes three and four. "Oh my goodness," she said as she opened volume three. "It's dated 1857. I'm not sure, but this may be the earliest Poe collection published here. Leta, see what it says in volume one."

My eyes wide, I carefully opened volume one to reveal the title page. The date was 1857. I looked at Beatrix and nodded. "The same."

It was as though a dam had broken. We all started speaking at once.

"Didn't they use his middle name back then? Why does it read Edgar Poe's instead of Edgar Allan Poe's?" I asked.

"He wrote all that?" asked Constable James. "I thought it was only a few stories."

"They must be terribly valuable," said Belle.

"I can't believe Teddy never told me he had these!" exclaimed Beatrix.

We placed the boxes and books on the desk, and Beatrix sat in the chair studying them, seemingly oblivious to anything else. I could appreciate they were rare and valuable, but I wasn't a collector. *Right this minute, I'm more interested in what else is in the safe.*

I turned to see what the boxes had been sitting on. It was an 8x10" burgundy leather notebook. Embossed on the cover in elegant gold script were the words "Teddy's Treasures", and lying beside the notebook was a gold-trimmed black Mont Blanc pen. Inside were ledger pages with column headers written in black ink—Item, Date, From, Price, and Where. I puzzled over the entries in the Where column for a few moments—BC, AL, M, W, US, and S. Then I realized they must indicate where to find the item, either in one of the binders—Bless the Children, Author Letters, or Miscellany—on a wall, in the umbrella stand, or on the shelves around the room.

I smiled as I pictured Teddy sitting at his desk documenting his acquisitions. The first was dated 7_5_1989, and the final entry was made in early April of this year. Beneath that entry was a yellow sticky. The scribble was difficult to read, but it looked like "Ask A / Twain / Barrie letter." *What does it mean?*

"Leta," said Belle, "You're grinning. What have you found?"

"It's the list of the items in Teddy's collection. With this, figuring out whether anything's missing will be easy as pie."

My last statement got Beatrix's attention. "A list?! Oh, thank goodness. My brain is fried from the mystery of the key —which, by the way, sounds like the title of a novel. Anyway, I could go for something easy. And, I could go for tea. Anyone else?"

When we all answered yes, Beatrix headed to the kitchen, and I followed her. She seemed to know her way around Teddy's cabinets and quickly located stoneware mugs. "Those china teacups he set out with the teapot are sweet, but not very practical. I need a large mug of tea, don't you?"

I nodded yes as Dickens came into the room and went to the French doors. "Looks like Detective Dickens wants to go out." I stepped outside with him. "Dickens, you've been awfully quiet. Are you okay?"

He cocked his head. "Just kind of bored. I was hoping Watson would be here, and I could introduce him to Christie."

Smiling, I kissed him between his ears and told him to see what he could find in the garden. I found a wooden tray and set the mugs and sugar dish on it. A sniff of the cream in the fridge told me it was still good, so I filled the matching pitcher and added it to the tray. When the tea was ready, Beatrix and I carried everything to the library.

Belle closed her eyes and sipped. "Hits the spot. Thanks, ladies. Tell me, when you were in the bedroom, did you see a cane?"

Beatrix, Constable James, and I looked at each other and shook our heads no.

"What made you ask that, Belle?" I said.

"I mentioned the sword cane to you, but when I was looking through the umbrella stand, I didn't see it. And logic tells me it should be near the bed. Teddy was like me in needing a cane to get around, even more so as the day goes on, so he would have used it to go to the bedroom Friday night. Perhaps it fell under the bed when the police were in and out."

I flashed back to when I was here Saturday. I didn't recall seeing it. Probably too distraught to notice. But I didn't remember seeing it Sunday either, and I'd been on my hands and knees looking under the bed. *Maybe it's shoved way up against the wall—not visible in the dark.* "Sounds like a job for me and Christie. She can help me search beneath the bed."

"Finally, a job for Detective Christie," she meowed as she leaped from Belle's lap.

She followed me to the bedroom. My memory was accurate. There was no cane between the bed and the nightstand. Christie stuck her nose beneath the bed skirt. "Eeew, dusty." She disappeared beneath the bed, and I got down to watch her progress. As I rolled over to grab my phone, her sneeze told me she'd encountered the dust bunnies. "Pfft."

I shone the flashlight on her and laughed as she stopped to clean her face. "Come on, Christie. You can bathe after you're done sleuthing. Look at the head of the bed near the wall. Is there anything lying by the baseboard?"

"Nothing, nada, zilch. Unless you want dust bunnies, you're out of luck." She crawled out and leaped on the bed to rub her nose on the comforter. I checked the closet to be sure the cane wasn't propped in there before I picked Christie up and carried her back to the library.

"No luck. No cane anywhere, not under the bed, not in the closet."

Belle frowned. "I don't want to jump to the conclusions, but unless the police carried it off, I think our killer did. We folks 'of a certain age' don't like to risk falling and breaking a hip. There's no way Teddy took himself to bed without a cane."

Constable James pulled out his notebook. "I'll double-check with the SOCOs. If they didn't bag it as evidence, we'll count it as missing."

Glancing from the binders on the desk to the elegant ledger book, I wondered how to proceed. "Beatrix, I think we need to take inventory, but I hate to make marks in Teddy's ledger. I could run to Bluebird Books to make copies so we can jot notes as we go. What do you think?"

Before Beatrix could respond, Belle piped up. "Could you pick up sandwiches too? It's going on 11:30, and if we mean to complete this task, we need to get on with it."

That settled, Constable James and Belle stayed behind with Dickens and Christie while Beatrix and I drove the short distance to the High Street. My friend wanted to treat us to lunch, so she went to the sandwich shop, and I went to Bluebird Books. I'd grabbed the pages of clues too. I thought they were clever and wanted to copy them to show Dave.

Fiona was at the front desk again today and smiled as I entered. "Hello, Leta. What brings you back so soon?"

I brandished the parchment pages and the ledger book and explained I wanted to use the copier.

"Why don't you let me do that for you so you can look around some more? I could tell yesterday that you're a book lover," she said.

Great customer service, I thought. *Probably a good salesperson too*. I accepted her offer and returned to wandering the shop. Near the counter was a wire stand with a sign labeled Staff Recommendations. It was written in the same script I'd admired the day before. Rhys Bowen's *Tuscan Child* was displayed, as was the latest Deborah Crombie mystery. I'd read a few of Bowen's Maggie Hope books but not this one, which was described as a standalone novel. I placed a copy on the counter and moved deeper into the store.

I was in the biography section when I noticed another movie poster, this one for *Can You Ever Forgive Me?* I recalled seeing the trailer at the theater and hearing the story was based on the autobiography of Lee Israel, an author who turned to forgery when her writing career dried up. I was surprised to see the poster was signed by Melissa McCarthy, who'd starred in the movie. *Wouldn't it be ironic if that signature turned out to be a forgery?*

Flipping through Israel's book, I thought about Dave and the research for his book, *Barrie & Friends*. At Edinburgh University and elsewhere, I knew he'd be focused on correspondence between Barrie, Tolkien, Arthur Conan Doyle, and their many literary friends. *I bet he'd be intrigued by the Lee Israel autobiography, given she was caught forging author letters.*

I took a copy to the front desk and put it with the Rhys Bowen book just as Fiona emerged from the back room. "You were too fast, Fiona. Given more time, there's no telling how many books I'd add to this stack."

Laughing, she placed the ledger book, the parchment pages, and the copies into a baby blue bag. "Hopefully, you'll return. By the way, I got a kick out of copying the loose pages. I'd forgotten writing those for Teddy. I never knew exactly what he did with them, but I could tell he was up to something and was enjoying himself."

"I should have known! I bet you calligraphed all the small signs around the shop too, right? They're lovely."

Beaming, she explained she'd taken a calligraphy class at the community center and enjoyed sitting quietly in the evenings writing signs and notecards and whatever else. She also occasionally addressed wedding invitations for customers. "Some people knit or cross-stitch to relax. I write."

With the bag of copies in one hand and a bag of books in the other, I exited the shop and found Beatrix leaning against the car in front of the sandwich shop. We were at the cottage laying out lunch in no time.

Constable James insisted on washing the dishes after lunch. "Thanks, ladies. That hit the spot. I don't often get a decent lunch." To me, he had the appearance of an overgrown child, one who could use a bit more meat on his bones, so I was happy we'd been able to treat him.

In the hopes of making our inventory go more quickly, I'd asked Fiona to make several sets of copies. My idea was for us to use the Where column as our guide. One of us could check for items listed as being on the shelves. Another could cross-reference the Author Letters binder with the ledger, and so on.

"If I get a choice," said Belle, "I want to work on Bless the Children, and I'll sit here at the kitchen table where the light is good."

I offered to take the walls and shelves, leaving Beatrix to start with Author Letters, and whoever finished first could move on to the binder labeled Miscellany. Christie chose to help Belle by curling up in her lap, and Dickens followed me around the library as I searched.

The items on the shelves varied from books to memorabilia—from extremely valuable to merely interesting. I checked off a first edition of Graham Greene's *Brighton Rock*, for which Teddy had paid £250 in 1990, and wondered what it would be valued at today. At the other extreme, he had an 8x10" framed print featuring first-edition covers of ten of P.G. Wodehouse's Jeeves & Wooster novels. He'd paid only £12 for the colorful arrangement in 1998.

I chuckled at the Jeeves collection. "Beatrix, do you recall the Ask Jeeves website from years ago? It never occurred to me the name came from Wodehouse's novels—maybe because I've never read any of them."

"Oh yes, and there was a BBC Jeeves & Wooster series in the '90s. Hugh Laurie was one of the stars. That was long before he became famous in the States as Dr. House."

"Wow, that's a blast from the past. Henry and I enjoyed that show, and I was always tickled at how much my friend Bev loved it. As an anatomy teacher, she was intrigued no end by all those obscure diseases and symptoms."

The figurines Dave and I'd noticed on Saturday were listed as being on the shelves. When I moved to that side of the room, Dickens yelped and stood on his hind legs with his paws on the shelf. "Look, it's a dog."

"Yes, Dickens, it is. That's Dorothy from the *Wizard of Oz,* and she's holding Toto." According to the ledger book, Teddy had paid next to nothing for it. The typewriter that had belonged to J.M. Barrie, on the other hand, had cost what in my book was a small fortune—£1075 in 2004. He'd discovered it on eBay of all places.

Beatrix was murmuring to herself, and I wasn't sure whether that was a good sign or a bad one. I was searching for a Sherlock Holmes pipe when Christie ran into the room. "Leta, you have to see this," she meowed as she turned and ran out.

I followed her to the kitchen, where she leaped into Belle's lap and stood with her paws on the table. She placed one black paw on a picture in the binder. "It's a black cat, and it's singing. I can sing, you know." With that, she gave a few high-pitched meows. I cracked up.

Belle laughed aloud. "I'm beginning to believe she recognizes cats, not just live and in person, but in pictures. Whenever I turn the page and find a cat on a book cover or page torn from a comic book, she stands in my lap—as though she knows what it is. Her reaction to this one, though, takes the cake. I think she's partial to Felix the Cat."

Christie turned around in Belle's lap and reached up to the collar of Belle's dress. "He's cute, don't you think?"

Too bad I can't tell Belle she's right. "Well, sure Belle, if you say so. Now, how are you doing with this binder? Anything missing?"

"Not a thing, but I've a long way to go yet. The good news is it's in chronological order. The bad news is I can't help reading the clippings and taking detours down memory lane, so I'm only about halfway through."

I assured her she could take her time, as Beatrix was still working on Author Letters and we hadn't started on Miscellany yet. I finished with my list of shelf items pretty quickly and turned to the few listed as being in the umbrella stand. These were all canes—the shot glass and gambler's canes I'd seen earlier—plus one with a compartment for cigarettes, another that opened to become a tripod, and as I should have expected, one that housed a pool cue. Many of these were quite pricey—anywhere from £500 to close to £2000. *The man was definitely passionate about collecting.*

Constable James had been quiet as Beatrix and I worked. I'd noticed earlier he'd picked up *The Monkey's Raincoat*, and I wondered what he'd think of the LA private eye Elvis Cole. I glanced his way and caught him with his head bowed and eyes closed. *Full stomach, comfy chair. It was bound to happen.*

There were only ten items listed for the walls and none appeared to be in the library. I returned to the only other room I'd spent any time in—the bedroom. Funny, I hadn't noticed an arrangement of five photos on the wall to the side of the dressing table. They were autographed pictures of actors who had played Sherlock Holmes through the years— Basil Rathbone, Jeremy Brett, Ian McKellen, Douglas Wilmer, and Stewart Granger. *Interesting that I don't recall the last two in the role.*

I'd also missed an arrangement near the closet. Three documents on yellowed paper were framed—typed on ancient typewriters, it appeared. I cross-referenced the ledger sheet and checked them off. I had two more items that were listed as being on the wall.

These two items seemed to be missing—"Agatha Christie to G.K. Chesterton re: the Detection Club 22_4_1935" and "Doyle to Twain 70th b'day tribute 5_12_1905". I was amazed at how little he'd paid for the Doyle letter—£125. Could that be right? He'd only purchased the Agatha Christie item a few weeks ago, though he'd had the Doyle letter for several years. *So where are they?*

I moved around the room, but I didn't see them. *Maybe they're in the sitting room*, I thought, but they weren't, nor were they hanging in the hall. A glance in the kitchen as I passed the door revealed not a thing. I returned to the bedroom. *All the other wall items are in this room. Shouldn't these other two be here too?* Puzzled, I moved from the Sherlock Holmes photos back to the closet. Upon closer inspection, I saw a faint shadow above the three frames. It was over my head so it was no wonder I hadn't noticed it at first. Standing on tiptoe, I saw a tiny nail hole. At some point, a frame must have hung there. So, I'd found eight, and a spot for a ninth, but no sign of the tenth.

Thinking I'd looked everywhere I could, I returned to the library. "Beatrix, I'm finished with the shelves and the walls. Shall I move on to the binder labeled Miscellany?"

She looked up. "I guess so. I haven't found anything missing in this binder yet."

"Okay, let me know if you need help." I tiptoed to the wingback chair opposite Constable James and got started on the Miscellany binder. He didn't stir.

This binder was mostly filled with newspaper clippings and playbills. Some of the clippings were original; others were copies. I laughed aloud at an article in which J.M. Barrie and Rudyard Kipling described their typewriters. According to Barrie, "nine-tenths of typewriter machines are vixens, and all of them have moments of malevolence." *I could say that about my laptop*, I thought, *though I'd call it a curmudgeon—not a vixen.*

Kipling humorously described his typewriter as doing the job for him, claiming to "start the cam action at the first line, pull open the throttle valve, and go out for a walk . . . [and return] to a poem of any desired length completed." If all the clippings were this entertaining, I'd never finish my task.

Several pages were filled with colorful postage stamps dedicated to authors or their novels—John Keats, Robert Burns, George Eliot, Charlotte Bronte's *Jane Eyre*, and Tolkien's *The Fellowship of the Ring*. There were playbills for *My Fair Lady* and *The Mousetrap* and many more London plays. As I scanned those, I noted he'd come by some by attending the play—he'd written notes on those—and others via flea market stalls.

I forced myself to focus on checking items off the list, knowing Beatrix would let me spend more time with the binders later. I could imagine her hosting an after-hours party at the Book Nook and inviting her friends to flip through the collection. With that image in mind, I sped through the cross-referencing. This binder appeared to be intact until near the end, where I encountered two empty plastic sleeves.

Examining the ledger sheets for items labeled as being in the Miscellany notebook, I found a notation for "T.S. Eliot notes on *A Connecticut Yankee in King Arthur's Court* 3_5_1924." Acquired only a few months ago, it was the next to the last entry for the Miscellany binder and it was quite pricey—£1025. Moving my finger up the sheet, I found another entry for which I had no corresponding document— "Twain/ on Arthur Conan Doyle for the Strand 23_7_1907." I thought this might be a copy of an article, as it was only £10.

I rose from my seat and moved to the desk. Dickens had fallen asleep at my feet, so now two males were dozing in the library. "Beatrix, I'm done, and I've discovered two things missing from this binder. I wonder whether they're among the papers piled here." I shuffled through the stack and found both documents. *That was easy.* The T.S. Eliot item was typed and scribbled across the top were the words 'possible subject for article.' I recalled seeing it on Sunday. *Why? Why was it pulled from the binder and discarded?* I had the same question about the other document, Twain's article for the Strand.

She looked up and frowned. "Are they there?"

"Yes, but I don't understand why they're not in the binder. No matter, that means I only have two things missing—both supposed to be on the wall." I read aloud the items that I couldn't find. "How's it going for you? All accounted for so far?"

"No, two are missing, and I'm not quite finished. And, best I can tell, he didn't pay nearly what I would expect—hundreds of pounds instead of thousands. It's a good thing he kept such good records."

"And whose letters are they? I mean, who wrote them?"

"Mark Twain. Look here where I've highlighted the entries on the ledger sheet."

I read aloud, "'Twain to Doyle on their meeting in America 29_8_1894' and 'Twain to Barrie on seeing Peter Pan in London 29_12_1905.' I always have to think about the dates when I see them written this way. In the states, we put the month first—so August of 1894 and then December 1905." *What is it about Mark Twain?*

Glancing at the still-snoozing Constable, I lowered my voice. "I'm not sure whether it will help or not, but I'm going to take pictures of the pages in the binders and the loose ones too. We may want to refer back to them, and I know Constable James isn't going to let us take them with us. This way we'll have the ledger pages plus what's in the binders."

"Okay, start with the Miscellany notebook so I can finish up here. I only have a few pages left. Then I'll check the desk to see if the letters are mixed in with the piles of papers." We went about our separate tasks, Constable James and Dickens snoozing all the while. We finished, checked on Belle, and were pretty much wrapped up when Dickens snorted and rolled over.

I knelt to rub his belly. "Dickens, did you have a nice nap? And, look, your companion is waking up too."

Constable James shook his head and turned red. "You won't tell DI Taylor, will you? If she hears I wasn't watching you ladies the whole time, she'll have a fit."

I mimed the lips-sealed sign. "Do you need to report back on our findings? Better get your notebook out." We told him about the four missing items and the two that turned up among the loose pages on the desk, and I handed him a set of ledger sheets with the items highlighted so he could show Gemma.

He frowned as he jotted notes. "So, we have a cane and a handful of letters missing. Hardly seems a reason for murder. Still, it establishes things were stolen, doesn't it?"

My thoughts were all over the place. "Yes, I think it means theft was involved. As good a recordkeeper as Teddy was, he would have noted the information if he'd sold anything. As for a reason for murder, maybe Teddy interrupted the thief. Except he was in bed. If he'd caught someone in the act, wouldn't we have found him in the library?"

Beatrix nodded. "The binders were in plain sight in this room. No reason for someone to even go to the bedroom. If Teddy had called out, whoever it was could have left without being seen. Unless . . . unless they still hadn't found what they came for. Could someone have killed him so they could keep looking? That's horrible. You wake a harmless old man and kill him? For what? A few pieces of paper?"

"Beatrix, two of the missing items were supposedly on the wall, and I think they must have been in Teddy's bedroom. If they were the objective, the thief would have been out of luck in the library and would have ventured into the bedroom to search."

Constable James shook his head. "I wonder why they only wanted those few items."

Tears came to Beatrix's eyes, and I put my arms around her. "Enough. Let's not think any more about this now. We've helped the police by identifying the missing items, and they can take it from here. You've got an appointment this afternoon. Let's get you on your way, and Belle and I can work with

Constable James to put everything back together and shipshape."

Sniffling, she agreed and asked that I call her if I had any sudden brainstorms. While Constable James put away the dishes in the kitchen and chatted with Belle, I returned the burgundy leather book and the grey storage boxes with the Poe books to the safe. I locked it, placed the key in the envelope, and tucked it back in *The Collector*. The copies of the ledger sheets I put in my purse.

"Belle," I said as I entered the kitchen, "I bet you're ready for your afternoon nap. Did this young man tell you he got one?"

Constable James ducked his head and smiled.

Dickens nudged Christie where she was curled in Belle's lap. "Me too. Did you get one?"

"Pfft. I was busy looking for clues, you silly dog. Good thing Leta brought me along."

Belle was all smiles. "When I get to enjoy interesting days like today, I can always forgo my nap. I hope I get to look through this binder again, and I'd love to show Ellie. She'll recognize many of the items, just as I did."

Patting Constable James on the shoulder, I thanked him for his help. "Your google skills were invaluable with the treasure hunt. I look up tons of things when I'm at my desk but don't always think about using my phone—wait, computer! Why didn't I think of that?! Teddy must have had a computer."

"He did. He had a Chromebook and the SOCOs have it. I don't think they've looked it over yet, and that reminds me, I need to ask about the cane. Hold on, let me ring them now." We listened as he placed the call. "No? You didn't pick up a cane? Then we need to add that to the list of missing items. We did a thorough inventory today, and I have a few more things to add. Hold on." He looked at me and asked what they should look for on the computer.

"If it's a Chromebook, he likely used it for email and surfing the internet. I'd say we need to know about any correspondence about rare documents and books—collectibles—plus internet searches for the same thing."

When he ended the call, I added, "With any luck, we'll discover that someone had an interest in the missing documents. That could lead us to the murderer or at least to whoever sent him—or her. I always have a hard time thinking of a woman as a murderer, but I guess I shouldn't. Anyway, if a collector wanted something Teddy had, they could have hired someone to break in and get it. It's hard to imagine some well-heeled collector of rare works breaking and entering."

"But not impossible, Tuppence," murmured Belle. "Miss Marple would never rule anyone out this early in the game."

Constable James looked from Belle to me. "Oh no, don't tell me . . . "

Belle grinned. "What? That the Little Old Ladies are on the case? Too late."

Chapter Fifteen

"Belle," I said as we parted company with Constable James, "Are you okay if we make a quick stop by Bluebird Books? I'd like to ask Fiona about the sword cane, to confirm Teddy took it to the bedroom Friday night."

"Sure. I wouldn't be averse to looking around the shop either. I've never visited this one."

When we reached the High Street, I turned toward the shop and found a parking place right in front. The only problem with making this stop was the need to once again get my four-legged companions out of the backseat. With Christie on my back and Dickens's leash in my hand, we all paraded into Bluebird Books.

Pris looked up as we entered. At least today, she was smiling, and when she spied Christie, a wide grin split her face. "Oh my gosh. Is that a cat peeking out of your backpack?" She rubbed Christie's nose and tickled her chin, which sent the princess into a paroxysm of purring and then loud meowing.

"I want to get down, Leta."

"No, Christie, I'm not putting you down. We won't be here that long."

Dickens all but stuck out his tongue. "But I get to wander anywhere I like."

The two animals had Pris chuckling. "So, what can I help you ladies with today?"

That reminded me I needed to introduce Belle, who explained to Pris she'd met Teddy Thursday night. They chatted about how delightful he was, and Pris pointed out some of the highlights of the shop. I learned that Teddy had been responsible for finding the movie posters I'd admired and that Watson the cat had been a hit with customers when he stayed at the shop.

"I swear no matter where I shifted the Sherlock Holmes selections, he'd wind up stretched out nearby. It was as if he knew, not that I believe that for a moment."

"Pris, is Fiona around?" I asked.

She looked at me quizzically before saying Fiona was upstairs. "There's an outside entrance and one from our store-room. Go on up the inside stairs and knock on the door. She won't mind."

With Dickens at my heels and Christie on my back, I made my way to the inside door and knocked. "Fiona, it's Leta and Dickens and another visitor. I hope we're not disturbing you."

She was grinning as she opened the door. "Dickens, come on in. You too, Leta."

Dickens put his front paws on her knees and licked her face when she leaned down. When she stood, she spied Christie and squealed, "A cat—in a backpack? Oh my! Could be a children's book like *The Cat in the Hat*."

We tossed rhymes around as I let Christie out of the pack. Fiona assured me the flat was too small for Christie to get lost.

The flat was compact yet inviting. The door opened to a sitting room, and I could see the outside door off the kitchen to the left. There were yellow and green flowered curtains over the sink and on the door, and a decoupaged key rack with several sets of keys hung on the wall. From what I could see, the short hall directly in front of me had a bathroom on the left and bedroom on the right. Fiona invited me to sit on a loveseat, but I declined the tea she offered.

"Sorry to arrive without calling first, but I wanted to ask you something. As we checked around Teddy's cottage today, we realized we didn't see his cane—the one he had Friday, the sword cane. Do you have any idea where it is?"

"When he went to bed, he always leaned it against the wall between the bed and the nightstand. That one or whichever cane he was using that day. Wasn't it there?"

"No. That's just it. We were sure he'd need it to get to bed and out again. We even checked beneath the bed, but it wasn't there."

"Well, it was for sure there when I left him for the evening. He was about to get up to fetch one of his binders, but I stopped him. He was stubborn like that, and I had to insist he let me get it for him. He already had a book to read but wanted his binder of letters to look through too.

"He had his odd ways. When his wife was alive, she never would have let him pile books on the bed. She'd have his head if she could see the state it gets in some nights—the *Telegraph*, the *Daily Mail*, a book or two, a binder, maybe even the day's receipts—all spread out on what used to be her side of the bed."

My mouth dropped open. "He had a binder in bed with him? Do you recall which one?"

"Yes, it was the Author Letters. It wasn't unusual for him to sit in the library of an evening and flip through one. When he was tired, though, like he was Friday night, he'd take one to bed. What with being out Thursday evening and at the festival most of Friday, he was pretty well knackered."

I was about to answer when someone hammered on the door to the kitchen. Fiona rolled her eyes and went to unlock the door. "Don't know why he has to knock so hard."

When a dark-haired young man burst through the door, I saw it was Albert. "Fi, can you lend me some dosh? I'm flat broke and I've got no petrol to get back to Dad's—oh. You've got company. Sorry, didn't know."

Standing, I held out my hand. "Hi, I'm Leta Parker. I saw you at the festival Friday when you were there with Teddy and again at the cottage Saturday. I'm sorry for your loss."

I could tell he was having difficulty placing me. "Um . . . yes. I'm going to miss him. Could talk your ear off, but he was a good 'un to work for." Christie chose that moment to rub against his ankles, and he squatted to pet her. "Is this your cat? She's a beauty."

Christie nudged his hand and meowed. "This one's pretty observant."

It seemed petting Christie made Albert think of Teddy's cat. "Do you know who has Watson? He must be upset about Teddy."

I explained where Watson was as Fiona looked through her purse and handed him some bills. "Now be off with you, and I expect to see that back."

He grunted goodbye and was gone.

"Is Albert your boyfriend, Fiona?"

"Boyfriend? That one? No, we were in school together in Manchester, but he went on to Oxford. Unfortunately, he got

KATHY MANOS PENN

sent down over a girl and that ended his shot at a University education. "

My protective instinct kicked in. "A girl? Please tell me he didn't attack a girl at Oxford?"

"Oh, no, no, nothing like that. He was head over heels, the poor sod, and did something stupid when she dumped him. Broke into her flat and took some things he'd given her, the way he tells it. Who knows the real story? It was enough to get him sent down, and he never had the heart to go back.

"Now, he does odd jobs here and there. He's forever low on petrol and petrol money because he's always on the road on his motorbike or in his dad's van, what with checking estate sales for furniture and books. 'Course, one of his best jobs was driving Teddy. Always said driving the Rolls was sweet."

"I bet it was. I don't know that Beatrix knows yet whether she'll keep it or not. She's got lots to think of right now. We spent most of today on the mystery of the key, as we're calling it, and then figuring out what might be missing from his collection."

"Beats me. Teddy sure loved those letters and clippings and figurines." She teared up. "I can see him now sitting in front of the fireplace thumbing through one of his Teddy's Treasures notebooks. Sometimes, he'd lift it so Watson could climb in his lap. Once the cat was settled, he'd open it again. I wonder where Watson will go long-term. Does Beatrix know he used to visit the shop? He'd make himself at home here all day and then go home with Teddy."

I explained the cat was one more thing my friend would have to figure out. She had Tommy and Tuppence at the Book Nook, so she'd probably be okay with having a shop cat at Bluebird Books—as long as he'd be well taken care of.

"Speaking of cats, Christie, it's time to put you back in

180

your pack." She wandered by at just the right time for me to scoop her up. I thanked Fiona and descended the stairs to the shop. Belle had a copy of *Dracula* on the counter and something in a small frame.

"Look, Leta. Since last week's book club meeting, I've been thinking about this. I bet you've read it, but I never have. I've seen lots of the movies, though."

"As long as you've got Peter or Wendy staying the night, you should be fine. It's not a book I'd want to read in my cottage by myself."

In unison, Dickens barked and Christie meowed. "What do you mean by yourself? We're always there." *My, my, something they agree on.*

"What's this?" I asked, holding up the small gilded frame. "Oh, it's a quote—'Age is an issue of mind over matter. If you don't mind, it doesn't matter.' – Mark Twain. Well, that's perfect for you."

"I thought so! Pris tells me Fiona does the calligraphy, and then they send her work to the print shop to be copied on sturdy card stock. A local frame shop does the rest. They're quite popular with the customers. You know what, I think I'll get one for Ellie too."

I held up the frame. "Who chooses the quotes?"

Pris beamed. "Oh, it's been a combination. Sometimes, it was Teddy. He particularly liked the one your friend is purchasing. Other times Fiona or Albert might see something and think it would be popular, and often it's me."

On the drive to Astonbury, I filled Belle in about my conversation with Fiona. "Your hunch about the cane was right. She confirmed he always had one by the bed. Just think, without you, we'd never have noticed."

Belle grinned. "That's what I enjoy about our cases—seeing

things others don't. That and folks telling me things they shouldn't."

"Now, what does that mean? Who's opened up to you now?"

"Pris Price, the manager. You think she'd have realized if I was friends with you, I must also be friends with Beatrix. Regardless, she let slip a few choice comments about Teddy leaving Beatrix the shop. She was already steamed he'd invited Beatrix to manage Bluebird Books this summer. And, I guess, like Beatrix, she had no inkling he'd decided who would get the shop."

"Hmm. Why wouldn't he have made that decision? Forgive me, but he was in his eighties, and he was right to have a will—the bookshop was a huge asset. Did she think it was up for debate?"

"I didn't get the whole story, but I gather there'd been some conversation about his stepping away from more than the day to day and leaving her to manage the shop entirely—the book signings, ordering—all of it. Could she have thought that meant he'd leave the whole kit and caboodle to her?"

Recalling what Beatrix had told me, Pris's version didn't seem to jibe. "Teddy described things differently. He wasn't sure she was up to the job as it was, much less taking on what he'd been handling. Interesting. Could it be he wasn't completely honest with her? As in, he didn't want to let on he had doubts? That could be why she was so upset about Beatrix suddenly taking over for the summer—and now completely.

"This whole thing reminds me of when I worked in Personnel. Managers were notorious for thinking they'd delivered a message about an employee needing to improve their performance when in fact they'd danced around it. I can't tell you how many folks were clueless their bosses were disappointed with their work."

Belle snorted. "Saw that time and time again as a nurse. Those hospital administrators had the hardest time shooting straight. Glad I don't have to worry about that anymore. So, do you think we should add Pris to our list of suspects?"

"List of suspects? I didn't know we had one!"

"Now, Leta, I'm sure you've started one in your head. If not, you're falling down on the job. Shall we brainstorm?"

Miss Marple is at it again. "Sure. Where do you want to start?"

"Might as well start with Pris. What's that list of motives you like—Lust, Loathing, Lucre—what's the other one? Love?"

Belle was cracking me up. "Yes, that's the list. What would Pris's motive be?"

"A burst of loathing, angry beyond words? Found out Friday morning she was essentially being replaced and worked herself into a lather worrying about it all day? Maybe she went by to have it out with him late Friday and lost her temper."

"Anything's possible, but why would she steal anything?"

"Tuppence, we don't have to figure it all out right this minute. We just need a list to start with."

Tuppence and Miss Marple. "Duly noted. In that case, how 'bout Fiona? I don't have a motive for her, but she does have a key to the cottage. And there were no signs of a break-in, so our murderer must have had a key."

"You know," Belle said, "I've not met the girl. I only glimpsed her at Dave's presentation. Do you have a motive for her or just opportunity? Means, motive, opportunity! Isn't that what Gemma would say?"

Dickens chimed in. "She's a sweet thing. Why would she hurt anyone?"

Trying to respond to Dickens and answer Belle at the same time was a challenge. "Yes, Gemma and every detective on TV would say that. I can't think of a motive for her, and based on what Beatrix told me, she seems to be an angel. But she has a key."

Christie had to have the last word. "Listen to you two, just because she's blonde and young—well, younger than Leta, anyway—doesn't mean she's an angel. Maybe we should ask Watson what he thinks."

Picking up on Christie's suggestion, I commented to Belle, "Gee, too bad Watson can't tell us what he thinks of all these folks. I understand Fiona put him out every night when she left, and Teddy let him in every morning. So, unless it was Fiona, he'd have been prowling the neighborhood when the murderer was there."

Now, Dickens was barking. "Wait, wait. What about that Albert person? He doesn't *look* mean, but he didn't pet me or talk to me—not any of the times he saw me. Could be he's not a dog person, but that's suspicious in itself, isn't it?"

Christie disagreed. "That's because he's a cat person—a very discerning cat person who thinks I'm beautiful."

When I laughed out loud, Belle looked at me. "What's so funny?"

"Um, just thinking about the cat knowing something. That reminds me, Albert was a big part of Teddy's daily life. I wonder what their relationship was like."

"That young man who brought him to the festival and picked him up?"

"Yes, that's the one. He came by the cottage Saturday morning while Dave and I were there with the police. He was scheduled to pick Teddy up. And today, he came by Fiona's flat to borrow some money while I was there."

Belle was quiet for a moment. "It would take some amount of strength to smother someone, wouldn't it? I don't know what his motive would be, but he'd be a more likely candidate than one of the women—as far as physical strength. I say we add him to the list."

Picturing Albert in Fiona's kitchen brought another thought to mind. "Belle, you know those plaques with hooks for keys? I saw one on Fiona's wall by the back door, and I bet both Albert and Pris have easy access to her flat—and to the key to Teddy's cottage. That makes three people with opportunity."

"Okay, duly noted. Anyone else come to mind, while we're in an accusing frame of mind?" She frowned. "I guess we have to put Beatrix on the list, don't we? She had the most to gain, though I don't think for a minute she did it."

That made me think of the conversation with the solicitor. "Hmm. I'd almost forgotten the solicitor said another individual was in the will, but he didn't say who it was. I guess if we'd asked, he would have told us. He emphasized Beatrix had gotten the bulk of the estate, so I wonder how significant a bequest this other person will receive."

"I'd say significance is in the eye of the beholder. If you live from one payday to the next, as I did when the twins were young and their father had just died, £500 could be significant. Now that Wendy's retired and we live together, it could fund a long weekend in an all-inclusive five-star resort—but it wouldn't mean as much."

"True. Well, at a minimum, I need to find out who that person is. I should be able to get that from Beatrix, since she's taking a copy of the will to her solicitor as we speak. Meanwhile, we've got who on the list? Pris, Fiona, Albert, Beatrix? And if we consider it being some avaricious collector who was desperate for something Teddy had, it could be someone we've no idea about. Just think, there was a literary festival in town, filled with book lovers."

Belle squinted and didn't respond right away. "Now that you mention the festival, you've made me think of Gilbert. After all, didn't he visit Teddy to see his collection? Could he have seen something he felt he had to have?"

Thinking about that possibility, I realized I didn't want to consider Gilbert a suspect any more than I did Beatrix. "I hardly know him, but somehow I think he'd offer money for whatever he wanted rather than break into Teddy's cottage to get it. Unless, he *did* offer to buy something and Teddy didn't want to part with it. My head is spinning. If it was Gilbert or anyone besides Teddy's employees, how did they unlock the door?"

As we pulled into the driveway to Sunshine Cottage, Belle yawned. "I think we've done good work today. Maybe Constable James will find something on the computer that will help. Or Gemma's come up with a fingerprint that will crack the case. You know, I think I still have time for a lie-down before Peter comes in."

I helped her into the cottage and got her comfy on her bed. Tigger came into the bedroom, stretching one paw and then another until he'd worked the kinks from all four. He leaped up beside Belle and curled up by her side, and I tucked a quilted throw around the two of them.

"Thank you, Leta. And Tigger thanks you too. He likes being beneath the cover. I'm sure we'll chat later."

By the time I drove the short distance to my cottage, I too was ready for a lie-down—or nap, as we Americans call it. I let Dickens inspect the garden while I put out fresh water for my furry friends. When he was back inside, we three retired to the bedroom, Dickens on the rug and Christie by my side. Maybe I'd wake up knowing who the villain was. *To sleep, perchance to dream ...*

Not a chance. I'd barely closed my eyes when Gemma called, and she didn't sound happy. "What were you thinking? Keeping my constable tied up for hours?! You know we have other crimes to solve!"

Good grief. What brought this on? "Gemma, what are you going on about? He's a grown man. He could have told us he needed to leave. And what crime could you have that's more important than a murder?"

She bulldozed right over my words. "And you took Belle! I didn't say you could have a party. Did you invite the neighbors too?"

At the best of times, Gemma ran hot and cold about my sleuthing activities. She could be snippy, rude, and downright insulting one minute, and then grudgingly—even nicely—ask for my help the next. "Excuse me, didn't you invite Dave and me to return to the scene of the crime and then ask for our help in studying the binders? What's gotten into you?" I wasn't usually this direct with her. I was usually the soul of politeness. But she'd rubbed me the wrong way one time too many.

"I'll tell you what! DCI Burton's been on the horn reading me the riot act about you dragging Belle into an investigation —yet again. Says the poor woman could be in danger because of you."

I guffawed. "Me *dragging* Belle? He's got to be kidding. She was putting together a list of suspects on the way home today. And what danger? We've been with Beatrix and Constable James all day. It's not like some crazed killer is going to commit mass murder in a Chipping Camden cottage. And if he's so concerned about Belle's safety, is he worried about mine too?" Now *I* was getting steamed.

"He's furious I allowed Beatrix to go to the cottage. Says she's a prime suspect."

"Seriously? Has he no respect for the local *bobby*—as in you —knowing her turf? I know she has to be cleared because she's the key beneficiary, but seriously?"

I heard Gemma take a deep breath. "He's on the wrong track, but there's no telling him that. He goes from wanting to bring Beatrix in for questioning to wanting to label it a random break-in—says the thief must've been surprised to find Mr. Byrd at home."

Could he possibly be that stupid? "What? Surprised to find him at home—an elderly man at home after 9 p.m.? Is he nuts? Has anyone even asked what time it was that Fiona left? It was probably closer to ten. And if he believes that, then he should clear Beatrix. She *knew* he was at home."

"Okay, okay, I admit he's not making much sense, but he's my boss. He's a—what do you call it—a micro-manager."

As was my nature, I defaulted to being polite—to being non-confrontational. Some people thrive on conflict. Not me. I spoke softly, which typically had a calming effect. "So, Gemma, what do *you* think? Do you think it was a random crime?"

Her tone shifted from furious to exasperated. "No. Nor do I see Beatrix as a suspect, but, of course, she doesn't have an alibi. She was in her hotel room alone. Too bad she didn't share a room like Belle and Ellie did."

"And this random crime thing? Has there been a string of break-ins in Chipping Camden?"

"Nope." She sighed and I could picture her shaking her head.

I reverted to my conflict management training from my corporate days. Not everyone I worked with agreed with my self-deprecating style, but it worked for me. "Gemma, I'm confused. Exactly why *did* you call me?" I thought I knew the answer. She'd been chewed out by her boss, and she was feeling defensive, but she was a good enough manager not to take it out on her constable. She had no qualms, however, about taking it out on me. Her response would be telling.

I sensed she'd spent her fury. "I . . . I'm not sure. I was beside myself when DCI Burton hung up on me. And I couldn't exactly talk it through with Constable James. That would have been unprofessional."

But she could blast me? Will the girl never learn? What she needs is a mentor. Instead, she has me. "Gemma, how do you think I feel?" *I should be getting paid for being a counselor,* I thought. *Never mind being a detective.*

"Point taken. How 'bout I hang up and call back—and start over?" That was as close as I was going to get to an apology. One thing Gemma never did was apologize.

It was my turn to sigh. Disaster averted. *Am I the only person in the world who thinks arguments are a disaster?*

"Let's pretend you did. Forgetting about our favorite DCI and what he thinks, am I correct in thinking Constable James has brought you up to speed on what we discovered at the cottage today?"

"Yes, pretty much. I understand there's a cane missing and some documents from the collection. It would appear our thief was looking for something or several things in particular. Otherwise, he or she would have carried off the binders, maybe even some of the rare books. Though hauling off more than a book or two could be difficult, I suppose. I wonder where they parked their car."

It was good to talk things over after letting my findings simmer a bit. "I wonder why they didn't just take the binders away to examine somewhere else. If you had access to a trove of rare documents, some valuable, some not so much, wouldn't you want to look through them? I mean if the motive was lucre—excuse me, that's what P.D. James says for money—why not take every bit and see what you could get for it?"

"I think you're rubbing off on Constable James. He asked something similar. Of course, for all we know, it was something else the thief was after, and they got distracted somehow by the binders. Couldn't have been the cane, could it?"

I thought about the ledger sheets. "I didn't pay close attention to what Teddy paid for it, but I think it was over £1000. I suppose it's possible he got it for a steal, and it's worth ten times that. Heck, they could have grabbed the umbrella stand and made off with the whole lot. Still, something tells me the target was rare documents or books."

"Aaargh. Don't tell me this is going to be another book collector drama. I can't see us having more than one of those in a lifetime in our little village. Besides, we locked up the culprit for that crime."

"Well, it's not exactly in Astonbury. It's in Chipping Camden, and it happened during a literary festival. Maybe it's not such a far-fetched idea. I wonder how many collectors were in attendance last week. Gilbert might know."

"Number one, I hope you're not serious. Number two, who's Gilbert?"

I was about to attempt an answer when another call came in. "Gemma, I've got another call. Ask your dad about Gilbert, and maybe we can catch up later." As rude as she'd been, I had no problem cutting our call short.

Hearing Dave's voice dispelled the lingering tension from

speaking with Gemma. "Thank goodness it's you, Tommy. I've had enough of talking with Gemma."

"Uh-oh," he said. "Does your calling me Tommy mean Tuppence is about to share tales of derring-do, or are you going to go straight to complaining about Gemma?"

I chuckled. "Never mind Gemma. No derring-do, unless you see looking through ledgers and bookshelves as particularly adventurous. Perhaps a tale of intrigue, though. You'll be sorry you missed the mystery of the key. We followed the clues, and we found it. And that's just the beginning . . ."

By the time I filled Dave in and heard how his research was going, any thought of a nap was gone. Besides, a trip to Sainsbury's was in order if I planned to cook dinner for Belle and Peter the next night. It occurred to me I should invite Ellie too.

I rang the Manor House, where Caroline, the cook, answered the phone. Before I asked for Ellie, I inquired about Caroline's dinner menu for Wednesday evening.

"No plans, Leta. Wednesday is one of my days to work at the Chipping Camden Café."

"Perfect. I called to invite Ellie to dinner tomorrow night, so that will work out well if her dance card isn't already full."

When Ellie came to the phone, there was no hesitation in her reply. " How nice. I don't often get to chat with Peter, and of course, I'm eager to hear the news about the Chipping Camden Affair, as I've dubbed it. I'm sure there's a bit of exaggeration in the comments posted on the Astonbury Aha!, and you can set me straight."

The Chipping Camden Affair, I thought. *Next, we'll be turning the tale into a mystery novel.*

Chapter Sixteen

Wednesday morning, I woke up thinking about Wendy, and my thoughts about my friend were a jumble. *Is she having a good time with Brian? If she's talking to Belle, how much of what she's hearing is she sharing with him? Surely, she doesn't think I've put her mum in danger. I wish I could call her, but that just wouldn't do!*

It was a typical spring day in the Cotswolds—cloudy and misty with a chill in the air. I imagined the weather was why the gardens in the area were so beautiful. Explaining to Christie that the mist wasn't conducive to a ride in the backpack, I grabbed my waterproof jacket, my ball cap, and a leash for Dickens. It would take a steady downpour to keep us from a walk.

"Dickens, what do you say we skip Martha and Dylan today and head to the High Street? Maybe have a latte and scone at Toby's?"

"Works for me. I bet Jenny will give me a snack, and there's sure to be someone there to rub my belly." He was right on all counts. It was rare we went anywhere that folks didn't exclaim over my boy and inquire about his breed, and if they knelt to pet him, he angled for a belly rub too. He had his routine down pat.

Midweek in the village was slow, but it would be bustling again when the weekend arrived, as the tourist season was kicking off. By late May, it would be busy every day, but for now, I could have my pick of tables at Toby's. I removed my ball cap and shook the water from it and then attempted to fluff my hair, without much luck.

Jenny greeted me as I approached the counter. "What will it be today, Leta? A caramel latte? Plus a snack? We've got blueberry scones." I settled on a skinny hazelnut latte and a plain scone with some of my favorite raspberry jam, and I ordered a bag of sugar cookies to serve for dessert that evening. As Dickens had suspected, Jenny came around the counter with a chunk of scone for him. *Spoiled rotten.*

I wanted to stop in the Book Nook before we returned home, so I didn't linger over my scone. The latte I could carry with me across the street. My phone buzzed with a text as I was pushing my chair back. Wendy wanted to know if I could talk. As soon as I responded yes, she called.

"Oh my gosh. Finally, he's gone out for a run. I've wanted to call you ever since I spoke to Mum and then heard Brian coming down on Gemma, but he's been glued to my side."

"I'm betting he had a few choice words about me, right? I heard from Gemma that I'd placed your mum in danger."

"Right. He chooses to believe you're a bad influence on her. You'd think he'd know better by now. I mean, he's been around Mum enough to know she has all her faculties and a mind of her own, but nooo, it's your fault. He even said, and I quote, 'It's a good thing you're far removed from the situation, love.' Seriously, he said that!"

"So, beyond the fact your best friend may soon be off-limits to you, how's your trip going?" I joked.

Wendy sighed. "That's a longer story than I have time for if I'm going to hear about the murder. I expect him to be gone an hour, and I want to take full advantage of my free time to get the scoop. Let's say it's going well enough that I'll be furious if he decides to cut the trip short to return to work. He acts as though Gemma's in over her head, and you know full well she isn't."

"Yes, I know. She lit a fire under the SOCOs and it spread to the coroner, so I'd say she's doing fine. And, she's been decent about my involvement, though, as so often happens with Gemma, she blasted me yesterday after speaking with your DCI."

"Aaargh. I can only imagine. Don't get me started. Mum says you spent half the day looking at rare documents, and I can't believe I'm missing the fun. Tell me more."

I explained as best I could what we'd found or not found, and I took great pleasure in telling her it had been Belle who started the list of suspects. I also promised to text her the video of opening the safe. "I could use your English teacher expertise on all this. A few of the missing documents connect to Mark Twain, but I haven't begun to figure out what the thief was looking for and why."

"I can't believe I'm not there to help. What are your next steps? I hear you're entertaining Mum and Peter tonight. Is there any way I can help from afar? Maybe you can text me questions about the authors, and I can google the answers for you. Or anything else you need me to research. I'm dying to help."

We agreed I'd contact her if I came up with anything, and she promised to let me know if she heard any tidbits on the case when Brian spoke with Gemma. Until Gemma was dressed down by her superior, she'd been open with me, but that could change in a heartbeat. Still, she couldn't deny that Beatrix, Belle, and I had come up with some vital information —like the missing cane and several missing documents.

Wendy yelped. "There he is catching his breath in front of the hotel. Got to go before I get caught fraternizing with the enemy." Somehow that comment didn't seem all that funny to me.

I grabbed Dickens and my latte and crossed the street to the bookshop. Beatrix's cats, Tommy and Tuppence, were lounging in the front window, and Trixie was straightening the books on the display tables. Beatrix stood behind the counter looking pensive.

She looked up as I entered. "How would you like a job in a bookshop?"

"I hope you're joking. You know I'd pretty much spend my entire paycheck on books. You *are* joking, aren't you?"

"Yes, but I'm soon going to be in the market for some help. First, I've got to wrap my brain around how Bluebird Books is doing and make some decisions. So much for spending the summer sussing out the situation. Just a bit much going on right now."

"Sounds overwhelming. Meanwhile, my brain is swirling with the why and who of what happened at the cottage— which makes me wonder about the solicitor's comment that Teddy also left a substantial bequest to someone else. Can you tell me who it is?"

Beatrix smiled. "Yes, and I feel good about it. He named Fiona in the will, and he's left her the flat above the shop plus a decent amount of money. The flat will go in her name, so no matter what happens with the shop or whether she chooses to continue working there, she'll have a place to call home. I think they had a very special relationship, and I'm glad he's taken care of her."

Of the three people we'd met who'd worked for Teddy, she'd seemed the most cut up over his death. My concern was that the inheritance gave her a motive. She had the opportunity, as she had a key to the cottage. And anyone who came across Teddy sound asleep had the means—the pillows lying there on the bed.

"By the way, Leta, Gemma called late yesterday to say I could now have free rein of the cottage and Constable James would be bringing me the binders sometime today. Guess her people have gleaned all they can from them. It strikes me that beyond fingerprints, you and I and Belle figured out way more than they ever could have."

Free rein? Now that's odd, especially after DCI Burton had chewed her out for allowing Beatrix access in the first place. I wondered whether this was Gemma's way of asserting herself. When he first arrived, Gemma pretty much told me she wasn't going to let him ride roughshod over her, but I imagined that was easier said than done.

"Well, that's good news. Do you plan to go through the binders again? Or do you have time for that?"

"No time at all. Trixie is itching to look at them, though. With her background in papermaking and printing, she can't wait to see the collection."

Hearing our conversation, Trixie came to the counter. "That's right, Leta. For you and Aunt Beatrix, it's all about the words on the page and what they tell you. For me, there's a bit of that, but I'm more intrigued by the texture of the paper, the ink, and the typeface."

I nodded as I had a thought. "Beatrix, is there any way

you'd let me study them a bit more after Trixie's had a chance to look through them? I took pictures of everything, but seeing the actual documents again would be much more helpful. There was so much to absorb yesterday, I couldn't begin to understand why certain things were missing. Could you?"

"No, other than Mark Twain cropping up more than once, which doesn't mean anything to me, not at all. Trixie, can you spend tonight with the binders and then let Leta have them for a bit?"

"Sure. You'll have them back soon enough and I can study them again. You know, there could be some quotes in those documents we could reproduce in my cards. The possibilities are endless."

That settled, I was almost out the door when I remembered the burgundy leather ledger book. "Beatrix, it would be helpful to have the ledger book too. Are you returning to Chipping Camden any time soon? Could you pick it up?"

Beatrix nodded yes. "I may be going tomorrow and can easily get the ledger. To my way of thinking, you're more likely to figure this mystery out than the Gloucestershire Constabulary. Can you imagine them sitting down trying to discern a pattern in the missing documents? Too bad your partner in crime is out of town. Wendy would be a big help, wouldn't she?"

She was right. "For sure! I may have briefly taught English, but Wendy taught the subject for over thirty years. This puzzle would be right up her alley. She was disappointed she missed the mystery of the key, though I think we did darned well on our own."

The mist had turned to rain, so I set a brisk pace on the walk home, Dickens prancing jauntily beside me. He had no issues with wet and cold weather—the colder, the better. The

Cotswolds climate suited him much better than the heat and humidity we'd endured in Atlanta. By late spring in Georgia, he could take walks only early in the morning or after dark, and he could most often be found stretched out on the cool tile floor in the bathroom during the summer months.

"Dickens, I'm remembering your refusing to join me on the screened porch on hot mornings. You'd look at me and say, 'Nope, not happening. I'll stay inside, thank you very much.' But take you for a walk in the rain, and you're a happy camper."

"That's me. Perfect weather for a walk."

As soon as we hit the mudroom, I toweled him off and wiped his muddy feet before letting him loose in the rest of my cottage. Fortunately, the flagstone floors downstairs were well-suited for a dog. I carried logs to the fireplace and stoked the fire that had almost gone out in my absence. I'd shopped and cooked the Bolognese sauce the night before, so I had several free hours ahead of me.

Christie strolled in and headed to the rug in front of the fireplace. She stretched to her full length as though she were trying to expose as much of her body as possible to the fire. I reached down to rub her fluffy black belly. "You're not quite the addict Dickens is, but you enjoy a belly rub from time to time, don't you?"

She purred. "And I like it when you rub your nose on my belly too. Let's take a nap, why don't we?"

"I'll squeeze one in later, maybe around two or three. For now, I'm trying to decide between starting a new book or working on the columns I never got to on Monday. I guess it will have to be writing. Are you going to stay here to nap or curl up in the office in the file drawer?"

The answer was obvious when she followed me with

Dickens right behind her. When we were settled in our respective positions—Dickens beneath the desk, Christie in her drawer, and me in my chair—I flipped open my notebook and read over the notes I'd taken the past week. I decided on Broadway Tower as the day's topic and made fast work of it since I'd taken such detailed notes. Another column about Martha and Dylan was easily dashed off. In no time, I emailed both to my editor plus the picture of Dave, Christie, and the donkeys.

The phrase 'work before play' popped into my head. In my corporate days, when I'd been certified in the Myers-Briggs Type Indicator—MBTI—that was the motto for my personality type. As an ISTJ, I always had a to-do list in my head and found it difficult to relax or 'play' until I'd ticked off most if not all of the items on my list. *Gee, is that why I seem unable to turn loose of a real-life murder mystery until it's solved? Maybe I should try that theory on Gemma as a reason for my being a nosy parker, as she calls me.* "Yup, I'll have to tell her that."

Neither of my companions responded to my comment. Heck, neither of them even stirred.

My cottage was filled with the enticing aroma of Bolognese sauce when Peter and Belle arrived. Ellie was right behind them, and the three made themselves at home in front of the cheery fire in the sitting room. As I carried in a tray holding a bottle of red wine and baked brie with pita chips, I admonished them. "Now, don't fill up on snacks. Dinner will be a hearty meal of salad, bread, and pasta plus cookies from the Tearoom. And, Peter, please no handouts for Dickens."

Peter chuckled as he poured the wine. "Don't fill up? Are you kidding? This will be the best meal Mum and I've had all week. After my cooking and a few nights of takeaway, she may never let Wendy leave again." He looked at Dickens. "Sorry, mate, maybe later."

Dickens barked and went to his bed by the fireplace. "Don't know why I can't at least have a chip."

Looking thoughtful, Belle sipped her wine and stroked Christie, who, as usual, had climbed in her lap. "Not to speak out of turn, but I'm not sure another trip with the silver fox, as Wendy calls him, is in the cards. I think he's gotten on her last nerve. I'm pretty sure we'll all get an earful when she gets home."

"I certainly got an earful from Gemma yesterday after Brian blessed her out over my 'leading you astray.' As if I could lead our resident Miss Marple anywhere!"

"Speaking of Miss Marple," said Ellie, "are you two going to fill us in on what you've been up to? I'd only just met the delightful Mr. Byrd, and I still can't believe someone killed the poor man. As distressing as it was, I could accept that he died in his sleep. If I get to choose, that's how I want to go. But murder? In Chipping Camden?"

"Mum hasn't told me much either. Said I might as well wait until we were with Leta tonight. So, let's hear it, ladies."

I looked at the Dowager Countess. "Ellie, you failed to mention you've dubbed the tale The Chipping Camden Affair. Sounds like the title of an Agatha Christie book, doesn't it? I can only hope it's wrapped up as neatly as one of her mysteries."

That comment made Belle laugh. "You know we're down one little old lady, Ellie. Perhaps you'd like to sub for Wendy. In fact, given your love of reading, you'd have been helpful with the mystery of the key." With that, Belle recounted how we'd spent our Tuesday at Teddy's cottage. She was in her element.

Not only did she explain the clues and our suppositions, but she also described the items in the Bless the Children binder. I could tell Ellie was getting a kick out of traveling down memory lane with her friend.

I excused myself to put the rigatoni on and ready the salad, and I was soon calling my guests to the dinner table. As Peter pulled out chairs for his mum and Ellie, Belle whispered something to him. He said he'd be right back and went to the car, returning with a blue gift bag he carried to the sitting room.

"Ellie, I keep thinking I should attempt to serve a meal like the one we enjoyed for your birthday in December—but I don't think I have five courses in my repertoire. And since I gave my staff the night off, the salad and pasta courses are being served together."

Among my Astonbury friends, Ellie was perhaps the only one who hadn't yet sampled my Greek salad. After a few bites, she asked if I'd be willing to share the recipe with Caroline.

I smiled. "I can give her the ingredients, but I don't have any exact measurements. Maybe I can come by one day and we can make it together. To me, the most important thing is good feta cheese, preferably made from sheep's milk."

When I asked my guests if they'd prefer coffee and cookies in the sitting room, they all agreed they would. I started the coffee maker and began clearing the table as they moved to the other room, but I wasn't fast enough to keep Peter from sneaking his plate to the floor for Dickens to clean. All I could do was shake my head.

Peter stayed behind in the kitchen as I put the dishes in the sink to soak. "How's Dave getting along in Scotland?"

"He says he's making great progress and may drive back tomorrow or Friday. If you're playing cricket in Stanway on Sunday, maybe we can see the match, but I'll have a better idea after we chat tonight. It's probably just as well he's away, given my sleuthing this week."

"Why do you say that? Because you'd be ignoring him?"

I stood with my hip propped against the counter. "Partly, but mostly because we had kind of a heart to heart about how much he worries about me—not all the time, but when my LOL adventures heat up. I guess, bottom line, he wishes I would cease and desist my sleuthing activities."

My friend looked thoughtful. "I guess I can see how he would. You *are* prone to placing yourself in danger—at least you have been in the year I've known you. It's a wonder you survived the episode in the river. I've never come right out and said it, but I worry about you from time to time. Funny, I don't worry about my sister getting hurt, but then she never does. It's always you. I can't say I blame the bloke. I think I'd feel much the same . . . if you were my girlfriend."

I blushed. Funny that Christie was always after me to think of Peter in that way. When I first moved to Astonbury, I wasn't ready for a boyfriend, and Peter was involved with someone else—though the relationship had been a secret. They say timing is everything.

I gave a weak smile and dodged that bullet by latching onto his comment about Wendy. "I think Brian Burton has worrying about Wendy covered—in all regards—and he also worries about your mum. Did Wendy tell you he had doubts about her being able to climb to Tintagel?"

That got a laugh out of him, along with an unflattering comment about his sister's boyfriend. By then, the coffee was ready, and Peter helped me by carrying the tray with the carafe and mugs while I got the bottle of Kahlúa and the plate of cookies.

In the sitting room, Christie was curled in Belle's lap, and

Dickens was lying at Ellie's feet. Both the ladies and my furry friends seemed content.

Dickens didn't move, but his eyes followed the tray of cookies. "I bet Peter will give me a cookie chunk if you let him." I knew he was right, so I cut Peter off at the pass by reminding him not to feed the dog.

As we sipped coffee, Belle offered the blue bag to Ellie. "This is a little something that made me think of you. I had to have one for myself too." I realized it was the small framed quote she'd found at Bluebird Books.

Ellie exclaimed in delight when she pulled it from the bag and read aloud the Mark Twain quote, "'Age is an issue of mind over matter. If you don't mind, it doesn't matter.' How apropos for two old ladies! Twain had a way with words, didn't he? I always loved his quote from the time a paper mistakenly printed his obituary: 'The reports of my death are greatly exaggerated.' I think I've heard he didn't say it exactly that way, but a biographer embellished it. Regardless, it's a great line. They should have sold these at the literary festival at the Twain session."

She was naming the Mark Twain books she had in her library when I interjected, "Oh my! The frame, the smashed frame."

Four pairs of eyes looked my way and Dickens barked, "What's wrong, Leta?"

"Belle, the missing frame from the bedroom—there was a frame in the wheelie bin, smashed. I forgot all about Dave finding it Saturday morning. There were two framed items missing, and I could tell from the shadow on the bedroom wall where one had hung. I never did find any indication there'd been a second one hanging anywhere."

"And what was in it, Leta? Was there a document?" asked Ellie.

"No, just a shred, a corner of a document. There was no way to tell what it was. It was a combination of you holding a gilt frame and the discussion of Mark Twain that brought it to mind because that was one of the missing items—a letter to Mark Twain from Arthur Conan Doyle."

Belle nodded slowly. "Mark Twain keeps cropping up, doesn't he? Were there more Twain letters or books listed in the ledger—items that *aren't* missing? Or was every last one taken?"

"I don't know for sure. I was only in charge of the items on the walls and shelves and in the Miscellany binder. Teddy had the usual books like *A Connecticut Yankee in King Arthur's Court* and *Huckleberry Finn* and *Tom Sawyer,* and they were all on the shelf. Two things were missing from the binder, but I found them on the desk. Beatrix went through the Author Letters binder, and I recall two Twain letters were missing, but there could have been more that weren't. Now my head's spinning."

Ellie's mouth dropped open. "I just realized I'm the only one here who attended the Twain session Wednesday evening. Matthew, Sarah, and I went and had dinner at the Chipping Camden Café afterward. We got to sample Caroline's new spring menu at the Café." Matthew and Sarah were Ellie's son and daughter-in-law—the Earl and Countess of Stow.

"Oh my goodness. That's what you meant when you said Twain session? I had no idea there'd been one."

"Yes. This year's festival was a departure from the norm. Typically, the conference hosts living authors. It's an opportunity for readers to hear them speak about their process, how they come up with their characters, and how their lives influence their writing. The new chairman decided to make this one historical, to bring in experts on authors of yore. That's why we had sessions on Arthur Conan Doyle, Graham Greene, R.F. Delderfeld, and such. Dave's discussion of J.M. Barrie was a perfect fit."

Peter looked amused. "So, could there have been some rabid Twain collector at the festival? You know my knowledge of this kind of thing is limited to the furor over Mum's rare J.M. Barrie book. Ellie, did you see any shady characters lurking in the conference room?"

Ellie laughed. "No, although I realized when I saw him at our book club that Gilbert Ward had been in the audience. He and another gentleman seemed to be competing for who could ask the most questions. The second man was accompanied by a woman in a wheelchair, and I could tell she was trying to get him to stop asking so many questions. We had an entertaining speaker, and she showed clips from both the Ken Burns special on Twain and Hal Holbrook's stage show. It was a marvelous evening. Instead of giving a canned presentation, she went out of her way to connect Twain to other authors who were represented at the festival. She even mentioned a letter Twain had written Bram Stoker thanking him for a photograph of Henry Irving, a famous British actor whom Twain admired."

I was itching to start jotting notes. "Ellie, do you have a program from that session? I'd love to see it and to sit down again with you to go over it in detail. I think Belle's right about you subbing for Wendy. Are you game?"

Ellie beamed. "I thought Belle was teasing, but I'd love to help. It sounds exciting." She offered to host us for brunch the next day. I wondered whether Ellie had any idea what she was in for. *Could it be that the Little Old Ladies' Detective Agency is about to expand?*

Chapter Seventeen

After seeing everyone off, I called Beatrix and explained I'd like to have the binders in time for my brunch meeting. I also asked if there had been any additional Mark Twain documents in the Author Letters binder.

"I plan to be in the shop around 9:30 as usual so why don't I run the binders by your cottage before that? As for Twain, no. I think those two missing items were the only ones listed for the binder I checked, but I could be wrong. What about books? Did Teddy have any of his books?"

"Yes, all accounted for. I can't help thinking that the Twain letters may have been the target of the break-in, though I think there was something from Agatha Christie missing too. I need to sit down with those ledger sheets and make a list before I get off on the wrong track."

"Leta, I can't thank you enough for looking into this. Any other time, I'd be right there with you trying to see a pattern —if there is one—but I've got too much on my plate right now to be of any help. By the way, Teddy's next-door neighbor called to tell me a Fed Ex package was delivered for him today, so I'll be making a quick stop by the cottage to get it, and I'll pick up the ledger book then."

"Thanks, Beatrix." I hesitated. "This may seem an odd question, but how much do you know about Gilbert Ward?"

She paused. "Not much. I was thrilled Dave sent him my way for our book club meeting, and, since I wanted to introduce him properly, I googled him. What's on the internet is mostly that he's a member of the Sherlockian Club, and that he's known for his entertaining presentations at various bookshops and clubs. I got the impression he's a collector of sorts, at least when it comes to Arthur Conan Doyle and Sherlock Holmes material. Why do you ask?"

I explained Ellie recalled seeing him at the Twain session a week ago, and that had piqued my curiosity. "Sounds as though he took in as many of the festival sessions as possible. I had to laugh when Ellie told me he had lots of questions for the woman who made the presentation on Mark Twain."

"Doesn't that sound just like him? He seems to be quite a character. Oh! I meant to tell you—I figured out why Albert, Teddy's driver, looked familiar to me. He used to work at his father's stall at the Bolton Flea Market. Was there most weekends until he went off to Oxford. He's grown up since I last saw him. I wonder how he wound up doing odd jobs for Teddy instead of something more in line with an Oxford education. Could be like Thom working for me last year. It's not always easy to find a decent job even with a degree."

"Um, I've got the story behind that."

She remembered him as a shy, polite young man and was surprised to hear about his being sent down from school. We agreed he was fortunate to have gotten his job with Teddy.

Next, I washed my face, changed into my PJs, and climbed in bed to call Dave. "You missed a good meal tonight," I said.

"Though the good news is I made enough sauce for us to have a meal when you get back."

"And didn't you tell me that a good Italian sauce is even better a day or two later? Something about the seasoning improving? I'll eat it any time you want to put it in front of me." He couldn't wait to tell me about driving to Kirriemuir to visit the house Barrie had grown up in. Thursday, he planned to visit the house on Picardy Place where Arthur Conan Doyle was born. The tours were welcome breaks from hours in the university library and might provide some colorful background for his book *Barrie & Friends*.

As I updated him on the progress, or lack thereof, on the literary angle of Teddy's murder, it occurred to me that I'd gone a day without hearing from Gemma. *Good news or bad?* I wondered.

Dave was intrigued by my idea that the killer, perhaps a collector, could have been after Twain material. "It's hard to imagine a literary festival as a hotbed of conniving collectors, but I guess anything is possible."

"Uh-huh, when Gemma blasted me yesterday, she expressed a similar sentiment—more along the lines of not wanting to believe we could once again have a murder connected to books or authors. Maybe it takes English majors and writers to find that idea believable. I wonder whether she'd get a kick out of that John Dunning series about book-sellers and book scouts. They're filled with murders. Maybe I should get her the first one, *Booked to Die*—only after she's solved this case, of course. I wouldn't want to distract her."

My boyfriend enjoyed a good mystery as much as I did. "Loved those books. Have you read all of them?"

"No, only two. Perhaps I'll get back to them after this. By the way, not that I see Gilbert as a conniving collector, but his name came up tonight. Ellie remembered seeing him at the Twain session Wednesday. As you would expect, she said he asked tons of questions. I wonder . . . is he as much an expert on Twain as he is on Doyle? Would he be able to help me understand the significance of these documents? Until my scholarly boyfriend wraps up his research trip and has the time?"

"Ha! He'd jump at the chance, expert or not. You know, beneath his showman exterior, he's amazingly well-read, even if he is careful to say he's no scholar. I'll text you his number and you can ask him. I can see him going all Sherlock Holmes on you. Are you ready to play Watson?"

I paused before responding. "Sure. But tell me, how well do you know him? Do you have any reservations about my involving him?"

"Now, where did that come from? Did you sense something unsavory about him? Or are you just being cautious?" He chuckled. "Wait, you cautious? That can't be it."

Not being sure how to take that last remark, I chose to ignore it. "I'm not sure where it came from. I need to be sure he doesn't share any details about the theft with anyone else since there's an ongoing police investigation. Maybe that's it."

Dave seemed to be finding this humorous, and I thought that was a good thing. "Don't want him to put the word out on the conniving collector grapevine? I think if you ask him, he'll keep quiet about it."

"Okay. I'll give him a call once you send me his number." We moved on to Dave's plans for the rest of the week. He was confident he'd be able to wrap up his research Thursday, get an early start for Astonbury Friday, and be back in time to take me to dinner. "Okey dokey, can you see me turning into a pumpkin?"

"Yes, I can. Goodnight, Tuppence. Love you."

"Love you back." I smiled as I turned out the light and snuggled beneath my comforter.

The next morning, Dickens was fired up at the prospect of seeing Ellie's Corgi. "I can't wait to see Blanche," he barked. "Wonder if she has some new toys?"

Thursday was one of Caroline's days at the Manor House, so Belle and I were treated to a leisurely meal of Eggs Benedict and fruit. I could tell I wouldn't need lunch. Dodging Dickens and Blanche while carrying two mugs of coffee, one for me and one for Belle, I followed my friends to the library.

Ellie stoked the fire, and I placed the binders on the large ottoman as Belle got settled. Seeing her prop her cane beside the easy chair reminded me of Teddy's missing cane. *Was it merely an opportunistic theft—nothing to do with the main goal of the break-in?*

Beatrix had placed the loose pages in their proper places in the binders with yellow sticky notes attached, so we'd know they'd been found on the desk. Though she hadn't recalled any other Twain material in the Author Letters binder, Ellie thought we should double-check, so that's where she started, cross-referencing to the ledger sheet copies as she went along.

I suggested that Belle flip through the Miscellany binder so she could see the two sheets that had been removed and replaced. Meanwhile, I pulled out the spiral-bound notebook I'd brought with me and, in large block print, listed the wall items I'd been unable to locate. When Ellie and Belle were done, the next step would be to check through the ledger sheets to find anything else identified as missing and complete the list.

Caroline arrived to refill our coffee mugs and bring home-made treats to the dogs. She had gotten their measure and asked them both to sit before handing over the treats.

As they followed her back to the kitchen, Dickens turned to bark, "Leta, we need some of these at home." For the moment, Caroline was his new best friend.

Ellie closed her binder. "I'm ready to dive in. How 'bout you ladies?"

Belle nodded her agreement, and I read aloud from my notebook. "Okay, here we go. Two author letters documented by Teddy as being on the wall are missing: 'Agatha Christie to G.K. Chesterton 22_4_1935' and 'Doyle to Twain 70th Birthday tribute 5_12_1905.' What do you have to add, Ellie?"

"Two pieces are also missing from the Author Letters binder. 'Twain to Doyle on meeting in America 29_8_1894' and 'Twain to Barrie on seeing Peter Pan in London 29_12_1905.'"

I nodded. "Your turn, Belle."

"Nothing missing because you found the two pieces among the papers on Teddy's desk, but we should probably make note of them. Why were they pulled out but left behind? We have 'T.S. Eliot/notes on *A Connecticut Yankee in King Arthur's Court* 15_3_1924' and 'Twain on Arthur Conan Doyle for the Strand 23_7_1907.' Is it significant that it's the only place T.S. Eliot shows up?"

I shrugged as I tore the page from my notebook and placed it on the ottoman so we could all study it. *There are common elements, but what do they mean?* "What do you think? I had the idea this all had to do with Mark Twain, but that doesn't seem to be the case."

Dickens and Blanche chose that moment to scamper into the library and skid to a stop in front of the fireplace. Each carried a rawhide chewy. *Spoiled rotten*, I thought.

Ellie shook her head at their antics and returned to the task at hand. She moved her finger down the page. "You're right, Doyle shows up almost as often as Mark Twain. In the stolen documents, he's noted two times to Twain's three. And J.M. Barrie appears once, as does Dame Agatha."

Leaning in, Belle spoke. "If you look at the pages that were removed, Twain shows up two more times. His name isn't mentioned, but we all know he wrote *A Connecticut Yankee in King Arthur's Court*. Plus, he appears as the author of an article on Doyle. Is it simply that these aren't valuable? But, then, I'd think anything by these famous writers would be worth a significant amount."

I kept coming back to the list. "I'm puzzled by what was taken and what remained behind, and I can't discern a pattern. If you bothered to pull pieces of paper from the binders to carry off, why not take all of them? Bottom line, we have four items that were stolen, so I'm thinking they must be of especially high value. When Wendy and I researched collectible books and letters last year, we were amazed at what they could go for. Last night, I googled the Edgar Allan Poe books that were in the safe. They're valued at £8575. Amazing."

Ellie laughed. "Stumped or not, talking about authors and books is fun, and at least we've got a complete list—four items. Where do we go from here?"

"I think we'll set this aside. I plan to contact Gilbert Ward later today to see if he can shed any light on these documents. Since he's a collector of sorts, he may have an idea. Are you ladies game to talk about suspects? Belle rattled off a list earlier this week."

Our resident Miss Marple beamed. "That's what the Little Old Ladies' Detective Agency does. We identify suspects and means and motive. Let's have at it."

As Belle and Ellie brainstormed possibilities, I wrote one name per page in my notebook. We had to set aside any reservations about the likelihood a person would smother an elderly man in his sleep. We didn't debate the names. I wrote any name thrown out. There weren't that many—only four.

Fiona

Albert

Pris

Beatrix

Ellie expressed her disapproval. "How can we suspect that sweet girl you tell me took care of both Teddy and his wife?"

"It's partly about opportunity, Ellie. Fiona has a key, and there was no sign of a break-in. She says it was her routine to let Watson out—that's the cat—and then lock up after seeing Teddy to bed. Plus, I've learned from Beatrix that Fiona has a motive. Teddy bequeathed her a substantial sum of money plus the flat above Bluebird Books."

"Okay, I can see that, Leta, but what's Albert's motive? What do you know about him?"

"I'm not sure I know all that much. It's mostly that he was in and out of Teddy's cottage almost daily, either delivering things or picking him up to drive him somewhere. In all that, I keep wondering whether Teddy could have given him a key at some point. And, as Belle and I discussed earlier, both Albert and Pris have easy access to Fiona's flat where the key hangs on a hook for all to see. And, well, he did steal some things from his girlfriend's flat when she broke up with him."

Ellie nodded. "So, he's taken things before."

I continued. "Yes. As for motive, who knows? Could it be that he figured out how valuable Teddy's collection was and thought he'd help himself to a few things?"

I paused as a memory popped into my head. "Wait a minute. Beatrix told me something I'd forgotten all about. Albert visits estate sales and flea markets looking for old furniture to refurbish, and Teddy told her Albert had also begun scouting for old books and magazines and always gave him first dibs. He *did* know enough to realize what Teddy had. Plus she mentioned off-hand that he looked familiar to her. She told me why last night."

"And," said Belle. "What?"

"She recalled seeing him as a lad working at one of the Manchester flea markets. You know how young boys change when they mature. It took her a bit to figure out who he was. Still, that means he could have connections for selling the documents if he took them. So, that's Albert. Belle, why don't you tell Ellie your ideas about Pris?"

Belle explained that Pris had picked the wrong person to open up to about her anger at Teddy's news he was bringing Beatrix in for the summer to manage the shop. It was Belle's belief she could have lost her temper and killed Teddy.

"And she stole things to make it look like a burglary gone wrong?" asked Ellie.

Belle encouraged her friend. "You've got it. Leta, what's that line Wendy quotes about evil in the hearts of men?"

Laughing at the memory, I lowered my voice. "Who knows what evil lurks in the hearts of men? The Shadow knows."

Ellie looked puzzled. "Seems appropriate, but who's the Shadow?"

"He's a character from a 1930s radio show. Some college stations brought it back in the States, and Wendy and I both listened to it in our younger days."

Quick on the uptake, Ellie knew right away why Beatrix made the list, but none of us seriously thought she was the killer. While we were discussing the suspects, I had noted their possible motives.

I looked at my team of sleuths. "I'd be the first to say we can't strike anyone from the list, but I'm struggling to convince myself any of these folks did it. I wonder whether we're missing someone. These are all people in his immediate circle, but he must have had business acquaintances, friends, fellow collectors, even customers who knew about his collection—if, in fact, that's even the motive. This could be the tip of the iceberg."

Belle smiled. "Maybe my son was on to something when he joked about a rabid collector last night."

Looking at Belle, I nodded. "Peter could be right. You know, I keep shying away from this idea, but I wonder whether we should add Gilbert to the list? He *is* a collector, and he specializes in Arthur Conan Doyle material."

My friends looked thoughtful, and Ellie spoke first. "I guess if you set aside having a key, that opens the way to consider Gilbert and plenty of others. But Gilbert's such a charming gentleman."

Belle laughed. "Ellie, I don't disagree. He's quite the character, but sometimes people aren't what they seem, and we only just met him."

Frowning, Ellie shook her head. "But wait a minute. What if theft wasn't the motive? Would that change the list? We added Pris and supposed she killed him in fury, and stole the documents as a smokescreen. What if someone else had a beef with Teddy? Someone we don't know about?"

"You know, Ellie, that's a good point," said Belle. "And my daughter better watch out. You could take her place on the LOLs." Belle looked at me. "Unless, of course, Leta can afford to keep all three of us on the payroll."

"Ha! As long as you're happy being paid in meals like I served last night, we're good."

That got a laugh from Ellie. "Sign me up, but tell me, do you ladies go on for hours doing this? I mean, how long does it take to have a breakthrough?"

I had a flashback to December, when my breakthrough had come just in time to keep the wrong person from being arrested for murder.

Belle cleared her throat. "It depends. Some clues steer us in the wrong direction, and we follow our noses down the wrong path."

I gathered the sheets of paper. "Right. It's not like the mystery novels we love or the BBC detective programs. Light-bulbs don't appear above our heads with the name of the culprit. If only. We've made a good start, but I, for one, have to sleep on things. And there's always Gemma to prod. I wonder if her folks found anything significant on Teddy's computer. She might tell me something if DCI Burton hasn't perma-nently sealed her lips."

As the founder of the Little Old Ladies' Detective Agency, I decided it was time to bring our meeting to a close and leave further sleuthing for another day, and we three promised to contact each other if we had any brainstorms. After placing the binders and notes in the car, I looked at Dickens. "Shall we take a stroll to see if we can find Basil?"

"Yes! I had fun with Blanche and her toys, but I want to see my big friend." Basil was the full-size version of my dwarf Great Pyrenees, and he guarded the flock of Cotswold Lions on the estate. I always thought of them as Raggedy Ann sheep because of the unusual way their fleece curled over their faces.

We walked past Matthew and Sarah's cottage and on toward the River Elfe where I saw the sheep grazing. Basil came bounding our way, his fur flying in the breeze. "Hey, Lil' Bit. I saw Leta's car and wondered if you'd stop by for a visit." It always made me smile to hear Basil use his nickname for Dickens. Despite being hugely sensitive about his size, my boy wasn't offended by Basil's affectionate term.

The two ran off, and I continued toward the river. On the opposite bank, the Olde Mill Inn with its distinctive water wheel was a quintessential Cotswolds sight. Seeing Gemma's cottage off to the side prompted me to give her a call.

"DI Taylor," was the clipped response. I realized it had been almost forty-eight hours since we'd spoken, and I hoped she'd made some progress.

"I spent the morning detailing exactly what was taken from Teddy Byrd's cottage. Shall I send you the list?" No need to mention my take on suspects just yet. I needed to gauge her reaction before I ventured down that path.

"Sure. I've already alerted my Oxford contact from my days on the Thames Valley force, the same officer I used last year when Belle's books were a target—told her I hoped to have a list of the missing items soon. I didn't want to put out the word with used bookstores and rare book dealers in the Cotswolds and Manchester until I knew what we were looking for."

This is sooo Gemma! I thought. She might not be buying into the book collector drama, as she called it, but she was already preparing to trace the stolen goods. What she wouldn't do was admit I was on the right track. *Typical*. "I hope they're knowledgeable about rare documents too because there aren't any books missing. "

"I have no idea. We'll just have to see. Constable James finally got around to searching the computer, once he had a day back in the office—except for a few hours being called out on a domestic. You know? The crimes he has to deal with when he's not babysitting a crew of book lovers?"

That was a dig, but I wasn't going to let her get me going. "I prefer the term bibliophile—much more erudite, dontcha know?" I could almost see her rolling her eyes.

"Whatever! When you come down off your high horse, you might want to know what he found."

Make nice, I said to myself. "You know I do. Did he find any threats from 'rabid book collectors' in the mix, to quote my friend Peter?"

"Ha! Mostly, he found correspondence about buying and selling. Mr. Byrd inquiring about buying and interested parties asking if he'd sell one thing or another. From what Jonas could gather, the old codger seemed uninterested in parting with anything in his collection."

"That doesn't surprise me. Think about it. He labeled his notebooks Teddy's Treasures, and I don't suppose he needed the money. So, no one badgering him to sell? All polite inquiries?"

Gemma paused. "All polite, but some more persistent than others, and I did recognize one name. You told me to ask my dad who Gilbert Ward was, and he told me about his Book Nook presentation and how much he would have enjoyed hearing the one he gave last Saturday at the festival. Dad seems to have taken a liking to the bloke. He exchanged several emails with Mr. Byrd about some Arthur Conan Doyle material starting midday Friday. He sent two Saturday morning. I'd label him persistent."

Phew. Those Saturday emails mean Gilbert can't be the killer, unless, of course, he was cleverly covering his tracks. Am I over-thinking this?

"Leta, are you there? Did I lose you?"

"Um, no, I was just thinking. Given that several of the missing documents concern Doyle, I'd love to know what Gilbert had to say. What are the chances you can have Jonas forward those emails to me?"

I heard what I thought of as an evil chuckle. "Oooh! Wouldn't that just stick in DCI Burton's craw? I might have to do it just to make a point with the meddling git. He called me three times yesterday to get an update on the investigation and a few other things."

This was the first murder investigation Gemma'd taken on since he'd become her DCI in December. I'd witnessed her solve two deadly crimes—with a bit of help from me, of course —without a DCI looking over her shoulder, and I wondered whether he seriously thought she'd solve this one any more quickly with him badgering her. Him acting like a jerk could play in my favor.

I chuckled. "You know I'd be happy to do anything to help put him in his place. I seem to recall you telling me he'd better not try getting in your face the way he got in mine. Aargh. My blood still boils when I think of him yelling at me at the Manor House. In my experience, it's best to nip that kind of behavior in the bud." I flashed on Barney Fife saying, "Nip it, nip it, nip it" on "The Andy Griffith Show."

"Still no love lost between you two? I thought since he was

dating your pal Wendy, you might have developed a fondness for him."

She couldn't see me shaking my head. "I guess stranger things have happened, but no, not yet. When he's back in the office Saturday, will you be handing him a list of suspects?"

"If that's your way of asking me who they are, yes I will. But I haven't had much joy with narrowing it down. It's either the locals he's closest to—Fiona, Pris, or Albert—or a significantly expanded list of who knows who! Maybe tracing the stolen goods will get us somewhere."

I was glad to hear Beatrix wasn't on the list. "That was pretty much my thinking too." Seeing Basil and Dickens jogging my way, I told her I needed to go and reminded her to have Jonas send me the emails.

Dickens stopped at my feet. "Leta, Leta, the lambs are cute and fuzzy. The older ones are growing fast, and there are a few new ones too. Come see." I followed the dogs and marveled at the sight of the youngsters. Pulling out my phone, I snapped a few photos to send Anna and Bev. My youngest sister and my Atlanta friend were huge animal lovers.

I rubbed Basil's head and scratched his ears as I watched the sheep. The gentle giant had held a special place in my heart ever since he'd pulled me from the river after an unfortunate mishap.

In his deep voice, he shared more news. "Do you know about the new cat at the inn? I'm used to seeing Paddington wandering across the way, but he's got a companion now—Watson." I explained that I'd met the striking cat with the green eyes. *I'll soon have to take Christie to meet him.*

Chapter Eighteen

C hristie was full of complaints when we returned to my schoolhouse cottage. "Where have you two been all this time? I thought it was only a breakfast date? And Dickens smells of sheep! Uh-huh, another adventure without me!"

She was right. Dickens had carried a faint aroma of sheep in the door with him. I might have to try some scented pet wipes on his coat. It wasn't warm enough to bathe him outside —my preferred option—and I wasn't up for the mess we made when we tried it in the tub. "If that eau de sheep doesn't fade in a few hours, Dickens, I may have to take you to the groomer tomorrow."

That statement sent him scurrying upstairs, as though he thought "out of sight, out of mind" might work. Now it was time to mollify Christie with some wet food. I made a cup of tea while I dipped dabs of food into her dish.

After four forkfuls, she looked at me and meowed. "Now, are you going to answer my question? Where've you been?" I did my best to explain my morning in a way that wouldn't tick her off even more.

It's time to call Gilbert. I need to trust my gut on this. "Tell you what, let's go to the office and get Gilbert on the speaker-phone, and you can listen in. Then you'll know something Dickens doesn't. Okay?" She knew being in the office also meant she'd get treats, so she sprinted to my desk.

After gulping her treats, she stretched out on the desk expectantly, her tail swishing back and forth across my keyboard. Her ears perked up when she heard the phone ringing on the other end of the line.

"Hi, Gilbert. It's Leta Parker. How are you today?"

"Leta, my girl, how are you? I'm at Broadway Tower. What an intriguing spot."

I thought he'd returned to London and hadn't realized he was still in the area. "Dave loved the Tower, and I bet you're enjoying the history as much as he did. I'd like to pick your brain, but I don't want to interrupt your tour. Can you call me back in a bit?"

He was on his way down the winding staircase and replied he'd call me when he reached the car park. To tour the Tower, you accessed each floor by climbing the stairs on the left, and you exited by coming down those on the opposite side.

When he returned my call, I learned that he'd scheduled two weeks in the Cotswolds for what he dubbed his spring break. "It's a nice getaway from the City, and of course, I get to visit the different places my favorite author haunted. Now, what can I help you with?"

Laughing, I told him he was right. I explained about the LOLs and my list of missing documents and how I could use his expertise—particularly as it concerned Mark Twain and Arthur Conan Doyle. After I swore him to secrecy, I gave him the highlights and offered to text him a shot of the list. I told him I'd rely on Dave for the items relating to J.M. Barrie.

"I say, Leta, I have a proposal for you. The text will certainly be helpful, but I'd like to discuss this over dinner if you're available. I can do a bit of research, and then we can talk about it in person. Bring Dave, of course."

"Dave will be disappointed not to spend time with you again, but he's still in Scotland. Perhaps I'll bring my friend Ellie Coates. You met her the other night at the Book Nook, and given her extensive collection of rare books, you two will hit it off."

He wanted to visit Stow, so I suggested we meet at the Old Stocks Inn, one of my favorite restaurants. As soon as we disconnected, I texted him the list and then called Ellie. She was excited about spending the evening with Gilbert on two counts—discussing their respective collections and continuing our investigation.

"Okay, Christie, what did you learn?"

"All I got from those calls is the fact you're leaving me again tonight to have dinner with some guy named Gilbert, and I bet you're taking Dickens too."

"No, I'm not. He's had a full day, and he can keep you company here. Now, let me text Wendy. She offered to help, and I've got just the thing for her."

When I texted my friend if she was up for a bit of research, she responded right away. "You bet."

I asked her to look up G.K. Chesterton to find out his relationship to Agatha Christie, since one of the missing documents was a letter she'd written him. I also teased her about her job being in danger now that we'd added Ellie to the team.

Instead of a text reply, she called me. "Hey, you better not replace me. It's killing me that I'm not there, though I've enjoyed our sightseeing. Today we're in Truro and we've toured the Cathedral of St. Mary. I'm only calling you because Brian's ducked into a sporting goods shop. He's a fiend for running clothes."

"You sound as though you're having a better time than when I last spoke with you. That's good."

"It took a bit of doing. I put my foot down yesterday after the third time he called Gemma. Told him I'd had it and got him to admit she could *probably* handle things on her own. Can you believe he had to hedge on that? Of course she can handle things without him! So far today, he's refrained from calling her, unless he's in the store doing it right now."

I got a kick from hearing that and wondered whether Brian was trainable. At least Wendy was upfront with him about her expectations instead of biting her tongue. I told her I'd text her the list of stolen items so she could stay up to date on our progress, but made her promise not to show Brian.

"Are you kidding? Show Brian? Hearing how involved you and Mum are would be too much for him, and I don't want to set him off. My lips are sealed." We left it at that. I was sure I'd get the whole story when she returned to Astonbury.

I had one last thing to do before I could turn off my detective brain, and that was to text Dave. I sent him a shot of the list too and asked if he could research the two documents referencing Barrie. As I suspected, he was in the library and said he'd get right on it and call me that night with his report.

I was applying my makeup when I heard a knock on the door. Hurrying downstairs in my robe, I found Beatrix with the burgundy ledger in her hands. "Hi. Are you going somewhere?" she asked.

I told her about dinner, and she apologized for interrupting me. "Sorry to be so late with the ledger, but I got tied up in Chipping Camden. I'd love to hear about your breakfast with Ellie and Belle, but I'm beyond late and I've got to run. Maybe tomorrow?"

Ellie pulled up in her Bentley at 7 on the dot. "Thought we'd go in style, since Peter's always telling me I need to take the car out from time to time and not let it sit in the carriage house too long. Matthew prefers his Range Rover, so I try to alternate between my Jaguar and this old thing."

Spoken like a true Dowager Countess. "No complaints from me. You can chauffeur me in *this old thing* any time you want." I was glad I'd dressed up a bit in a black dress and boots topped with a red pashmina.

Dressed in his signature waistcoat and bowtie, Gilbert was already seated at a table near the fireplace when we arrived. A bottle of red sat on the table along with an appetizer of red pepper burrata for us to share. He stood and gave us each a peck on the cheek.

His delight was obvious. "Ladies, I can't tell you how intrigued I am by your inquiries and how much I'm looking forward to our chat. Mark Twain, Arthur Conan Doyle, G.K. Chesterton—all the greats. I'm honored that you think I can be of assistance. I suggest we place our orders first, and then I'll share my assessment."

We agreed and made short work of choosing our entrees— duck for Ellie, sirloin for Gilbert, and for me, what had become my favorite fish, hake. Ellie and I were eager to hear what Gilbert had to say.

"Now, I don't claim to be an expert on any of the authors whose letters are represented—even Arthur Conan Doyle— but it's not difficult to uncover the facts if you know where to look. I focused on two items. First, there's the tribute Doyle sent Twain on the occasion of his seventieth birthday celebration. Twain's birthday is November 30th, but his friends hosted a party for him on December 5th at Delmonico's in New York City. Were you aware the Delmonico brothers opened the restaurant in 1837 and it's still a renowned dining establishment today? This is what I love about research. One can find the most amazing facts.

"As for the celebration, letters and telegrams came in from across the country and from England. After Twain gave his speech, the tributes were read aloud, beginning with one from President Teddy Roosevelt. The rest were read as the evening progressed including one from Joel Chandler Harris. The telegram that will interest you is the one from the Brits—many whose names are unfamiliar today. It read, 'The undersigned send Mark Twain heartiest greetings on his seventieth birthday and cordially wish him long life and prosperity.' Some thirty-odd names were listed, among them Arthur Conan Doyle, Gilbert—or G.K. Chesterton, as we know him, and Rudyard Kipling."

Ellie interrupted. "But Doyle also sent a letter on his own, right?"

"That's the thing. He didn't. The letters and telegrams were printed in *Harper's Weekly Magazine*, and there is nothing from Arthur Conan Doyle. The article in *Harper's* is the official record." He paused. "Now, Leta, what are you frowning at?"

"I'm frowning because I don't know what it means. Could the magazine have gotten it wrong?"

Shaking her head, Ellie chimed in. "I think it means no such document exists. Or if it exists, it was created out of whole cloth—it's a fake."

Gilbert looked quite pleased with himself. "Precisely! You ladies have stumbled upon a forgery, or perhaps I should say the existence of a forgery, since you don't have the piece of paper."

"A forgery," I repeated. "I guess whoever took it will be disappointed if they try to sell it."

Pouring more wine, Gilbert made an interesting observation. "True, but remember someone sold it to Teddy, and he was none the wiser. The thief could have similar luck passing it along. Now, shall I tell you what else I discovered?"

My mind was already racing, trying to make sense of what Gilbert had just shared, but I nodded yes.

"The first document was alleged to be from Doyle *to* Twain. The second was the opposite, a letter from Mark Twain *to* Doyle. The listing says 'Twain to Doyle on meeting in America,' and I saw that letter in Teddy's binder when I visited him Friday morning. In it, Twain thanks Doyle for the hours he spent with him in Hartford and is effusive about how much he enjoyed meeting him.

"I told him then I was all but certain the two men never crossed paths, but couldn't swear to it without checking further. I forgot all about that conversation until I saw your list. I can now tell you categorically that no such a meeting ever took place. The year Arthur Conan Doyle visited America, Twain was in Paris."

Nearly choking on my wine, I spluttered, "You mean it's a forgery too?"

"Ladies, it would seem so. I didn't want to steal Dave's thunder, so I held back from digging into the item concerning J.M. Barrie, but I have to wonder if it's also a forgery."

Stunned into silence, I thought it was timely our food was served right then. I nodded yes when Gilbert asked whether we'd care for a second bottle of wine and Ellie suggested we enjoy our meal while digesting Gilbert's revelations. As was always the case at the Stocks Inn, dinner was superb.

We slipped into small talk and covered the topics of how I'd come to relocate to Astonbury from Atlanta and what Gilbert had seen so far during his visit. Ellie offered to show him her library and to have Matthew give him a tour of the brewery at the estate.

"Gilbert, you should take her up on both of those offers. Her son Matthew brought that brewery back to life, and Astonbury Ale is popular throughout the Cotswolds. And, of course, you'd enjoy seeing Ellie's book collection. Plus, when will you get another opportunity to take a tour led by the Earl of Stow?"

We all declined dessert and opted instead for coffee. Staring into the fire, I had a sudden thought. "It's nearly nine, and Dave's likely back in his room, typing up his notes. Why don't I give him a call to see if he can shed any light on the Barrie document?"

The phone rang a few times before Dave answered. He said he'd had to dig among his pages of notes to uncover the phone, and I pictured him sitting at the desk in his hotel room, laptop in front of him, and papers spread on every surface—the desk, the floor, and the bed.

I gave him a synopsis of Gilbert's findings, and he said he wasn't surprised. "If I hadn't discovered a similar scenario, I might have been shocked. I sat in the library at the university and pored through the Barrie collection. Twain's supposed letter about Peter Pan? Everything I've read tells me Mark Twain wasn't in London at any point in 1905. He saw Peter Pan on Broadway and was very complimentary about it. Hold on, let me find that piece of paper." I heard shuffling. "Here it is. He wrote, 'It is consistently beautiful, sweet, clean, fascinating, satisfying, charming, and impossible from beginning to end.' Twain liked it and liked Maude Adams, the actress who portrayed Peter Pan.

"So, it seems this is another fake, perhaps not made up out of thin air, but at least derivative. Twain could have written to Barrie about enjoying the play, but he saw it in New York City, not London. And I can't find any reference to Twain corresponding with Barrie about it at all. Amazing."

"Dave, let me tell Ellie and Gilbert, and see what they think." My companions listened attentively and wondered whether Twain could have also seen the play in London, but at a later date.

Despite me having my hand over the phone, Dave heard the question. "Leta, I wondered the same thing but couldn't find any indication he did."

I went back and forth between Dave and my dinner companions to be sure we understood everything Dave had found. I wrapped up the call and told him I'd call him later.

I was pretty sure the expression on my face mirrored what I was seeing around the table. "We're talking about forgery, but why would someone break in to steal forgeries? I realize we haven't looked into the Agatha Christie letter, but it must be a forgery too, don't you think?"

Gilbert sat back and hooked his thumbs in his vest pockets. "It would seem so. And I have the same question you have —why steal forgeries when there was a room full of genuine letters, books, and memorabilia?" None of us had an answer.

When Gilbert walked us to the car, he gasped as he caught sight of the Bentley. "If I visit Astonbury Manor, might you take me for a ride in this beauty?"

Ellie laughed and promised she would. The drive home was unusually quiet, and I surmised Ellie was as puzzled as I was.

As I said goodnight to her in my driveway, she said, "You mentioned sleeping on things earlier today. Let's hope that works for sorting out what we heard over dinner. Good night dear."

If only it were that simple. Something tells me finding the key to this mystery will take more than a good night's sleep.

Chapter Nineteen

No lightbulbs hung suspended above my head when I awoke Friday morning. No sudden ah-has about the theft or the murder had sprung to mind. *Time for yoga for me and an appointment at Posh Pets for my still fragrant dog.* I snagged Dickens a spot at 8 a.m. and was able to drop him off a few minutes early.

He whined as we entered the shop. "I don't think I smell bad at all. Can't I skip the bath and just get a new bandana?"

I ignored his plea and gave him a quick hug before dashing to Let It Be for class. The intense focus required for holding yoga positions was just what I need to clear my mind.

Toby's Tearoom for a cup of ginger tea and a lemon scone was my final stop. Home by 9:30 with nothing on my schedule other than picking Dickens up after his bath, my goal was to relax quietly in front of the fireplace until Dave arrived late in the day. I surfed Facebook, played Words with Friends, and sent the sheep photos to Bev and Anna.

Trying hard not to undo the calm of yoga, I only glanced at the message from Constable James with the emails Gilbert had sent Teddy. My thought was that Dave could study those later. During my "unfortunate sleuthing adventures," as my sister Sophia had labeled my activities, I always seemed to reach a point when I questioned what the heck I thought I was doing. I was there now. It was usually Wendy who convinced me our services were invaluable, and she wasn't around this time.

Christie stretched on the rug in front of the fireplace and meowed. "Nice to have you home. Here I come." She jumped onto the couch and settled in my lap as I began *The Tuscan Child*, the book I'd picked up at Bluebird Books. I was several chapters in when my phone pinged with a text from Wendy. She briefly explained that G.K. Chesterton was the author of the popular Father Brown series and that he and Agatha Christie had been members of the Detection Club. Chesterton had been the club's first president. *Right! I have a framed copy of their rules, The 10 Commandments of the Detection Club.*

My return text was a brief thank you with a promise to give her a full report when she got home. *Now she's done it,* I thought. I flashed on the conversation with Dave, and the word forgery popped into my brain and lodged there. I managed to read another chapter in my book but kept having to reread entire passages. In frustration, I laid the book by the lamp, dumped the cat from my lap, and wandered to the kitchen.

A cup of tea in hand, I stared out the kitchen window while my brain swirled. Where was that book I'd bought for Dave? The one that became a movie? It would have made sense for it to be with the Rhys Bowen book I'd bought the same day, but it wasn't. I finally found it hidden beneath Teddy's burgundy ledger on my desk. *Can You Ever Forgive Me? Memoirs of a Literary Forger* was a slim paperback, only 129 pages, and the temptation was too great to resist. *I can read it in no time.*

By the time Posh Pets called to say Dickens was ready, I'd skimmed the book and was once more in full on sleuthing mode. As I drove the short distance to pick him up, a gazillion questions bounced around in my head. Could it be that someone like Lee Israel, the New York City forger in the book, was making a living from selling clever fakes? Was it one person or several people who had forged the missing documents? How had Teddy wound up with a handful in his collection? Could there be still others in his binders that we were unaware of? No matter the answers, the bigger question was why anyone would steal them—and kill a harmless old man?

Dickens barked a happy hello when I opened the door to the shop. "Look at me! Don't you love my bandana? It has lambs on it."

He was never enthusiastic about visiting Posh Pets, but he was always well behaved. As I paid, the owner told me she wished her other clients were more like him. "He's such a sweetheart, so calm he sometimes falls asleep while we brush and dry him." I felt like a proud parent. He pranced to the car, and he was right. I *did* love his bright blue bandana with the fluffy lambs.

Though Dave looked exhausted when he pulled up at three, he insisted he'd be good as new after a short nap. He'd made reservations for eight at a special place—as a surprise for me—and there was no arguing with him.

Christie was vocal as she followed him to the bedroom. "I think he needs me to warm his feet, don't you? And Dickens, now that you smell better, you can come too."

When I looked in on them ten minutes later, they were all sound asleep. Even after I showered, blew my hair dry, and got dressed, no one had stirred. Wherever Dave was taking me, I doubted it was more than a thirty-minute drive, so I figured he and the menagerie could snooze until 6:30 if they wanted.

Reading in the sitting room with Frank Sinatra on the CD player, I smiled when I heard the shower going and Christie came yawning down the stairs, followed by Dickens. She glanced in the sitting room and went to the kitchen, and he barked at the door, "Out, I need to go out, Leta."

Both of my four-legged friends ran to Dave when he came to the kitchen—even Christie, who continued to tell me Peter was the better choice.

Dave enveloped me in a hug. "How I love waking up to the smell of your perfume. Shalimar, right?"

"It's been my favorite for years. Are you ready for a glass of wine?" In typical Cotswolds fashion, the day had turned warm after a cool misty start, so we took our glasses outside to the garden. Dave showed me photos from Scotland and grew more animated as he told me of his research and how it had fueled new ideas for his book. It had been a successful trip for him.

I grabbed the blue gift bag containing the Lee Israel book as we left for dinner. I knew he wouldn't mind that I'd read it before wrapping it for him. He still hadn't told me where we were going, but I could tell he was quite pleased with his choice. When we parked near the Wheatsheaf in Northleach, I knew why.

He turned and kissed me on the cheek. "Do you remember? This is where we had our first date. I wasn't in town for our six-month anniversary, so I hope a seven-month celebration will do."

"I remember our date, but I must admit I'd lost sight of it being seven months since that auspicious occasion. You have an amazing memory."

He'd reserved the same spot by the fireplace where we'd shared our first dinner, and a bottle of champagne in an ice-filled bucket sat on the table. I beamed as the server filled our glasses and Dave tapped his glass to mine. "Here's to my very own brown-eyed girl."

I couldn't help myself. "Oh hell, I love you!"

We both laughed as we sipped champers, as Wendy called it, and shared happy memories of our long-distance relationship—visits to New York City and London and the quiet times here in the Cotswolds.

I placed the blue bag on the table. "I'd like to say it's an anniversary gift, but I've already confessed my memory isn't as good as yours. I picked it up thinking you'd find it intriguing, and it's turned out to be a very timely choice."

When he pulled the book from the bag, he knew right away what I meant. "You're kidding. I saw the trailers for the movie but never went to see it, nor have I read the book. Did you get this after last night's conversation?"

"No, I bought it days before I had any inkling about the forgeries. Quite the coincidence, don't you think?"

We agreed it was strange how things had transpired, and Dave laughed when I explained I'd read it that afternoon before wrapping it for him. I shared the highlights from my afternoon of reading, explaining how the author had turned to forgery in desperation when her previously successful writing career had fallen apart and she was nearly destitute. "Of course, her documents weren't handwritten. They were created on a variety of ancient typewriters because she was crafting fake letters by authors and celebrities from the '50s and '60s."

"But, she had to forge the signatures, right?"

"Yes, she did that by tracing authentic signatures. Her real talent, though, lay in making up real-sounding letters—by taking lines from existing documents and mingling them with her own words. She studied the works of her targets—Lillian Hellman, Dorothy Parker, Edna Ferber, Noel Coward, and others—and then wrote convincingly in their voices."

"Wow! This little book will have to be my bedtime reading tonight. I haven't studied the history of forgery, but I've read some interesting stories in the years I've been writing literary articles. William Henry Ireland was famous in the late 1700s, I think it was, for forging letters allegedly written by Shakespeare. Until then, the only piece of writing surviving the great man was his signature. Ireland was even so bold as to produce a play written by Shakespeare. I think that was his undoing. Anyway, he eventually confessed what he'd done. The astonishing part of the story is that he was never remorseful. Instead, he was proud of his accomplishments."

I shook my head. "That may be a common theme among forgers. Lee Israel was also proud of her work—at least the initial stage. I think she used the words 'larky, fun, and totally cool' to describe her letters. What she regretted was later spiriting authentic letters from libraries and replacing them with her fakes."

We placed our orders, and I laughed at the two of us ordering the identical items we'd eaten on our first visit. I chose the lamb, while Dave went with the beef tenderloin and requested a bottle of Cabernet Sauvignon to accompany our entrees.

Dave drummed his fingers on the table, a sign he was thinking. "The forgeries taken from Teddy's home are a horse of a different color because they aren't likely to be typed documents. Sure, Barrie and Doyle and their peers typed their work in later years, but they still wrote their letters in longhand."

"What kind of background would someone have to have?

To be able to imitate someone's handwriting for an entire letter? An artist . . . or . . . maybe a calligrapher. Oh my goodness. Fiona at the shop! She does wedding invitations and small framed quotes in lovely script."

"That's one part of it, Leta, but whoever is crafting the letters a la Lee Israel would also have to dream up believable content. That would take research—a literary mind."

A thought popped into my head. "I wonder . . . Could Albert have supplied her with the words? He was bright enough to get into Oxford. Could he have enough of a literary mind to come up with the content?"

"That's a thought. Of course, Fiona could also be well-read since she works in a bookshop. And with her exposure to Teddy and his collection . . . well, let's just say anything's possible."

I wondered whether he realized he was getting caught up in the puzzle just as I had—that this was how things evolved once the LOLs set out to solve a mystery. I sipped my wine. "Changing the subject, what would you like to do tomorrow? We could tour Gloucester Cathedral. We haven't done that yet. Or we could take a boat ride on the River Severn or have a quiet day at the cottage or anything else you'd care to do."

"Why don't we go to Manchester to explore the flea markets? That way we can take Dickens and make a day of it. I don't plan to buy anything, but I'd like to see what's out there in the way of Barrie items."

"Are you sure? It sounds like fun, but it's an awfully long drive for you, especially after your round trip to Edinburgh this week."

He grinned. "It probably is, but if we split the driving, it won't be too bad. With my research fresh in my mind, I'm eager to explore. Wouldn't it be amazing if we stumbled across something in the wild, so to speak—a treasure that hasn't made its way into university collections like the ones in Edinburgh and at Yale?"

We agreed we'd set out early the next morning, and the conversation shifted to possible outings for the following week. Unusual for me, I wasn't sleepy when we got home. I tended to the animals while Dave stoked the fire. He poked his head into the kitchen and asked whether I was up for an after-dinner drink and reading in front of the fireplace before going to bed. "I checked with Dickens and Christie, and they think we should have a wild night and stay up past eleven," he joked.

I grinned at him. "I'm game, but only if I can change into my robe and slippers. I'll be back down in a sec."

When I returned, Dave was engrossed in his new book. He'd placed my glass of amaretto on the side table nearest the fireplace and was seated on the opposite end of the couch sipping his. Christie was purring in his lap. "I think I'll get the ledger book and the copies we made and look at them more closely," I said.

I wish I could tell what the notes in the From column stand for. Knowing that might get us a step closer to the forger. As I studied the book, I turned one of the copies over and began to jot down the different abbreviations. Some were obvious, like eBay, and I assumed AZ meant Amazon. Others meant nothing to me. *Duh! My brain must be addled with alcohol. I should start with the notations for the four missing documents.* That was easy enough. Three of the four were listed as being from BF/AA. The Agatha Christie note said AP.

I'd narrowed it down but still didn't know what the notes meant. Flipping through the book again, I saw that the bulk of his recent acquisitions came from eBay, AB, and Bib. Beyond that, most were from BF/AA, BF/CC, BF/TT, and AP. I'd gone far enough in the book that I was now staring at blank ledger pages, but I continued flipping and thinking until suddenly I reached the last page. It wasn't blank. It was the key to the abbreviations.

BF stood for Bolton Flea Market, and the letters that followed BF seemed to be for names of individual dealers like Alastair's Attic, the China Closet, and Tina's Trinkets. "Aha! The figurines must have come from those last two."

I didn't realize I'd spoken aloud until Dave looked up. "What? Last two what?"

"Flea market stalls. I found the key to the notes in the ledger, so I know where the items were purchased. AP is Albert Porter." I scooted toward Dave and showed him the page at the end of the book.

He ran his finger down the page. "AbeBooks and Biblio . . . They're respected dealers. I'll bet he got the Edgar Allan Poe books from one of those. For a purchase like that, you'd want to know the provenance had been established. You don't want to spend thousands of dollars or pounds unless you know for sure a book or document is authentic."

I turned back to see what Teddy had paid for the missing documents. "Maybe this is how he wound up with forgeries of the letters, then. I recall Beatrix saying he didn't pay nearly what she thought they might be worth—hundreds of pounds instead of thousands. If they were real or if they'd come from AbeBooks, would they have cost lots more?"

"Absolutely. And Lee Israel says in her memoir she thinks she got away with her scheme for so long because her prices were low—$40 and $50 apiece. The dealers she sold to turned around and priced them at hundreds of dollars, sometimes thousands."

I pointed out that the missing documents had come from two sources, Alastair's Attic and Albert Porter. "Albert was Teddy's driver and also did odd jobs at Bluebird Books. And Alastair? He's the man who gave you the business card after your presentation, the one with the cravat. Funny, I bumped into him earlier this week in Chipping Camden while I was with Beatrix. I think his stall may be our first stop tomorrow."

"Yes. I'd forgotten his name, but it was the conversation with him that gave me the idea to visit a flea market or two. How 'bout we see if Gilbert wants to meet us in Manchester? With his knowledge of collectibles, he'd be a big help. I can call him first thing tomorrow."

A grin spread across my face. "Does this mean the game's afoot, Sherlock?"

Chapter Twenty

The aroma of coffee brewing woke me Saturday morning. That told me Dave had quietly rolled out of bed and started his day. I pulled on my robe and joined him in the kitchen.

"Good morning, Sleeping Beauty. Ready for your coffee?"

Yawning, I took the cup he handed me and took note of Christie nibbling her dab of food. "It appears you've gotten the hang of feeding the princess. How many times have you had to fluff her food this morning?"

Before he could answer, Christie looked up and meowed. "He's pretty good at it, maybe better than you are."

"Oh, only five or six rounds of fluffing have been required. Dickens is much less demanding. I tossed him a treat as he ran out the door, and he's been contentedly checking the corners of the garden for the last thirty minutes. By the way, I've already spoken with Gilbert and he leaped at the chance to shop the markets in Manchester."

"Super. I'll give Beatrix a call to see if there are any particular stalls she recommends, since she's a regular." She visited the Manchester flea markets monthly to stock up on used books for her shop and occasionally stumbled upon a find like the first edition of a J.M. Barrie biography she'd sold me. *Hide-and-Seek with Angels* came out in 2006, so it wasn't as costly as first editions from the 1900s.

"Too bad she can't join us. Can you imagine the education we'd get shopping with both Gilbert and Beatrix?"

I swung into action, as Dave had told Gilbert we'd be there before noon and we had a three-hour drive ahead of us. We fixed to-go cups of coffee, snagged two protein bars, and were on our way. It was another beautiful day, crisp and sunny, and we marveled at the spring flowers bursting into bloom along the way.

Dickens barked greetings to sheep and dogs and horses for the first part of the drive and then snoozed on the back seat. One of the many things I loved about my new life in England was being able to take Dickens everywhere I went.

Pulling out my phone, I rang Beatrix and put her on speaker. "Guess where we're going? To Manchester to explore the flea markets—and Gilbert Ward is joining us."

"Oh! I'm jealous. Which ones do you plan to visit? I'd recommend the Bolton Flea Market as your first stop. Well, I suppose that depends on what you're looking for. If you're after books, that's the best. If you're looking for fashion like hats and scarves, try the Radcliffe Market."

I told her our priority was books and memorabilia and explained what I'd discovered from the index in the burgundy ledger. "I think we have to nose around Alastair's Attic, don't you?"

"Because some of the missing items came from there?"

"Oh my gosh, Beatrix. I just realized I haven't spoken to you since Ellie and I had dinner with Gilbert. I haven't told you about the forgeries!" Together, Dave and I told her how we'd established that at least three of the missing documents were fakes and had been purchased from Alastair's Attic. And then we told her about the Lee Israel book.

"Lee Israel? Of course, I read her memoir. But forging handwritten letters would be much more difficult than what she did. I want to say it's an outlandish idea, but I guess it isn't."

Dave shook his head and responded. "I think it's the only explanation, Beatrix. When you look at the facts, the letters have to be fakes. The question is, why steal them? *Who* would steal them?"

"I don't have an answer for that, and it surprises me that the forgeries came from Alastair. I've always found his merchandise to be top-notch, though I've never been in the market for things like letters. I'm not sure I'd know whether one was authentic or not.

"Anyway, I hope you get to meet his wife Bonnie. I've always liked her. By the way, remember I told you that young Albert used to work for his dad at the flea market? It's Alastair who's his dad." Funny, how she thought of someone in his thirties as young, but I guess I did too.

I got a bemused look from Dave. "Well, that's interesting because Albert was the source of one of the missing documents. Which one was it, Leta?"

"It was the Agatha Christie letter, the one that was supposed to be on the wall."

Beatrix interjected. "Well, it's no longer missing. Teddy sent it off to be framed, and that's what was in the FedEx package the neighbor called me about. Guess that means only three items were taken—and according to you, all three were forgeries. I wonder . . . What if they were stolen because the person who created them was afraid of being found out?"

At first, I couldn't see it, but then I had a flash. "You know . . . maybe that's it. Could the forger have gotten wind of the fact Teddy was entertaining two experts? First Gilbert, an Arthur Conan Doyle expert, and then Dave, somewhat of a Barrie expert on Saturday."

Dave repeated, "*Somewhat* of an expert?"

"You know what I mean! It seems the forger was successful in pulling the wool over Teddy's eyes, but what if he or she was worried the two visitors would immediately see a problem? That the crime would be discovered? Is that what you're thinking, Beatrix?"

"Yes . . . but why was the forger so careless in the first place? Didn't he know he'd gotten the facts wrong? Good grief! This is complicated. I wonder how good Alastair's records are. Maybe he can tell you where he got them before he sold them on to Teddy."

Nodding, Dave agreed with her. "Since he invited me to visit, I should be able to ask him about his sources. I mean, I don't want to offend him, but if he thinks I'm a serious collector—now that's a laugh—he would expect me to be curious."

We told Beatrix we'd report back today or tomorrow and signed off. I looked at Dave. "A serious collector and somewhat of an expert. How good an actor are you?"

When we parked, Dickens leaped from the car with his nose up in the air sniffing, and I imagined he was anticipating all kinds of delicacies. "Oooh, Leta. Do you smell that? I think it could be sausages."

Leaning down to attach his leash, I whispered in his ear. "Don't you go scarfing every last thing you find on the ground, young man."

We texted Gilbert we were at the entrance and received an immediate reply he'd be right with us. Today he was sporting a fedora with his waistcoat and bowtie.

He grasped Dave's hand in a firm handshake and gave me a peck on the cheek. "This place promises to be a collector's paradise. I'm glad you thought to invite me. Plus, it's a bit of a quest, right? To find a forger, or at least the seller of the forgeries? I have an idea for how to approach Alastair." His plan involved the two men taking the lead.

He is such a hoot. I had no doubt we'd have an enjoyable day, whether we got any further along in our investigation or not. The China Collection was near the entrance, so we ducked in there first. I could see why Teddy had purchased so many figurines there. The place was huge, as was the assortment, and Dave had to tear me away from the Disney selection. I was a sucker for Disney paraphernalia and had several coffee table books on the early animated features.

Gilbert stopped to look at pipes at the same time as I spied a stall with scarves and hats. Handing Dickens's leash to Dave, I tried on a black checked rain bonnet. "No, not quite right, but look, here's a red one." That one I had to have.

We made slow progress but eventually found our way to Alastair's Attic, where the proprietor recognized us right away. He greeted us with a smile and asked how we'd enjoyed the rest of the festival. As I looked at books, I heard Dave telling him about Gilbert's presentation and the ones on R. F. Delderfeld and Graham Greene.

"I've got books by both authors in stock—nothing of fine quality, mind you, but good reads." As we'd agreed earlier, Gilbert had hung back and came in a few minutes later.

He cocked his head and looked at Alastair. "I say, you're

the chap who was in the audience for the Mark Twain session. You asked almost as many questions as I did. And we spoke again at the Barrie presentation." They shook hands and talked about how much they'd enjoyed the festival.

I was wondering whether his wife was there when Alastair called, "Look here, Bonnie, you must meet these book lovers." When I looked around to find her, I realized I'd missed her because she was seated behind the counter, almost hidden—in a wheelchair. *So, she was the woman Ellie had seen with Alastair at the Twain session.*

Alastair leaned over and planted a kiss on her head, and I stepped forward to introduce myself after the men had shaken her hand. "Bonnie, I'm Leta Parker, and I'm a friend of Beatrix Scott. She said I should be sure to meet you."

It turned out Bonnie and Beatrix were well acquainted, and we chatted about the Book Nook and books while the men disappeared to the back of the stall. *Now, what are they up to?*

Hanging behind the counter and around the large stall were oil paintings in gilt frames. Most were landscapes of the Cotswolds. I was especially taken with one that depicted sheep grazing. "Bonnie, these are beautiful. Who's the artist?"

She smiled. "Those are mine. I studied art, and when we lived in London, my work was available at Spitalfields Arts Market and Camden Market. Once we moved to Manchester and this chair became part of my life . . . well, the larger works got to be too much for me to tackle. These days, I do more of these." She pointed to a rack of matted 8"x12" abstract water-colors on parchment.

I was struck by how delicate they were—an entirely different style from the landscapes. The colors were translucent. In some, faint lettering was visible beneath the glaze of colors. In others, I glimpsed what looked like sheet music. It was like looking through a sheer curtain at a blurred image. The word gossamer came to mind . . . or diaphanous.

I was trying to picture the grazing sheep hanging in my sitting room and one or two of the watercolors elsewhere in my cottage when Dave reappeared. I showed him the watercolors. "What do you think? Maybe a pair in my office?"

He studied the two I was holding up. "Either on a stand in your bookcase or framed on the wall? I could see them one over the other to the right of the big picture window." I placed them on the counter and asked Bonnie about her technique. Her explanation was above my head, but I understood something about using a fine calligraphy brush, then a wash to fade it, and finally the watercolor.

"Alastair and Gilbert are negotiating, or should I say haggling, over a signed first edition of *Moriarty*. I don't know enough about it to be interested. Now, if it were a signed copy of a book or play by Barrie, that would be different."

Bonnie heard Dave's comment and looked up. "Too bad. We've had the occasional letter to or from Barrie, but I don't think we have anything right now. Shall we keep an eye out for you?"

Dave did his best to beam. His acting skills were quite impressive. "That would be great. I'll be returning to New York soon, but Leta could come by to see it."

I paid for the watercolors and told Bonnie I wanted to think about the landscape. After Dave gave her his business card, we looked around for Gilbert. I wondered if he was seriously considering a purchase or playing Sherlock. When he emerged from the back room with a parcel wrapped in brown paper, I still wasn't sure.

When we were far enough away from Alastair's Attic, I stopped to look at my companions. "Alright, you two, you look like the cats that ate the canaries, and I've got a glimmer of an idea too. Can we sit down and talk over lunch?"

Dickens barked, "Leta, Christie would never eat a canary, would she?"

My escorts thought lunch was a grand idea, and we chose a booth that offered savory pies and had available tables. Both men ordered ciders, but I knew my brain would be shot for the day if I had one.

I pointed to Gilbert's package. "Okay, you first. What did you buy?"

"I've started adding modern-day pastiches to my Sherlock collection, so I had to have this Anthony Horowitz book. He's the only writer authorized by the Arthur Conan Doyle estate to carry on the Sherlock story. They chose well. If you didn't know better, you'd believe the tales came from Doyle. Plus I got it for a song—only £40. I've seen it online for as much as £100."

I wondered whether Gilbert's collection ran to the type of material Teddy had, with items priced in the thousands of pounds. "Okay, based on the prices I saw in Teddy's ledger book, that sounds quite reasonable, but I know it's not the same as finding something from the last century."

"Right you are, but more importantly, my genuine interest in the book helped move the conversation along. Dave and I were being careful. We went in thinking Alastair'd been taken advantage of as Teddy had been, but we couldn't take any chances." Gilbert chuckled. "For all we know, he's the frontman in a scheme to pass forged documents. Anyway, Dave and I tag-teamed."

The two grinned as Dave picked up the story. "As Gilbert shopped the available papers and books, he mentioned how he enjoyed seeing the variety of material housed in Teddy's cottage, so it was easy for me to bring up the fact I'd found Teddy's body the day I was supposed to be viewing the collection. Alastair was suitably shocked. I don't suppose he knew anything beyond the fact Teddy had died.

"I mentioned I'd been helping Beatrix assess what she had —like I have any idea—but he doesn't know that. When I explained items were missing, he looked surprised and asked how we knew that. That's when I told him about the ledger book. I explained you were friends with Beatrix, and we'd been leafing through the binders Teddy kept trying to figure out what was what."

Gilbert crossed his arms. "Yes, I think he was quite taken aback at that news. Not sure why. I think most collectors keep records of their acquisitions. I certainly do."

Looking pleased with himself, Dave continued. "He asked if I knew exactly what was missing—books or papers or heaven forbid, the typewriter. He said most Barrie collectors knew about the typewriter and quite a few were jealous Teddy had beaten them to it.

"And then, Gilbert clapped his hand to his brow and said, 'I say, Dave, didn't you tell me a few of those letters came from here?' His act was priceless. And, it was natural for me to add we were shocked to find the missing documents were forged."

I tilted my head. "Didn't he wonder how you knew something was forged when you'd never laid eyes on it?"

"Yes, that was his first question. I told him the truth. The descriptions in the ledger were detailed, we noticed some inconsistencies, and we checked some facts. I shared the example of Mark Twain seeing *Peter Pan* in New York City, not London."

They were having fun with this. "Okay, I can tell you two

are ready to take your act on the road, but before you do, can you tell me what you found out?"

I knew Dave could sense my impatience. "Right. We went back and forth, and I finally pulled out my notepad and told him what the items were. When I asked Alastair whether he'd gotten them from one person or several, he said he wasn't sure and would have to check his records, that it sometimes happened that a person would arrive with a trunk from their great-grandfather's attic that held a treasure trove. More often, it was a pile of worthless moldy books."

I frowned. "So, he was unable to give you information about their origins. They could have come directly from the forger or they could have changed hands multiple times before they got to Alastair and then to Teddy."

Gilbert leaned back in what I recognized as his favorite position, thumbs hooked in the pockets of his waistcoat. "Except, I have this sense Alastair knows more than he's letting on. Call it my collector's nose. In this business, you learn to pay attention to hunches."

It was my turn to share. "I also have an idea of sorts. Let's see how my observations about Bonnie's artwork fit with your sixth sense. I was quite taken with her landscapes, but it was her watercolors that started me thinking."

I unwrapped the two I'd purchased. "Aren't they lovely? Look at the faint letters that appear beneath the colors. What do you remind you of?"

Gilbert studied one, then the other. "Something from a manuscript . . . perhaps written with a fountain pen . . . or these days, a calligrapher's quill dip pen."

"Uh-huh," I said. "And, the script in each of these is differ-ent. Could be simply an artistic choice . . . "

Dave finished my sentence. "Or it could be an indication

that she's capable of a variety of styles. Leta, are you going where I think you are with this?"

With a gleam in his eye, Gilbert grabbed my hand. "Sherlock would say, 'There is nothing more deceptive than an obvious fact.' Bonnie Porter quite likely has the talent to be a forger."

"But," asked Dave, "does she have the knowledge, the literary background, to put the words together—to write a letter that *sounds* like Mark Twain or Arthur Conan Doyle? She's an artist with oil, watercolor, and ink, but can she mimic the way Arthur Conan Doyle would craft a tribute to a friend?"

At that moment, the proverbial lightbulb flashed over my head. "Dave, it's what I said last night, only I was thinking of Fiona and Albert. It's two people! It's a partnership. Alastair comes up with the text, and Bonnie puts pen to paper. Or it could be their son Albert, with his Oxford education, however brief . . . maybe he feeds his mother the words. Maybe they both feed Bonnie the words."

Gilbert picked up the thread. "And where do they get the paper so it looks authentic? From those trunkloads of moldy old books that are worth next to nothing. I can picture them carefully cutting the blank endpapers from them and turning them into coveted rare documents."

Prone as I was to second-guessing myself, I had to ask. "Is my hunch reasonable? Or am I leading us astray?"

We went back over what we knew and decided the idea was both plausible and probable. It could be a husband and wife partnership or a family affair. What we didn't have was proof. And, as Dave pointed out, we still didn't know who took the forgeries and smothered Teddy.

Once we made the leap to the Porters being white-collar criminals, it was tempting to think Alastair or Albert had broken into the cottage, taken Bonnie's forgeries, and killed Teddy. Who else would have chosen those particular documents to take?

Why am I reluctant to see Albert involved in this? I have to admit my track record for fingering the right person is less than stellar, and I barely know him.

No matter whether it was Albert or his father, why steal the documents? What had happened to make them want to get them back? Alastair had attended the Twain presentation and, according to Gilbert and Ellie, asked lots of questions. Did he learn something that alerted him to the inaccuracies in the forged documents? Even so, those mistakes had so far gone unnoticed. Why act now?

Dave rubbed his chin. "It's like we discussed with Beatrix. They somehow knew Gilbert and I had been invited to view the collection, and that worried them. But how did they know?"

Reflecting on the events of Thursday and Friday, I thought of Teddy's two employees. "When Fiona came over Thursday night after Peter brought him home, he probably told her about meeting us and the invitations he'd extended. Either she mentioned it to Albert or Teddy did. Regardless of whether Albert's involved or not, he might have mentioned the information to his dad. With Albert a book scout, and Alastair a dealer in rare books and documents, it would be natural for them to have a conversation about it."

I could tell my idea resonated with Gilbert. "That has to be it. Two things happened. First, Alastair heard disturbing details at the Twain presentation. Second, Albert told him about Dave and me visiting. The convergence of those two events led to the break-in. It was the perfect storm."

And we three landed in the middle of it.

Chapter Twenty-One

Despite there being plenty more to see, none of us were inclined to stroll idly through the market after our discussion. When we'd set out to discover where Alastair had acquired the fake documents, we hadn't anticipated that the forgeries originated with him. Nor had we foreseen getting so close to unmasking the killer. We knew it wasn't Bonnie, but was it Alastair . . . or Albert?

We sat and pondered our next steps, and Dave and Gilbert wondered whether they'd said anything to Alastair that he would see as a threat to his enterprise. Or worse, did he think it was only a matter of time before they put two and two together and saw him or his son as the killer?

Had the father or the son or both of them planned to kill Teddy or had the elderly man woken up to see someone in his bedroom, removing a frame from the wall or a binder from his bed? Had the killing been a spur-of-the-moment act? Or had it been cold-blooded and premeditated?

By this time, the men were on their second round of cider and I'd given in and joined them. Dickens had enjoyed numerous chunks of pie crust and was snoozing quietly beneath the table.

Surprised neither of them had suggested it yet, I said, "It's time to involve the police, I think."

Though the situation wasn't funny, the look on Gilbert's face made me laugh. "The police? Surely you jest. Just when we're close to solving the case on our own? What was it Ellie called it—the Chipping Camden Affair?"

I looked meaningfully at Dave. "Well, I've been in some sticky situations because I failed to do so soon enough in the past."

"She's right, Gilbert. Leta has a contact in the constabulary, and I think it's time we put her in the picture."

Gilbert wasn't buying it. "Her? It's a woman? Not that it matters one way or the other, but I think we need to have the tale all ticked and tied before we involve anyone else."

Hmmm. Does my new friend have some male chauvinist tendencies? "How do you suggest we tick and tie, Gilbert? Do you have the real Sherlock waiting in the wings?"

"If only. No, but I can speak with some friends in the business to see if there's even a whiff of doubt about Alastair's integrity. I should be able to tell pretty quickly whether we're on the right track or have gone completely off the rails."

Dave looked from me to Gilbert. "Leta, what do you think? You can always contact Gemma later. How long will that take, Gilbert?"

Gilbert spoke first. "The first bit won't take long at all. I should get some answers before the day is done. If there's a whiff, so to speak, I'll ask those friends and others if they've purchased anything from Alastair lately and then go from there."

I shook my head. "I guess I should be relieved you're not

planning to sneak into Alastair's Attic under the cover of dark-ness. If you'll promise to update us tonight, I'll wait to hear what you sniff out before I reach out to Gemma, but I need to tell her soon."

Looking at Dave, Gilbert asked, "Is she always this stubborn?"

It was a long drive home in more ways than one. I was itching to call Gemma to ask her to do a background check on Alas-tair. I had no idea whether there'd be anything to find, but if he was the kind of person we thought he was, this might not have been the first time he'd been involved in something nefarious.

Dave, on the other hand, seemed energized at the prospect of what Gilbert might uncover. Why I wasn't sure. Given his feelings about my getting involved in amateur sleuthing, he was oddly excited about doing the same.

The good news was I had Bolognese sauce in the fridge, so dinner was an easy affair. When Dave uncorked a bottle of red, I was more than ready to put my feet up and relax. It was his toast that caught me off guard.

"Here's to Tommy and Tuppence."

"So, you see yourself as Tommy now, do you? After a week engaged in staid library research, you're eager to explore the dark side of literary forgery?"

He was downright jolly. "Aw, come on, Tuppence. Admit it, we had fun today, piecing the clues together. I can see how you and the Little Old Ladies' Detective Agency get caught up in the chase, but trust me, I have no intention of snooping around dark alleys. Let Gilbert check with his contacts, and then you can call Gemma. I'll confine my sleuthing to studying those binders more closely."

We didn't have a bad evening, but it was by no means as pleasant and relaxing as our time together normally was. There was an undercurrent. Dave was excited, but I was worried, and not a little put-out with him. *Tommy and Tuppence, my foot.*

I had a restless night and woke before him Sunday morning. Wrapped in a fleece blanket, I took my coffee to the garden. Dickens explored as I sat deep in thought. We hadn't heard from Gilbert last night, and when Dave tried to call him, it went to voicemail.

Oddly enough, the person we heard from was Alastair. The reason for the call seemed to be twofold—one was to inquire about our Sunday plans. He'd gotten a lead on some Bram Stoker documents and wondered if Dave would like to join him on the outskirts of the village of Lower Slaughter to check it out. The other was to let me know Bonnie was willing to drop the price on the landscape and he could have Albert deliver it to me sometime next week if I was interested.

I'd listened to Dave's side of the conversation. "Sunday? We're attending a cricket match. Yes, a friend is playing. Right, so I hear. That's why we're packing a picnic lunch. Really? Darn. I hate to miss an opportunity to be a book scout for a day. Maybe another time. Okay, here's Leta."

I told Alastair I was interested in the landscape but wasn't ready to make a decision yet. He was a good salesman and explained that the lower price wouldn't be on offer beyond Friday, and I promised to let Bonnie know my answer by midweek.

That conversation gave Dave a taste of how you could be convinced of someone's guilt one minute and then second-guess yourself when you had an innocent conversation with them. We both wondered why, if Alastair was the guilty party, he'd be so chummy with us.

And now, I was sitting here thinking something had to be done, but what? I was pretty sure Dave still wanted me to wait to hear from Gilbert before contacting Gemma, but the longer I waited, the more likely she'd be furious with me for not involving her sooner—despite the fact that she'd ridiculed my idea the crime had to do with rare documents.

As I was sipping a second cup of coffee, my phone pinged with a text from Wendy. "Tell me you can talk. I may do myself bodily harm if I can't speak with you soon." *Oh my. This has to be about Brian.*

I called her. "Dave's still asleep. What's going on?"

Wendy didn't miss a beat before launching into a ten-minute tirade about Brian Burton. The adjectives she spat out included sexist, condescending, arrogant, and controlling, and the list went on. She concluded with, "Can you believe when I told him it was over between us, he wouldn't accept it? He said something about liking how fierce I was. Said he knew I was angry with him, but that all relationships had moments like this. How can he be a successful DCI and be so obtuse?"

"Whoa. It must have been an awful week. When did you deliver the message? Not on the drive home, I hope."

"No, I knew better than that. I waited until last night and called him. Can you believe he chuckled? That's when he delivered the line about loving me for my independent spirit and my feistiness. It beggars the imagination!"

I listened to her vent for a few more minutes. When she ran out of steam, I said, "It's not the same situation, but I also have a boyfriend who's having a hearing problem. It's a new phenomenon with him."

"Oh no. Don't tell me that. Are you two on the outs? Say it isn't so."

I explained it was nothing we couldn't work out, but I was at a loss as to what to do. "Maybe I'll tell him you have a Brian situation and I need to hold your hand. What do you think?"

"It that works, go for it. I'm here."

When I found Dave in the kitchen, he was feeding Christie. "She told me you were ignoring her and she was starving."

"Uh-huh, and you fell for it. Well, she may be starving, but she doesn't have the boyfriend problem Wendy has. I just got an earful. Are you okay if I leave you on your own for a bit and head to her cottage?"

My boyfriend was nothing if not the soul of patience. "Sure, leave Dickens with me, and we'll take a walk to see the donkeys."

"Me too, me too," meowed Christie as I ran upstairs to change. I was on the road in a flash.

Wendy and Belle were sipping coffee in the kitchen when I arrived at Sunshine Cottage. Surprisingly, talking through the events that had led to our Saturday visit to Manchester took very little time. Though Ellie had already given Belle an update on our dinner with Gilbert, she sat patiently through the summary.

Wendy had no problem following. "Okay, I'm with you so far. Who would have thought this was about forgeries? It sounds like you and Mum and Ellie did some fine work with a little help from Dave and Gilbert. So, what does Gemma have to say about this new angle?"

"That's just it," I said. "I haven't told Gemma."

She gave me a surprised look. "You haven't? Well, I guess it wouldn't it be the first time we didn't go to her right away, like when we felt we had to have more facts to give her . . . she *does* tend to brush off our ideas. Still, I predict she's going to be irritated with you because you didn't give her a chance to reject your idea."

"That is so well put. I'm sure she will be, even though she's already pooh-poohed my theory about rare documents. Maybe that's why I didn't share what we'd concluded about forgeries. But that's only the tip of the iceberg. Wait until I tell you about our visit to Alastair's Attic."

As I described the interactions with Bonnie and Alastair and the purchases we'd made, both mother and daughter nodded and commented that the visit sounded harmless enough. It wasn't until I got to our lunchtime breakthrough that they reacted strongly.

My sleuthing partners looked at each other and Wendy spoke first. "Wow! That's quite a leap, but it seems plausible when you lay it all out."

Belle nodded thoughtfully. "It makes sense that someone with an artistic background would be involved."

Bringing the coffee carafe to the table, Wendy paused. "You've had two major ah-has, and you still haven't called Gemma? What's going on with you?"

"Um, I blame the delay on Dave and Gilbert. I tried to tell them we needed to call her."

I wasn't sure how to interpret the expression on Wendy's face. Indignation, maybe? "*Tried* to tell them? What does that mean?"

That's when I told her Gilbert insisted on checking with the collector crowd but seemed to have gone AWOL, and that Dave didn't seem concerned.

"So, that's what you meant about Dave's hearing problem. And you haven't heard from Gilbert this morning?"

"Not unless he's called Dave while I've been gone. I think I'll have to risk making Dave angry and give Gemma a call when I get back. I don't think Gilbert being incommunicado means anything's wrong. It's just that he's put me in an uncomfortable position."

Wendy sighed and put her chin in her hands. "I can't believe I missed all this. A literary mystery, for goodness' sake. Did you hang sheets of paper on the wall as you mapped out suspects and clues? The way you and I usually do?"

I laughed. "Not quite, but we were pretty methodical, weren't we Belle?"

"Yes, we were. We made sure to capture the details of the missing documents and the names of the people we saw as suspects."

"Your mum's right. There wasn't much to write down. It wasn't until yesterday in Manchester that the pieces flew together. It happened so quickly, there was no need to map it out. Now, let me get back home. Speaking with you two has made it all the more clear that I need to call Gemma, and then I need to prepare the picnic lunch to take to Peter's cricket match. You ladies are going, right?"

"Oh yes, we try never to miss a match, though I often have to run Mum home before the match is done. Six hours is a long time for her to sit anywhere, especially if it's too warm or too cool. Today looks to be a warm one."

I passed Dave, Dickens, and Christie on the road as I drove home and was in the kitchen when they came in. Dickens ran into the room barking. "Donkeys, you missed the donkeys."

From Christie I got a snub, and from Dave a huge hug. "Did you solve Wendy's romantic woes?"

"Well, that remains to be seen. She thinks the romance is

over, but Brian isn't convinced. I didn't let on that I agree with every complaint she has about the man, in case they kiss and make up."

"You're a wise woman, Leta Parker."

"So wise that the next thing I'm going to do is call Gemma. Have you heard from Gilbert yet?"

"As a matter of fact, I have. He met up with friends last night in Chipping Camden and over-imbibed, as he describes it. He sounded a bit worse for the wear this morning." He laughed. "I had a vivid image of him clutching his head or lying in bed with a cold rag on his forehead as we talked.

"Anyway, the upshot is there does seem to be a miasma—another Gilbert term—of uncertainty around Alastair. It's only developed over the last five or six years. Gilbert spoke with several fellow collectors and found that two of them had gone back to Alastair with their purchases, demanding a refund. One with an autographed Graham Greene book, another with an alleged Virginia Woolf letter. In both cases, there were questions about the authenticity of the items."

As we talked, I pulled tuna from the pantry and mayonnaise and celery from the fridge. "Is that typical in the business?"

"Not according to Gilbert, but he did say Alastair was a gentleman in both instances. He apologized for not vetting his sources more thoroughly and issued full refunds."

"Okay then. Let me make the tuna salad, and I'll call Gemma. I trust our friend has no further objections to involving the police?"

That got a laugh. "I think he might have, but he's in no condition to pursue any leads, so we're released to proceed."

I told Dave that Gilbert would never make it as one of my Little Old Ladies. We were made of stronger stuff—or at a minimum, we didn't overindulge and find ourselves under the weather when time was of the essence.

I put Dave to work cutting the crusts from the bread in preparation for making finger sandwiches, and I rang Gemma. It was a toss-up as to whether I'd get a positive response or a dressing-down.

She sounded chipper. "Hallo, Tuppence. What is it today? Do you have a fresh lead you can't wait to share, or do you want something from me?"

So far so good. "If you've time to hear me out, I'd like to tell you a story. It will be worth your while."

"Right. I can't wait. Are you still on the trail of rare and hitherto unknown documents? Or do you have a more down-to-earth scenario?" Typical Gemma, she had to get in a subtle dig.

I put her on speakerphone so Dave could chime in. He nodded as I described how we'd ascertained which documents were missing and enlisted the help of him and Gilbert to help us understand why they might have been taken. When I explained they were forgeries, Gemma balked.

"Forgeries? Okay, if you say so, but why would someone break in to steal forgeries when there was a treasure trove of valuable books and documents there?"

Dave took over. "Gemma, we wondered the same thing, and thought at a bare minimum, we should to go the source of the fakes. And that's what we did."

Gemma groaned. "Do I even want to know what that means?"

Dave told her about the index in the burgundy ledger, our trip to Manchester, and the playacting he and Gilbert engaged in.

If anything, the groaning got louder. "Bloody hell, please tell me you didn't make a scene."

She might prefer a scene over what we have to tell her next.

When I laid out how we'd arrived at the Porters being the forgery team, she guffawed. More harebrained notions! If you were convinced you were on the right track, you'd have called me sooner. Gilbert has a *nose* and you have a *hunch?* You see watercolors leading to forgery? Is that what I'm hearing?"

"See?" I mouthed to Dave. I just knew she was rolling her eyes, but I plowed ahead. "Before I tell you who we think's responsible for the break-in and the murder, tell me, do you have a theory of the case? Do you already know the motive for the break-in and the killing of Teddy Byrd?"

I got the response she'd give the media if they asked. "You know we're pursuing all possible leads."

My voice rose. "Right. Well, can I at least get you to plug the names Alastair and Albert Porter into your database to see if either one has a record? Let's assume there's a team that produces the forgeries—husband and wife or mother and son or all three. I doubt this is their first illegal venture. I don't think someone wakes up in their mid-fifties and turns to a life of crime, do you?"

"White-collar crime, maybe . . ." Her voice grew faint and I could tell she was talking to someone in the background. "Sorry, my boss is here, back from his vacation in Cornwall. If I get a chance, I'll try to ring you later."

I looked at Dave. "Ugh, getting Gemma to cooperate is iffy at the best of times, but having Brian back on the scene makes it even trickier. I'm going to take a chance and ring Constable James. He's the one who'd be searching the database for Gemma anyway."

When I reached him, I learned he didn't start his shift

until noon, but he promised to check on the Porters for me. I could tell he was intrigued by the conclusions Dave and I had drawn and was eager to help.

Hanging up, I commented, "There's more than one way to skin a cat," which got a screech from Christie.

Dave chuckled and picked her up. "She didn't mean it, girl."

It's time to take a day off from sleuthing and turn our attention to cricket.

Chapter Twenty-Two

I'd learned how fickle the weather in the UK could be, so I dressed accordingly. Though the day had begun to warm up, there was no telling how long the pleasant temperature would last. I chose a pair of lightweight ankle-length jeans, my red Sperry topsiders, a red tank top, and a hip-length crisp white linen top. I could roll the sleeves up or down and layer on a windbreaker as need be. I surveyed my straw hats and chose one with a broad brim. Heaven forbid I get any sun on my face.

Dave watched, fascinated, as I laid my ensemble out on the bed. "For you, half the pleasure of an excursion is the outfit, isn't it?"

"Absolutely. Now, we only need to pack the picnic basket and we'll be ready." With tuna sandwiches, cheese and crackers, fruit, and biscuits—as I was learning to call cookies—we were set. We took my taxi, Dave driving, and Dickens in the backseat. It was a twenty-minute trip to Stanway and the nearly 100-year-old cricket pavilion where Peter's team was playing.

KATHY MANOS PENN

Dave reminded me of the structure's history as it figured prominently in the book he was writing about J.M. Barrie. After spending summers at Stanway House during the 1920s, the author had the pavilion built for the village.

Visiting the rustic building located adjacent to the Cotswold Way was not something I did very often. Though I tried, I could never approach it without remembering the dead body Dickens and I had stumbled across behind the building.

Today, I smiled at the sight of friends setting up deck chairs and small picnic tables. Wendy and Belle waved as we approached and motioned to the spot they'd saved for us. I saw Peter in the distance with his teammates. They'd dubbed themselves the As in honor of Barrie's team and his gift of the pavilion. In this day and age, using Allahakbarries, the original name, was deemed politically incorrect.

We were soon joined by Ellie and her son and daughter-in-law, Matthew and Sarah. As he did for so many local events, Matthew had brought a pony keg of Astonbury Ale to share with the small crowd.

Dave helped him set it up on a table and tap it in time for the match at eleven. He returned to our chairs with cups for both of us. "Though I can't follow this game as well as I do baseball, I still enjoy it. What a glorious day!"

The conversation among the spectators was chock-full of cricket terms, not all of which I understood—bowled, stumped, googly, leg-side, and more. Like Dave, I mainly enjoyed the time outdoors with friends. Dickens was having a good day too. When he wasn't visiting our friends and getting handouts, he followed the shade, seeking cool patches of grass.

By two, I was closing my eyes behind my sunglasses. I thought no one had noticed until Dave leaned over and whispered in my ear. "Engrossed in the game, are you?"

I opened one eye. "Oh yes, I can't wait to rehash the action with Peter and tell him how impressed I am with his cricket prowess."

A shadow fell across me, and I glanced up to see Wendy. "As predicted, it's time I took Mum home. It's unseasonably warm today, and she's about done in."

Dave stood. "Wendy, I know you follow the game more closely than either me or Leta. Why don't we take Belle home so you can stay and see the rest of the match?"

"Oh! That would be marvelous. You've made my day, Dave."

Gathering our chairs and the picnic basket, we packed the car before returning for Dickens and Belle. At Sunshine Cottage, I helped her inside and poured her a cold drink. She was more than ready for her afternoon nap, and I was looking forward to the same thing at my home.

When we passed the Ploughman Pub, I suggested we either have dinner there later or get takeaway. Cooking wasn't in my plan for the evening. We saw two cyclists turning into the Olde Mill Inn and a couple feeding the donkeys. Crossing the stone bridge over the River Elfe just down from my cottage, I noticed a motorbike on the verge and pictured someone taking advantage of the sunny day to do a spot of fishing. Everyone was out enjoying the good weather.

I yawned. "Let's leave the chairs in the car and tend to them later. I'll get Dickens unlatched while you grab the picnic basket."

Dave called over his shoulder as he opened the door to the mudroom. "Uh-oh, I think we went off without locking the door."

Huh, I guess when I handed the car keys to Dave, I forgot. I shooed Dickens to the garden and followed Dave to the kitchen. I saw him place the basket on the counter and jerk toward my office. "Who's that?"

He moved past the stairway, calling, "Who's there? What are you doing?"

Plowing into Dave's back, I grasped his jacket and caught sight of Christie crouched on the back of the easy chair to the left of the doorway.

With the burgundy ledger in his hands, Alastair stood on the opposite side of the room in front of the picture window overlooking the garden. Teddy's three binders were peeking from a leather knapsack on top of my desk. "Stop right there!" He glanced nervously at the two of us.

Dave tried to block me from moving any further into the room, but I squirmed past him and cried, "What are you doing? Why are you here?"

He clutched the burgundy ledger to his chest. "Why aren't you at the cricket match?"

Pushing me behind him, Dave took a step forward. "Alastair, I don't know what you think you're doing, but this is a mistake." He sounded so reasonable.

"I'm protecting my family, my livelihood, that's what I'm doing. You, with your snooping around . . . "

Dave inched toward him. "What are you talking about, Alastair? We visited your stall. Leta bought some artwork—"

"Don't come any closer!" In one quick movement, he dropped the ledger, grabbed the cane propped against my desk, raised it in the air, and pulled a sword from it. *Teddy's cane!* "Now, back up, both of you . . . slowly."

Dave held his right hand in front of him with his left hand behind his back gripping my arm. As we backed from the office, I was aware of Dickens barking outside. When my hips pressed against the kitchen counter, I groped for a weapon.

The wooden block with the knives was too far away. The picnic basket was useless. And then I felt it.

Ducking around Dave's right side, I aimed the canister at Alastair's face and sprayed three short purple bursts. He screamed and jerked back just as Christie launched herself from the chair to his chest. The cane flew from his hand as Dave barreled into him and they fell to the office floor, where Alastair alternated between attempting to pry Christie from his neck and trying to defend against Dave's frontal attack.

Grabbing the sword cane with one hand, I found my phone with the other and dialed 999. As I spoke to the operator, I stood with the cane at the ready, but Dave and Christie had the situation well in hand. Alastair's face was bloody, swollen, and purple, and he now lay motionless on the floor. Dave stood near the chair—Christie's launching pad—well enough away from Alastair to avoid any sudden moves. Christie was backed against the bookcase, hissing and spitting, and I glimpsed Dickens outside hurling himself against the window.

Handing Dave the sword, I sank into the easy chair as tears sprang to my eyes. He knelt beside the chair and took my hands. "It's over. It's okay now."

"I felt so helpless. All I could see was him running you through with the sword."

"Shh, shh. I bet that thing is dull as a butter knife." Half pushing and half lifting, he put me in his lap, where I leaned my face into his shoulder. I had no idea what he was murmuring. I only knew it was comforting. That's how Constable James found us when he flew in the house, followed by Dickens. He'd been just up the road between Bourton-on-the-Water and Astonbury when the call came in.

When our dazed and subdued intruder was handcuffed and

propped against the bookcase, Dickens stood on his legs and growled in his face. "You better not have hurt them."

Christie leaped to the floor and nudged her canine brother. "Where were you? I could have used some help." Dickens told her the story of being stuck outside, frantic to get in. *Poor fella.*

From cricket to crime. So much for a day off.

The next several hours were tedious, nerve-wracking, and draining. I thought the afternoon would never end. Officials paraded in and out of my cottage, as Dave and I sat stunned in the sitting room. Tending to Alastair, the paramedics decided he didn't require a trip to the hospital. They cleaned Dave's bloody and bruised knuckles and bandaged his hands.

Gemma arrived and called in a third officer to assist with transferring the prisoner plus the Scene of Crime Officers to ensure that she got all the evidence she needed to throw the book at our intruder, at least for breaking into my cottage. If I never again saw a white-clad SOCO, it would be too soon.

In his semi-conscious state, Alastair had babbled briefly to Constable James but clammed up when Gemma arrived. He'd said enough for her to apply for a warrant and dispatch officers to Alastair's Attic to search for evidence, interview Bonnie, and possibly make another arrest or two.

It was my neighbor Deborah Watson who comforted us with cups of brandy-laced tea—the British cure for whatever ails you. She'd seen the hubbub outside my cottage and come running. Meanwhile, Dickens wandered from room to room, alternating between comforting me and seeking attention from all the visitors. Christie had retreated to goodness knows where.

The next person I saw was decidedly less comforting. Gemma had interviewed me first, and now it was Dave's turn to meet with her in the kitchen. That meant I was alone in the sitting room when DCI Burton arrived. Tears pricked my eyes when he sat next to me on the couch and grabbed my hands.

He shook his head and spoke softly. "Leta, are you okay? I understand you weren't attacked, but I'm sure finding an intruder had to be harrowing."

When I mumbled Dave and I were alright, he released my hands and gave me his handkerchief before rising from the couch and moving to the fireplace. His tone shifted as though he'd flipped a switch from nice to nasty. "You realize you may have jeopardized this entire case, don't you? That once again, your meddling has gotten in the way?"

I couldn't believe my ears. I scrambled off the couch and put my hands on my hips, prepared to do battle. "*Your* case? What case? If it weren't for me and Dave and my friends, you wouldn't have a *case!*"

In response, he thundered, "My people were on the way to getting there in the *right* way—methodically—the way good police work happens. Not in a slapdash, reckless manner."

Slapdash! Was he serious? "You have no idea how we figured out—"

He shook his finger in my face as he spoke over me. "And let's not forget you endangered yourself *and* Dave this time, not to mention Belle and Ellie." *That again?*

By now, Dave, Gemma, and my animals had heard us and come running—Dave put his arm around me, and Gemma stood near her boss. Dickens growled and Christie gave a low hiss.

I was trembling with rage. "How dare you accost me in my

home! How dare you accuse me of endangering Dave or anyone else! I want you out of my house, now!"

Gemma looked from me to her DCI and hesitated. The silence was palpable. Finally, she placed her hand on his arm and nodded toward the door.

He resisted for a moment but must have thought better of it. As he exited, he called over his shoulder, "This isn't over by a long shot." *He had to have the last word. How like him.*

Dave looked at me with an expression of disbelief. "Did I just witness a verbal assault? Did he *really* accuse you of—what do you call it—reckless endangerment?"

"I believe he did. He was even more obnoxious than he was the last time he reprimanded me."

"Is that what you call it? A reprimand? He was way out of line."

I blinked and smiled. "I'd say we need to call the police . . . except they were just here."

Chapter Twenty-Three

On Monday morning, it was apparent the Astonbury grapevine had been in full swing. It was a good thing I'd turned my phone off before I fell into bed, as it was filled with texts, and my voicemail was full to overflowing.

Downstairs, Dave was on his phone. I picked up that it was Gilbert calling to see if Dave wanted to join him on his brewery tour. "I don't think I can make it, Gilbert. Let me tell you what happened here yesterday." Dave rolled his eyes and made the yakking sign with his hand. It seemed Gilbert wanted all the details. I was sure I'd have the same problem when I got around to speaking with Wendy.

Dave was hanging up when Gemma rang me. "Are you awake enough for an update?"

I asked her to let me pour a cup of coffee and I told Dave who it was. He followed me into the sitting room and stoked the fire while I put us on speakerphone.

"First, let me say how sorry I am for how you were treated yesterday. That's twice now you've gotten a dressing-down from my boss."

"I know it's not your fault, Gemma. What would you say: 'He's a right git?'. I can only hope I never have to see him again."

"Yes, well, it probably doesn't help, but I've been on the receiving end of several similar rants. After each one, he reverts to normal and acts as though it never happened. Anyway, let me tell you where we are with the Porters."

The upshot was that she had the husband and wife on the forgeries but not yet for the murder. Once Bonnie heard that her son Albert was under suspicion too, she confessed that it was only she and Alastair who partnered on creating the documents—that Albert was neither involved nor aware. Our initial supposition about a team of forgers—one as the author and one as the artist—was on target. Gemma didn't have much more than that.

I sighed as I hung up. "It seems like we should be doing something, doesn't it?"

"Like what? Something beyond taking it easy and recovering from being attacked by a murdering forger? Think about it—we solved the case, Tuppence."

I studied him. For a man who'd been so worried about the activities of the Little Old Ladies' Detective Agency, he seemed amazingly calm. "That we did," I said, "and it feels pretty good, doesn't it?"

He grinned and nodded. "Sure does."

"So, you're fine with how it all worked out? You don't think we took any unnecessary risks?"

Dave was quick to see where I was headed. "Oh, we're going back to our disagreement, aren't we? No, I don't think we did. Especially since we were careful to stick with each other or with friends. Had I accepted Alastair's invitation to go book scouting with him, I guess that could have been dicey. I wonder what he had in mind?"

"That's just it, Dave. If we hadn't been busy, you would have been tempted. You'd have thought, no harm in looking at books. The danger isn't always obvious, at least not in my experience."

"Point taken. Doesn't make me worry any less about you, but I'm beginning to understand. Once you start asking questions, once the wheels in your head start turning . . . well, it's hard to turn back."

"I know, and believe it or not, I'm telling myself this is it, never again—but I've said that before."

Dave touched my chin with his finger and turned my head toward his. "Oh, I get it. I'd be lying if I said I wasn't hooked. But thinking of you taking risks . . . I'd also be lying if I said that didn't scare the heck out of me."

I smiled. "I think it was Eleanor Roosevelt who said, 'Do one thing every day that scares you.' Maybe I could try for every other day."

"Uh-huh. And, since Mark Twain figures so prominently in this adventure, let's remember he said, 'Twenty years from now you will be more disappointed by the things you didn't do than by the ones you did.' Well said, right? Except I don't think he had confrontations with killers in mind."

"Enough! Two word nerds sitting on a couch. We could keep this up for hours."

Dickens must have thought the same thing, because he came to the couch, put his paws between us, and barked. "Are you two done? Can we go see the donkeys? We could even take Christie."

Dave scratched Dickens's ears. "What's up, fella? Need to go out?"

"He just wants attention. Here's an idea. Why don't you go on the tour with Gilbert and take Dickens with you to hang out with Basil? I'll be fine here by myself. And, maybe tonight, we can go to Burford for a quiet dinner."

Once he was sure I was fine, he agreed. "I'll call Gilbert and then I'll fry up some eggs for breakfast, okay?"

While he was gone, I played Words with Friends, straightened the mess two people can make, and wrote an email to my sisters and my friend Bev to let them know about the latest happenings. I could pretty well predict their responses. My youngest sister Anna would have a conniption about my putting myself in danger again. Sophia, my middle sister, would tsk-tsk a bit, and immediately request more detail about how my friend the dowager countess had been involved. Bev would be suitably concerned about my well-being, but would refrain from chastising me.

Christie followed me from room to room and crawled into my lap when I finally sat on the couch with my phone and a book. She purred her approval.

Before I could settle down to read, I knew I had to call Wendy. She'd left two messages Sunday and sent a text this morning. I was surprised she hadn't shown up at the door.

She answered on the first ring. "Thank goodness. I thought I'd never get to talk to you. Are you okay? Is Dave?"

"Physically, I'm fine, but the stress has worn me out. Dave has bruised knuckles, but that's about it. He seems to have already gotten over the fact that a man threatened him with a sword. How much do you know? And how do you know?"

"As soon as I saw the note Deborah posted on the Astonbury Aha!, I called Libby. You know she got the scoop from Gemma. I can't believe that man broke into your cottage, much less pulled out a sword. Mum and Peter told me all about the cane. What if you'd been alone when you found him?"

She was asking the question that had been on my mind. What if Dave hadn't been there? What if he hadn't supplied me with defensive spray and alarms? Then again, if Dave and Gilbert hadn't spoken with Alastair at the flea market, maybe none of this would have happened. Too many what-ifs to consider.

"By now, you may know more than I do. Dave recalled mentioning that we were helping Beatrix with the binders, so that explains how he knew we had them. And because Dave told him we'd be at the cricket match, he expected the cottage to be empty. I guess he was counting on us staying the entire time. Still, it seems to me that breaking into my cottage in broad daylight was awfully risky."

"Well, I do know that he parked his motorbike by the bridge hoping no one would see him. Surely, one of your neighbors would have noticed it in your driveway."

I recalled seeing it at the river and thinking it belonged to a fisherman. I wondered whether he'd borrowed it from his son.

"Wendy, are you there?"

"Um, yes. I was thinking I don't mean to make light of the sword attack, but I'm maybe even more upset about the way Brian treated you."

As well you should be, I thought. "So, Gemma shared that with her mum too? Have you spoken with him?"

"No! He's rung me twice, but I've ignored the calls. I've already told him I don't want to see him, and I've nothing more to say. The way he treated you is just the icing on the cake. I don't believe a person can have two different personalities. If he treats you and Gemma that way—which Libby says he does—he's bound to do it with me sooner or later. Remember the lesson I gave you on British terms for jerks? He's all of those—git, plonker, prat, and some I can't say aloud."

Phew. At least she and I agree he's a jerk, or whatever British term she wants to use. "So, I don't have to worry about you bringing DCI Burton the next time I throw a party? Is that what I'm hearing?"

Wendy spluttered. "You got that right. I'm well-shed of him. Now, I'm going to let you get back to recovering from yesterday. Let's take a yoga class later this week, okay?"

I was reading when Ellie called. "I'm dying to know the full scoop, but I've gotten most of the story from Dave and Gilbert, so I'm not going to push you for more detail. I've spoken with Belle, and we have a proposal. We'd like to invite the usual suspects to dinner here at the Manor House and fill everyone in on how the Little Old Ladies, plus Dave and Gilbert, of course, unmasked the culprit. And, as a part of the evening, we'll honor Teddy's passion, his generosity, and his wit. Just think. Sharing the mystery of the key will be a wonderful example of who he was. What do you say?"

I wasn't sure about the plan, but then, it wasn't up to me. If Ellie and Belle wanted to tell the tale, who was I to get in the way? I'd done something similar after the murder at the cricket pavilion. Not exactly a Hercule Poirot denouement, but close. I'd grown weary of telling the story over and over again to everyone I ran into, so it had seemed a good idea.

"I say yes, and I'll get the binders back to Beatrix in case she wants to showcase them that night. Is there anything else you'd like me to do?"

"Just be here with bells on Friday evening—with your beau, of course."

Dave and I had a quiet week. We walked. We drove to Gloucester and toured the Cathedral. We had lunch at the Swan Inn in Swinbrook, once owned by the last of the Mitford sisters. We read and sat by the fire.

We heard nothing further from Gemma until Thursday morning. Once again, I put her on speakerphone. "I have good news. We have a confession from Alastair. He says killing Teddy Byrd was an accident, but the courts will have to decide whether that's true or not."

"Are you any the wiser as to why? Why he wanted the documents? Why he broke in?"

Gemma sighed. "It's not a pretty story. You were right about Alastair having a record. As a young man, he went to prison for burglary. Upon his release, he returned to his wife and young son, turned his life around, and kept his nose clean —until the financial crisis, when his flea market business almost went under. That's when the couple turned to forgery, a lucrative venture for them. Fast-forward to a local literary festival and three occurrences that led to a desperate act.

"One, at a presentation about Mark Twain, Alastair realized he'd sold Teddy Byrd several *obviously* fake documents referencing Twain, Arthur Conan Doyle, and J.M. Barrie. He was in charge of getting the facts straight for the forgeries his wife created, and he'd messed up. Two, the very next night, Teddy met Gilbert and Dave, experts on Doyle and Barrie. What were the chances?

"Three, Alastair tells us Teddy pulled him aside Friday at

the festival and told him Gilbert had questioned at least one of the documents Alastair had sold him and that he was meeting with Dave the next day and would ask his opinion on a few others. He also mentioned speaking with other collectors about their authenticity. Alastair saw his forgery scheme unraveling and prison looming. Worse, he pictured his wheelchair-bound wife in prison too. He panicked."

"Desperate times call for desperate measures? He thought he had to get the fakes back or they'd both wind up in prison?"

"Yes. He was right about *his* situation—because of his record, he'd get a prison sentence for sure—but he was wrong about his wife. Almost certainly, she would have remained free with a suspended sentence, a stiff fine, and community service. Still, it seems it was panic, pure and simple, that led him to break into Teddy's home."

Dave asked, "How did he get in? Did he have a key?"

"The same way he got into Leta's cottage. He picked the lock, a skill he'd learned in the old days."

I was nodding and thinking. "But how do you accidentally smother a helpless old man?"

Gemma raised her voice. "You don't. Not in my book. There's no way he's getting away with that. The judge may buy that it wasn't premeditated, but it was no accident. Teddy woke up and saw him, and he killed him."

This was a lot to absorb. "But his wife had no idea? So she won't be charged with anything to do with that?"

"Not for murder. Like I said, she'll likely get a suspended sentence for the forgeries as a first offender, but her husband's rash and violent actions have brought the walls tumbling down around them."

The more I heard, the angrier I got. "And his final move was to break in here. What was the point?"

Dave thought he knew. "More than anything else, he wanted the ledger, because that—coupled with the contents of the binders—would lead to him. I'm betting the few forgeries we found are only the tip of the iceberg. Beatrix may want to get an expert to analyze all of it."

I looked at my boyfriend. "Did he even think about what he'd do if we came home? What would he have done if we hadn't gotten the drop on him? Killed us both? He couldn't very well leave us alive once we'd seen him. Panic, desperation? Call it what you will. In my book, he's evil."

Gemma agreed. "It's clear to me he *did* think about what he'd do if you surprised him. That has to be why he brought a weapon with him to your cottage. I mean, who walks around with a sword cane, and who attaches one to a motorbike? I'd call that premeditated, even if he was hoping he'd never see you two."

Dave shook his head. "I keep thinking of Hercule Poirot saying, 'There is evil everywhere under the sun.' It certainly fits."

The plane trees lining the long driveway to Astonbury Manor sparkled with raindrops from the shower we'd had earlier in the day. Since Ellie had decided to hold her small dinner party outdoors, it was fortunate the clouds had given way to bright sunshine. I glimpsed the tent in the distance, a bright blue and yellow pennant with the Earl of Stow's crest flying from the center pole. Dave let Dickens out of the car, and I grabbed the backpack with Christie in it. I hadn't planned to bring the princess until Ellie requested her presence.

With Christie on his back, Dave turned to me and grinned.

"You know, this is my first dinner party hosted by a dowager countess. First a brewery tour with an earl and now this."

As we approached the tent, I took in the cheerful tableau. I saw flowers centered on each table, torches positioned in the ground around the perimeter, and Teddy's binders with a selection of his figurines displayed on a table. Fiona was speaking with Deborah Watson and Wendy. Several of the men—Peter, Toby, Gavin, and Gilbert—were standing by the keg. My neighbor John Watson had his head thrown back laughing at something Sarah Coates was saying, and her husband Matthew, the Earl of Stow, stood chatting with Libby, Rhiannon, and Gemma. Belle had just hugged Constable James, and Ellie was conferring with her chef, Carolyn.

I noticed Libby pointing to the edge of the tent and turned to look. "Dave, is that Watson?"

"Sure looks like him, but what's he doing here?"

When we asked Libby that question, she laughed. "Well, he keeps showing up over here, and if you can believe it, hanging out by the kitchen entry to the manor house. Smart cat, I'd say."

Dave was surprised. "But how does he get across the river?"

"That's easy. He has a choice. He can cut through the donkey pasture to the bridge over the river, or he can cross by the waterwheel behind the Olde Mill Inn. There's a spot where the branches from the trees on either side stretch nearly to the middle. For now, which way he chooses is his secret."

Ellie joined us and chimed in. "It's nice having a cat around. Carolyn's let him in the kitchen a few times, and he's a little gentleman, though Blanche doesn't seem to know what to think of him. Beatrix has agreed he can stay here and become the manor cat."

Based on how Christie's eyes were following the handsome cat, I wasn't sure she knew what to make of him. *Wouldn't it be interesting if he visited Schoolhouse Cottage? I'd love to see Christie's reaction to a gentleman caller.*

I left Ellie conferring with Dave when I heard Belle calling my name. "Leta, do we have a surprise for you! Look what we came up with." She handed me a pamphlet, its cover emblazoned with the words *The Chipping Camden Affair*.

"Oh my goodness. And what's inside?" I turned the page to a table of contents—A Life Well-Lived, The Mystery of the Key, Never the Twain shall Meet, Gilbert and Sullivan, All's Well that Ends Well. For each topic, a speaker was listed, and I was thankful *not* to see my name. Dave's was listed, though.

Looking at Belle, I grinned. "Does this mean Dave and Gilbert are going to sing?"

Gilbert walked over and answered that question. "Not a chance, but we promise to demonstrate our acting ability."

When I returned to Dave's side, I glimpsed a shiny gold medal attached to my backpack. "Oh my goodness! Hero Cat? Is that what it says?" Christie preened and purred.

Dave explained that that's why we had to bring Christie. Ellie wanted to be sure she got the recognition she deserved.

It wasn't long before Matthew went to the display table and got everyone's attention. "Dear friends, Mum and I want to thank you for joining us this evening. We've lost a fine gentleman, and tonight we plan to honor his larger-than-life personality. Beatrix and our new friend Fiona knew him better than any of us, and they assure me he'll be looking down and enjoying our camaraderie."

Beatrix took her place in front of the table and motioned to Fiona to join her. Together they told the story of how they knew Teddy and what he'd meant to them. They spoke of his passion for literature and collecting and how he'd opened Blue-bird Books later in life. Taking turns holding up the binders, they described a few of the documents inside.

As they spoke, Matthew made the rounds pouring champagne into the flutes arranged on each table. Beatrix lifted her glass as did Fiona, and together they said, "Here's to a life well-lived." Most of the guests knew the bare bones of how Teddy had died and that his death had resulted from someone breaking into his cottage, but not much beyond that.

Peter walked his mother to the display table and pulled a chair up for her. Belle sat and chuckled. "It's storytime. Please open your programs to The Mystery of the Key. Teddy was nothing if not fun-loving. That meant Beatrix had to embark on a treasure hunt to find the key to his safe. He couldn't just leave it for her. Instead, we had to follow the clues to find it. Even Constable James got in on the act with Ellie, Leta, and me. First, Leta stumbled across the safe hidden behind a false cover to the book *Safe Haven*, and then the fun began. Inside the cover was a note—***You found me! Now you must find my key.***

Each clue led to a book—except the one that inspired us to look beneath the bed—until, finally, we located the key. I won't tell you the answers, but you can follow along in your program as I read the clues aloud. By the way, the lovely calligraphy is compliments of Fiona."

When Belle closed her program, Wendy called to the owner of the Book Nook and now Bluebird Books. "Beatrix, this sounds like so much fun. Can we use the clues to do a treasure hunt at your shop for our next book club meeting? Say yes, please."

Beatrix nodded and agreed. "Who knows? We might get a bigger crowd if we advertise the event. And we could have a drawing to win the books. Great idea. Teddy would be pleased to know he inspired us."

It was Ellie's turn to stand by the display table. "Never the twain shall meet. Thus ends the first line in Rudyard Kipling's poem 'The Ballad of East and West,'" but in this case, I've used it to reference Mark Twain.

"First, Beatrix, Belle, and Leta inventoried the items in Teddy's collection to identify missing pieces. Next, I assisted Belle and Leta in double-checking the list and trying to ascertain a pattern. Wendy, I was delighted to act as your substitute in the Little Old Ladies' Detective Agency.

"We determined that one thing the missing documents had in common was Mark Twain and that each one was also connected to either Arthur Conan Doyle or J.M. Barrie. What did it mean? We turned to Gilbert and Dave to help us figure that out. Those two saw right away the documents had to be . . . forgeries." When the audience gasped, Ellie curtsied and invited the pair to come forward.

I looked around. Our friends seemed enthralled. *I guess when you're not privy to the investigation along the way, hearing how the puzzle was solved can be intriguing.* Gilbert and Sullivan, a.k.a Dave, did not disappoint as they explained how we'd concluded Bonnie and Alastair, or perhaps Bonnie and her son, were a team of forgers. The audience erupted in laughter when Gilbert re-enacted the scene where he slapped his forehead and exclaimed, "I say, Dave, didn't you tell me a few of those letters came from Alastair's Attic?"

Gemma and Constable James were the last to take center stage. "Ladies and Gentlemen," began our local Detective Inspector, "It took several days for all the pieces of the puzzle to come together. As Alastair Porter was caught in the act, we could easily charge him with breaking into Leta's cottage, and with his wife's confession, we were able to charge the couple with forgery.

"It wasn't until yesterday, though, that he confessed to murdering Teddy Byrd." There were shocked gasps all around. Several guests wondered aloud why he would kill Teddy. Briefly, Gemma laid out the sordid saga of what led the proprietor of a flea market stall to murder an elderly man. The lighthearted atmosphere gave way to shocked silence. "Now, let me turn things over to our very own Constable Jonas James for the rest of the story—the part that ended well."

Our young constable smiled shyly. "As we've heard tonight, many of you had a part in unraveling this crime. The Chipping Camden Affair didn't start in Astonbury, but it ended here, just across the lane at Leta's cottage.

"Our killer had to get his hands on those binders Beatrix and Fiona showed you, and he thought the coast was clear at Schoolhouse Cottage. After what he'd already done, breaking into Leta's home was nothing. It was his misfortune that Dave and Leta came home early from the cricket match and caught him in the act. When Alastair Porter came at Dave with a sword, our friend single-handedly got the better of him . . ."

When Constable James paused, Dave stood and took a bow, and the crowd went from gasping to laughing. "What he meant to say was that Leta single-handedly painted the guy purple. And just in case that didn't do the trick, her attack cat nailed him." Pointing to Christie in the backpack, Dave pulled me to my feet, and I did my best to emulate Ellie's elegant curtsy.

"And so," Gemma concluded as she raised her glass, "Though I'm once again none too pleased with their inter-fering ways, many thanks to Tommy and Tuppence and the

Little Old Ladies. As the Bard would say, All's well that ends well."

Book V

It was supposed to be a relaxing vacation. Now this legendary location could be hiding a killer in its battlements.

Read *Castles, Catnip & Murder* and join the Little Old Ladies' Detective Agency as they search for a murderer in the legendary birthplace of King Arthur.

Have you read the earlier books featuring Leta and her friends?

Find them on Amazon!

Receive a download of Leta's Family Recipes when you sign up for the Dickens & Christie newsletter. And be the first to know when new books are available.

Visit kathymanospenn.com for Dickens & Christie news and pics, and if you're reading a paperback version, that's where you can sign up for the newsletter.

Don't miss out on Leta's Family Recipes.

Psst... Please take a minute...

Dear Reader,

Writers put their hearts and souls into every book. Nothing makes it more worthwhile than reader reviews. Yes, authors appreciate reviews that provide helpful insights.

If you enjoyed this book, Kathy would love it if you could find the time to leave a good, honest review . . . because after everything is said and done, authors write to bring enjoyment to their readers.

Thank you,

Dickens

*Be sure to look for the recipe at the end.
**Click here to purchase and download other books in the series. Or visit Amazon for the paperback.

Recipe

Pastitsio

Servings: 8
Ingredients

- 1 stick unsalted butter
- ⅓ cup all-purpose flour
- 4 cups warm or hot whole milk
- 1 tbsp kosher salt divided
- ¼ tsp nutmeg
- ½ cup grated Romano cheese (optional: an extra ½ cup for top of casserole)
- 1 ½ lbs lean ground beef
- 1 cup diced onion
- 3 large garlic cloves, minced
- 6 tbsp tomato paste
- 1 ½ tsp ground cinnamon
- 4 large eggs, beaten
- 1 lb ziti or elbow macaroni

Preparation:

1. Grease a 9x12 baking dish. Preheat oven to 375 degrees. Bring a large pot of water to a rolling boil.

2. For the béchamel sauce, heat a large pot on medium heat. Add butter.

3. Once the butter melts, whisk in the flour. Cook for one minute.

4. Take the pot off the heat and slowly whisk in warm or hot milk, making sure there are no lumps.

5. Return the pot to the heat and whisk in 1 ½ teaspoons salt and the nutmeg.

6. Bring to a boil and reduce to a simmer. Simmer until thickened, about 8 minutes, whisking along the way.

7. When mixture is thickened, remove from the heat and whisk in grated cheese. Season to taste with salt and pepper. Set aside.

8. While béchamel is thickening, heat a large non-stick skillet on medium. Add ground beef. Start to brown the beef, breaking it up with a wooden spoon.

9. When beef is halfway done cooking, drain fat if necessary. Add onion, garlic, and remaining 1 ½ teaspoons of salt. Continue to cook beef until it's browned all the way through and onion is soft.

10. Mix in the tomato paste and cinnamon. Cook for 1-2 minutes. Set aside.

11. When the meat sauce is almost done cooking, drop the pasta into the boiling water. Cook until it's just **under** al dente. Drain.

12. Slowly add ½ to 1 cup of the warm béchamel sauce to the beaten eggs so that eggs don't curdle.

13. Whisk the egg mixture into the béchamel sauce in the pot.
14. Add the pasta back to the pot you cooked it in. Toss with half of the béchamel and half of the meat mixture.
15. Construct the casserole:
16. Layer half the pasta mixture into the prepared casserole dish.
17. Cover with remaining ground beef mixture.
18. Layer remaining pasta on top.
19. Pour remaining béchamel sauce on top of the pasta.
20. *Optional:* Sprinkle another ½ cup grated Romano on top.
21. Bake in the oven until lightly golden brown and bubbly, about 30-40 minutes. Let it rest for 5-10 minutes before cutting into squares and serving.

Tips:

- Adjust the recipe to your taste. There are a variety of pastitsio recipes. Leta's sister Anna doesn't use tomato paste or anything tomato in hers. Some cooks use pureed tomatoes or tomato sauce. Some, though not many, use a combination of lamb and beef.
- For the béchamel sauce, be sure it is thickened but still thin enough to pour over the casserole.
- You can make the meat sauce ahead of time and reheat it when you prepare the casserole.

Would you like to know when the next book is on the way? Click here to sign up for my Newsletter, or visit KathyManosPenn.com to sign up there.

Books, Authors and Series Mentioned in Collectors, Cats & Murder

Books & Plays

- *Peter Pan* (J.M. Barrie)
- *Jane Annie* (J.M. Barrie and Arthur Conan Doyle)
- *The Sherlockian* (Graham Moore)
- *The Once and Future King* (T.H. White)
- *The Mists of Avalon* (Marion Zimmer Bradley)
- *Morte D'Arthur* (Thomas Malory)
- *The Third Man* (Graham Greene)
- *The Quiet American* (Graham Greene)
- *The Bookman's Tale* (Charlie Lovett)
- *Alice in Wonderland* (Lewis Carroll)
- *The House of Silk* (Anthony Horowitz)
- *Dracula* (Bram Stoker)
- *Arthur Conan Doyle: A Life in Letters* (Charles Foley, Daniel Stashower, and Jon Lellenberg)
- *The Crystal Cave* (Mary Stewart)
- *The King Arthur Trilogy* (Rosemary Sutcliff)

- *Long Summer's Day* (R.F. Delderfeld)
- *Post of Honour* (R.F. Delderfeld)
- *The Green Gauntlet* (R.F. Delderfeld)
- *Treasure Island* (Robert Louis Stevenson)
- *Hamlet* (Shakespeare)
- *Pride and Prejudice* (Jane Austen)
- *Persuasion* (Jane Austen)
- *Murder on the Orient Express* (Agatha Christie)
- *Howards End* (E.M. Forster)
- *Key to Rebecca* (Ken Follett)
- *Chitty-Chitty-Bang-Bang* (Ian Fleming)
- *Lie Down with Lions* (Ken Follett)
- *Eye of the Needle* (Ken Follett)
- *The Big Sleep* (Raymond Chandler)
- *In Cold Blood* (Truman Capote)
- *Lost Book of the Holy Grail* (Charlie Lovett)
- *A Midsummer Night's Dream* (Shakespeare)
- *The Interpretation of Dreams* (Sigmund Freud)
- *The Book Thief* (Markus Zusak)
- *How to Find Love in a Bookshop* (Veronica Henry)
- *The Readers of Broken Wheel Recommend* (Katarina Bivald)
- *The Diary of a Bookseller* (Shaun Bythell)
- *The Collector* (John Fowles)
- *The Tuscan Child* (Rhys Bowen)
- *Can You Ever Forgive Me?* (Lee Israel)
- *Brighton Rock* (Graham Greene)
- *The Monkey's Raincoat* (Robert Crais)
- *A Connecticut Yankee in King Arthur's Court* (Mark Twain)
- *The Cat in the Hat* (Dr. Seuss)

- *The Adventures of Huckleberry Finn* (Mark Twain)
- *The Adventures of Tom Sawyer* (Mark Twain)
- *Booked to Die* (John Dunning)
- *Hide-and-Seek with Angels* (Lisa Chaney)
- *Moriarty* (Anthony Horowitz)

Authors

- J.M. Barrie
- Arthur Conan Doyle
- P.G. Wodehouse
- A.A. Milne
- Jerome K. Jerome
- Rudyard Kipling
- H.G. Wells
- Bram Stoker
- Dorothy L. Sayers
- Margery Allingham
- Agatha Christie
- Patricia Wentworth
- Josephine Tey
- Graham Greene
- Michael Dobbs
- Robert Louis Stevenson
- Oscar Wilde
- Ngaio Marsh
- R.F. Delderfeld
- T.S. Eliot
- Mark Twain
- Lee Childs
- Quentin Jardine

- Robert B. Parker
- Ian Rankin
- J.K. Rowling
- Beatrix Potter
- Nancy Mitford
- Jane Austen
- E.M. Forster
- William Faulkner
- Edna Ferber
- F. Scott Fitzgerald
- Sigmund Freud
- Ian Fleming
- Ken Follett
- Edgar Allan Poe
- Deborah Crombie
- G.K. Chesterton
- John Keats
- Robert Burns
- George Eliot
- Charlotte Bronte
- J.R.R. Tolkien

Series / Related Books

- Peter Wimsey
- Albert Campion
- Tommy and Tuppence
- Russell and Holmes
- Sherlock Holmes Bookshop Mysteries
- Mrs. Bradley Mysteries
- Spenser series

- Bosch series
- Inspector Lynley Mysteries
- Maggie Hope Mysteries
- Jeeves and Wooster
- Father Brown

About the Author

Kathy at her desk when she was four years old.

As a corporate escapee, Kathy Manos Penn went from crafting change communications to plotting page-turners. Adhering to the adage to "write what you know," she populates her mysteries with well-read, witty senior women, a sassy cat, and a loyal dog. The murders and talking pets, however, exist only in her imagination.

Years ago, when she stumbled onto a side job as a columnist for a local paper, she saw the opportunity as an entertaining diversion from the corporate grind. Little did she know that her serendipitous foray into writing "whatever struck her fancy" would lead to a cozy mystery series.

How does she describe her life? "I'm living a dream I never knew I had. Picture me sitting serenely at my desk, surrounded by the four-legged office assistants who inspire the personalities of Dickens & Christie. Why is Dickens a fiend for belly rubs? Because my real-life dog is.

The same goes for Christie's finicky eating habits and penchant for lolling on top of the desk or in the file drawer. She gets it from my calico cat who right this minute is lying on the desk swishing her tail and deciding which pen or pencil to knock to the floor next."

—Kathy

Visit www.KathyManosPenn.com to contact Kathy, read her blogs, and more.

Would you like to know when the next book is on the way? Be sure to sign up up for her newsletter here or on he website. https://bit.ly/3bEjsfi